SUPERNATURAL™

WAR OF THE SONS

ALSO AVAILABLE FROM TITAN BOOKS:

Supernatural: Heart of the Dragon
by Keith R.A. DeCandido

Supernatural: The Unholy Cause
by Joe Schreiber

SUPERNATURAL™

WAR OF THE SONS

**REBECCA DESSERTINE
& DAVID REED**

Based on the hit CW series SUPERNATURAL created by Eric Kripke

TITAN BOOKS

Supernatural: War of the Sons
ISBN: 9781848566019

Published by
Titan Books
A division of Titan Publishing Group Ltd
144 Southwark St
London
SE1 0UP

First edition August 2010
10 9 8 7 6 5 4 3 2 1

Visit our website: www.titanbooks.com

Did you enjoy this book? We love to hear from our readers. Please email
us at readerfeedback@titanemail.com or write to us at Reader Feedback
at the above address.

To receive advance information, news, competitions, and exclusive Titan
offers online, please register as a member by clicking the "sign up" button
on our website: www.titanbooks.com

HISTORIAN'S NOTE

This novel takes place shortly after the season five episode "My Bloody Valentine."

PROLOGUE

This guy's not from around here.

The thought occurred to Caleb as soon as he saw the man's car. It was almost silent, drifting up the long driveway to the camp with no engine noise, the only sound the crunch of gravel under its tires. The gunmetal-gray frame came to a halt in the grass field adjacent to the camp that was too-generously labeled "Parking Lot."

Caleb stared as the driver's door opened and a tall man got out. The stranger's appearance was immaculate—every hair perfectly in place—but something was off. Caleb figured it was probably the Hawaiian shirt.

"Where is Justin Black?" the man intoned, without preamble.

Despite Caleb's considerable strengths as a camp counselor, actually keeping track of the children was a remarkably low priority for him. *We're in the middle of the woods,* he told himself, *where are they gonna go?* For that reason, the Hawaiian-shirted man had caught him off guard.

"Uh… at camp?" Caleb said, and regretted the words as soon as they spilled from his mouth. *Is Justin Black the fat one with the Harry Potter birthmark*, he pondered, *or the creepy little one who was always trying to give out free hugs?*

"My son. His location." The man paused for effect. "I require more specific information."

Caleb glanced into the open window of the activities building, hoping that he'd happen to see the boy in there.

Nope.

"I'll find him. He's out by the lake, I think," Caleb said, putting on his best reassuring voice. *He'd better be*, he thought, *or this is going to be awkward.*

"No," the man said. "I'll find him myself."

The man walked purposefully toward the forest path, and Caleb quickly followed. There was something off-putting about the guy, and Caleb didn't recognize him from parents' night. *Could have been the weed, though*, he thought. Actually, wasn't it Justin Black's dad who'd brought the weed?

Caleb hurried to catch up to the man's long strides.

"Is there a problem?" he asked. "Usually Justin's mom picks him up—"

"No problem." The man cut him off. "I just need to speak with the boy."

Yup, he's a pervert. Who else calls their son "the boy?" Caleb sped up his pursuit.

"What was your name again?" Caleb asked, hoping it would jog some memory of this guy. "I didn't catch it before."

The man turned, slow and deliberate.

"Don. Call me Don."

The camp counselor was certainly annoying, but it was by no means the worst thing Don had had to put up with in his long and storied existence. His former profession had brought him into contact with the absolute worst of the worst, the darkest blights on the fabric of humankind that ever walked the Earth. *I'm like Jerry Springer without the fame*, Don thought, amused by his own analogy. After his previous occupation, it didn't take much to amuse Don. *Well, the fame part is about to change.*

Losing the counselor in the forest was a simple matter. One moment, the kid was an arm's-length away. The next, Don was a quarter-mile ahead of him. The path wound its way down a hill, dense thickets of forest obscuring the view. It would all be over before the counselor caught up.

The lake itself was pristine and beautiful, its glassy surface rippling with the slight breeze. An amazing summer day, one like Don hadn't seen in… too long to remember.

"Ew! Don't touch it with your bare hands!"

Don's head turned an unnatural degree to find the source of the shout. It had come from a girl, about ten years old, running away from a boy of the same age.

Justin Black.

"You're gonna get warts!" the girl cried, desperately dodging away from the frog in Justin's outstretched hands.

"No I won't," Justin said, "my brother said frogs give you herpes."

"What's that?" the girl asked innocently.

"I dunno. Why don't you ask the frog?" Justin thrust the amphibian at her, only to have it leap out of his hands and into the bog at the lake's edge.

"Great, now you made me lose it," Justin complained.

He reached down into the bog to find the lost creature, but another pair of hands got there first. Don lifted the frog out of the swampy water, holding it delicately, as if the slightest pressure would shatter it.

"It's not lost, my boy," Don said, a warm look on his face.

Justin took a step back, confused.

"Dad?"

"No, Justin, not exactly."

The frog croaked loudly, startling both of the children. Justin's brow furrowed.

"Mom said you're not supposed to come see me. She said the police wouldn't let you."

"My boy, that was the old me. There's a new set of rules, now." Don held out the frog to Justin, trying to bring the boy closer.

"You like frogs, don't you?"

Caleb's mind was racing. Where had the man gone? Should he call the cops? How the *hell* had he got so far ahead? He began to run, hurtling down the path as he started to panic, stumbling over the uneven ground. Then he felt his foot hit a rock, sending him tumbling down the slope and slamming into a tree.

"Damn it!" he groaned, as the pain shot through him, bringing tears to his eyes. Wincing, he shifted into a sitting position and peered at his leg. His pants were ripped and a trail of blood was seeping down his thigh.

Crap.

He pulled himself up, took a step forward, and collapsed. *Oh God, I can't stand. Maybe it's broken.*

Fear filled his mind. Fear of what would happen to the kids at the lake, fear of what would happen when his boss found out about his inattentiveness, and fear of dying slowly of bloodloss out in the woods where no one could find him.

Calm the hell down, he thought, *this isn't even that bad. It's barely even bleeding.* That realization helped him get back to his feet. He had managed to hobble a few steps forward when he heard it.

The blood-curdling scream of Justin Black.

ONE

I can feel it, Dean thought. *The sky is falling.* It wasn't a new feeling. In fact, the sky had been falling on Dean Winchester since he was four years old. The difference, of course, was that this time could very well be the *last* time. *And this is where it all ends? The Apocalypse is gonna go down in the ass-edge of nowhere?*

Dean let out a tired sigh as he gunned the Impala onto County Road 6. There was nothing on either side of the asphalt except cornfields, cattle, farms and farmers—the very Americana that Dean and his brother Sam fought to protect. For a moment, Dean's imagination took hold, and the clouds on the horizon became pillars of smoke, spilling from unseen tongues of flame. The rotting wooden beams of a decrepit barn became the last remnants of humanity. Dean shook the vision out of his head, and the clouds were once again clouds. The barn was, once more, just a barn.

For months, Dean and Sam had been on the suicide mission to end all suicide missions—to hunt down and kill the Devil. Though the weight of the task seemed unbearable, the brothers knew that they were the only ones who could shoulder it. It was, after all, their fault that right now Lucifer walked the earth.

No. Sam's *fault.*

Dean shoved the thought to the dark recesses of his mind. It wouldn't do him any good to dwell on it. His younger brother—the boy who Dean had practically raised since their mother died—had broken the Final Seal. In a moment of weakness, Sam had killed the demon Lilith, unintentionally popping the lock on Satan's cage. Now, after nearly a year of chasing him, they were no closer to shoving the bastard back into the lock-up.

But that wasn't even the bad news. The angels, ostensibly protectors of humanity, had in fact been behind Satan's jailbreak.

"They *wanted* you to break the Seal," Dean had explained to his brother in the moments after Lucifer's rise. "They're sick of waiting around in Heaven. With Satan out, they get to bring on the prizefight. Winner takes *Earth.*"

The angels already had a plan in motion—according to the winged bastards, the only way to defeat Lucifer was for Dean to be the host for the archangel Michael, the most powerful weapon in Heaven's arsenal. They even had an overdramatic pet name for Dean: the Michael Sword. Every fiber of Dean's body rebelled against the idea. The battle between Michael and Lucifer would have the minor side effect of destroying half the Earth. A "planetary enema," Zachariah had called it. The douche.

Lucifer's final vessel was to be Sam. *The symmetry must be funny to someone upstairs,* Dean thought. Michael and Lucifer were brothers, one of them following closely in their father's footsteps, the other... Well, just like Sam, Lucifer had always wanted to go his own way.

However, the one thing neither Heaven nor Hell could control was human will. While on Earth, angels—both righteous and fallen—had to take a willing human host. If Sam and Dean didn't say "yes" to Lucifer and Michael, the battle couldn't happen. The archangels would have to putter around in their alternate, non-ordained meatsuits, tearing their lesser vessels apart while they waited for Sam and Dean to come around to the party line.

The Winchester brothers weren't going to fight each other. There *had* to be another way.

But every time they thought they had Lucifer within their sights, fate slapped their faces again. They had tried their old standby: straight-up violence, attempting to kill Lucifer outright. First with the Colt, a gun so powerful it was said to be able to kill anything, but that had barely given their Adversary a headache. They had Ruby's demon-killing knife, but that was just as impotent against an archangel. The only chance they had left was to catch Lucifer by surprise. No small feat.

"Take a right at Camp Dakota Road," Sam directed.

"Really? Couldn't have figured that one out, Sam," Dean shot back. "Since we're going to a *camp*."

Sam had been getting under his skin recently. Actually, *everything* had been getting under his skin. The endless hours on the road had proven useless thus far, and Dean was beginning to doubt that they would be able to win this war.

Can't fight something you can't find, he thought. But he also had doubts about his role in the battle to come. *Even if I'm doing everything in my power to find another way… can someone change the role they're destined by fate to play?* Avoiding destiny is what Dean and Sam had been doing so far. *But how much longer can we keep that up?* They were flying under the angels' radar, and for now, that was enough.

It had to be.

A week ago Sam had started tracking the local news from a small town in South Dakota. It had been lighting up with apocalyptic signs like an end-of-the-world Christmas tree.

Maybe we're finally getting a freakin' break, Dean thought hopefully.

Their first stop was a kids' day camp. A gas station attendant a couple of towns over had told them about it. The scruffy dude had said he didn't rightly know what had happened, but his cousin's girlfriend's mom had told him that it was like something out of the Bible and children had been harmed. That alone was enough to warrant a visit.

Dean pushed the accelerator to the Impala's firewall, his hazel eyes glinting with anger. Every second they were delayed, Lucifer got another step ahead of them.

Sam threw a sideways glance at Dean. Thanks to all the years they had spent on the road, Sam could read his older brother's mood just by the way he tightened his grip on the steering wheel or blew his breath out through his nose in short staccato bursts.

Dean's pissed about something again, Sam thought. *And probably for no good reason.* Sam felt the constant burden of his brother's anger and expectations. Chief among them was the expectation that they'd do things Dean's way—or, more accurately, John Winchester's way. The pressure to fit into their father's shoes had always been immense—doubly so since his death—and Dean was the poster child for Daddy's boys. He dressed like John Winchester, drove his car, listened to his music. He even walked like John. Sam, on the other hand, had tried time and time again to get free of his father and everything that he represented. Now, Sam realized that Dean felt like his brother had strayed *too* far off the path, at times even irretrievably. He had dealt with demons, using the power that their blood gave him... all things that John would never have allowed. Despite all of that, Sam was fine. *He* knew that, he just wished that Dean would realize it too. For the most part, Dean seemed to trust him, but that didn't mean they would always get along.

The final battle is looming, and we're stuck smack dab in the middle of it. Sam pursed his lips together—he felt like they were coming to the end of something. He just didn't know *what.*

Preoccupied, Sam glanced out the passenger window just as the Impala careened by the split log sign for CAMP WITKI NIKI.

"There!" he shouted, a little too loudly, pointing at the sign.

"G-and-an-H crap!" Dean yelled, as he turned the wheel quickly to the left, fishtailing the Impala's tires, a spray of gravel hitting the trees on both sides of the deeply rutted driveway. "Inside voice, inside voice!" Dean spat. He opened his mouth to say more, then clearly decided to drop it.

The Impala bumped its way over the gravel.

"Okay," Dean said. "So what are we walking into?"

Relieved his brother's outburst was over, Sam grabbed his laptop.

"From what I can find, a bunch of creeped out parents, but no dead kids. Guess our gas station buddy was overstating that part." Sam pulled up the *Grenville, South Dakota Tribune* webpage and scanned the article.

"There's this posting on a comment board written by some totally hysterical mother named Nancy Johnson. Something huge happened yesterday, but she doesn't say what, just that a strange man walked into the camp. It scared the bejesus out of all the parents, but there's nothing in the police report, so technically no crime was committed. This woman writes, 'Considering the highly sensitive nature of the children at Witki Niki, it is of the utmost importance that each child be under an adult's care at all times.'"

Dean brought the Impala to a stop on a grass field. Pulling on the hand-brake he turned to Sam.

"We're here because some berserk Betty on a mommy-blog vents that a 'strange guy' walked into little Timmy's day camp? Are you effing kidding me, Sam?" Dean paused for a moment to let his frustration sink in. "What, so if somebody farts in Yankee stadium, we run it down as a demon?"

Sam sighed. Sometimes he felt as if he could never to do anything right for Dean.

"There are apocalyptic omens here. The attendant says

it was straight out of the Book of Revelation… You don't think that's worth looking into?"

Sam pushed open the car door. Then he heard *it*.

"What the hell *is* that?" Dean growled, emerging from the other side of the Impala.

A cacophony of what sounded like a thousand dying car horns emanated from behind a grove of trees. Sam and Dean looked at each other, the edginess of the last twenty minutes now dropped.

Sam sprang into action. Ears stinging from the piercing noise, he ran round to the back of the car, popped open the trunk and lifted up the false bottom to reveal their secret stash of weapons and materials. Dean reached in and backhanded Sam a revolver, taking a sawed-off for himself. He slipped the shotgun down the back of his worn Levi's with practiced ease.

Sam palmed a quart bag of salt and slipped it into his breast pocket. *Never be caught off guard*, he thought, hearing his father's words as if John was standing two feet away.

They strode through the grass with deliberation, the strange noise getting louder and louder. As they reached a rocky path that led down a slope, they heard a high-pitched voice call out, "Hey! Stop! I said *stop!*"

The Winchesters turned and were accosted by a freckled, red-haired youth, several inches shorter than Dean and several years younger than Sam. He came limping toward them, an elaborate-looking air cast on his left leg.

He managed to get within a few yards of them before he had to start hopping on his good foot. Dean looked the young man up and down, eying his lime-green cast.

"Wow, that's some injury there. You get that playing World of Warcraft, or doing some major texting on lonelygeek dot com?"

Sam saw the guy's face immediately sour. *Smooth, Dean.*

"I got it on duty," the young man squeaked out.

"Really. On duty?" Dean said, smirking. "What do you do, exactly?"

"I'm head junior counselor. Who the hell are you?"

But Dean had already lost interest and was making his way down the hill.

"Don't worry about it, kid."

Sam glanced at his brother's retreating back, then smiled at the young man. "We're just checking some stuff out. Were you here yesterday? I'm sorry, what's your name?"

The young man looked embarrassed and Sam could see sweat bead on his upper lip, despite the breeze.

"Caleb. It wasn't my fault," he stuttered. "The EPA said it was just a freak explosion—"

"Explosion?" Sam interrupted.

"Yeah, freak explosion of the population."

"The population of what?"

His answer didn't come from Caleb, but from the tree line.

"FROGS!"

Sam turned to see Dean holding up a large frog. Dean took one of the amphibian's front legs between his thumb and forefinger and made it wave at his brother to join him. Sam thanked the kid and headed down the hill to meet Dean.

"Can you believe this?" Dean said, gesturing toward the sea of frogs that were hopping around the forest floor. "Guess Kermit and Miss Piggy have been busy."

Sam walked past him toward the lake.

"Okay, you got your frog-sex joke in, but now are you going to tell me I was right? I mean, this is about as apocalyptic as it gets."

"I guess so." Dean gently put down the frog and caught up with Sam. "Remind me what the deal is with frogs and the Apocalypse?"

Sam looked toward the lakeshore, where every kid in the camp was sprinting around with buckets, bags, milk crates—anything that could carry more than one frog. He spotted several makeshift frog-racing sites, as well as kids trying to make frogs play badminton, kids having frog tea parties, a couple of kids trying to have frogs play basketball—there was even one lonely kid that had set up frogs for a mock trial. Deep inside him, Sam again wished his childhood had been more normal. The kids here were having a ball, despite the biblical overtones of the situation.

Sam turned to his brother.

"In Exodus, God rained frogs down on the Egyptians as punishment for not letting the Israelites free. 'And if thou refuse to let them go, behold, I will smite all thy borders with frogs.'"

"Okay, so frogs are bad. But these kids are going apeshit over them. Doesn't look so terrible to me."

Sam shrugged. He didn't have all the answers.

Caleb tottered down the hillside and caught up to them.

"Excuse me, I still didn't get your names," he said.

Dean scowled at him.

"Why don't you tell us how all these frogs got here."

Caleb threw his hands in the air, exasperated.

"Like I told Mr. Butler! How many times do I have to explain this?"

"Who's Mr. Butler?" Sam asked.

"My boss," Caleb said with a hearty eye-roll. "Justin Black's father showed up out of the blue yesterday. I didn't exactly realize he wasn't supposed to see his son. Guy was acting kind of strange, and the next thing I know he's down at the lake with the kids. Then all hell broke loose."

Dean surveyed the children running around in near-hysterical, frog-induced mayhem. A few tired-looking counselors were trying—and for the most-part failing—to keep some kind of control.

"Where *is* Justin Black?"

Dean and Sam made their way toward a large rectangular log cabin dining hall. Inside, little Justin Black sat at a long table. He was pudgy, and wore a striped shirt a size too small and cargo shorts five inches too long, Dean could tell that Justin wasn't the most popular kid at Camp Witki Niki. Dean himself would have made fun of this kid.

Justin's face was red and splotchy from crying. A large frog sat in his lap, and his fingers stroked its flat head like it was a golden retriever.

"Justin?" Sam said gently.

The boy looked up suspiciously.

"Justin, hey. I'm Sam, and this is my brother Dean."

Dean gritted his teeth. *Aliases, Sam, aliases. Guy has such a soft spot for kids.*

"Justin, we know that your dad came to see you yesterday. Was that the first time you'd seen him in a while?" Sam made his way to the bench next to Justin, and the boy nodded his head.

"Not supposed to see him till he pays my mom all the supports," he murmured, and then sniffed and wiped his dripping nose with the back of his hand.

"You mean child support?" Sam asked.

"Yeah," Justin said, keeping his eyes on the table.

Sam scooted toward Justin a little.

"You know what kind of frog that is?" he asked.

"It's a *Rana catesbeiana*, American Bullfrog," Justin said with a short snort.

"Oh, of course," Sam said, gently touching the frog's head. "Justin, did your dad seem… normal yesterday?"

"Umm. What do you mean?" Justin moved the frog away from Sam's reach.

"Did you recognize him right away?" Dean probed. He pressed his hands on the table and leaned toward the boy. Sam gave him a warning stare, indicating that he should take it easy.

"He's my *dad*," the boy responded.

"No, I know that, but did you notice anything different about him?" Dean persisted.

"Well. Like maybe…" Justin trailed off as he inspected his frog.

"Like maybe what?"

"Maybe he wasn't like usual... like... mean." Justin's large wet eyes met Dean's.

"Do you think that *was* your dad, Justin?" Dean asked, crouching so his head was level with the boy's.

"Of course. He brought me my favorite thing." Justin rearranged himself on the bench.

"What's that?"

Justin looked at Dean like he was a complete idiot.

"*Frogs.* What else?"

Sam and Dean got back into the Impala.

"Okay, so the kid's father shows up, hasn't seen him for a while. Guy used to be a dick, now he's bringing Justin a butt-load of his favorite apocalyptic omen? What, the store was out of Super Soakers?" Dean pressed his fingers into his forehead, soothing a building headache. "Who *is* this guy?"

TWO

Later that day, the Impala rumbled its way through the small town of Waubay, South Dakota. Like so many American factory towns, the place seemed mostly deserted.

"Keep your eyes open, we may be walking into Hell's favorite fishing ground," Dean said as they parked. He tucked the shotgun underneath his worn leather jacket.

The brothers walked side by side down the empty streets. The facades of the small mom-and-pop stores were mostly run-down. Paint peeled off the clapboard, giving everything a rag-tag look.

An obnoxiously loud rumble broke the silence, causing Dean and Sam to swivel on their heels, only to see a jacked-up pick-up truck swing around a corner and disappear. No one else was around.

Then someone screamed. The boys looked at each other.

"Where did that come from?" Dean exclaimed, sweeping the streets, wide-eyed. They still seemed to be alone.

They heard another scream. Sam cocked his weapon, aiming at a nearby intersection.

"This way," he said.

The boys took off, their heavy boots pounding the pavement as they turned the corner and heard it again. Sweat ran down their faces as they skidded to a halt in front of—

The Waubay Community Swimming Pool. The pool was empty and several old women were wandering around in bathing caps and large tent-like bathing suits. Dean looked at Sam, who just shrugged.

"What just happened here?" Dean called out, one hand shielding his eyes from the bone-chilling display of geriatric flesh.

Despite his best efforts, Sam was also having trouble dealing with the half-naked old women. He spied a young-looking guy in sweat pants, holding a whistle, and moved toward him.

"Can you tell us what's going on?" he asked.

The guy, whom he assumed must be a swim instructor, squinted at Sam in confusion.

"I have no idea," he said helplessly. "I was giving our regular aquatics class, and the pool just started bubbling."

"Bubbling like… boiling?" Sam asked.

Joining them, Dean smirked.

"You sure one of these lithe young ladies didn't lay one?" he said.

The instructor tilted his head sideways at Dean, a look of surprised irritation Sam had seen directed at his brother with some frequency. Without another word, Dean walked away, wisely leaving the interrogation to Sam.

"Was anyone hurt?" Sam asked, trying to brush past the instructor's annoyance.

"No," the man replied. "No one gets hurt on my watch. It's just like I said: the pool started bubbling, scared the scream out of everyone here. Who are you guys anyway?"

Sam smiled. "Inspectors Antilles and Solo, we're with the NPSS, National Pool Safety Systems. Have you had your filter updated to the latest safety standards?"

"Of course I have," the instructor answered, scowling. "What kind of community pool do you think I'm running?"

Sam took a step back.

"Fantastic, we're always happy to see a dedicated guy like yourself take responsibility. Pool safety is…" Sam trailed off. "…important. I guess. Thanks for your time."

Sam joined his brother, who was interviewing a large woman with a bellowing voice. Dean nodded at Sam's approach.

"Myra, could you tell my partner here what you just told me?" Dean asked.

Myra pulled her robe tighter around her.

"We was just doing our morning routine when the water started getting bubbly," she boomed. "Slowly at first and then more and more, then it got hot. Real hot, but not enough to boil you. The weird thing was, Eunice and me were just saying that the pool was way too cold to be in it."

Sam cocked his head. "Wait, you just said you were cold, then the water got warmer by itself?"

"Uh huh," Myra said, nodding her bathing cap-clad head.

Thanking Myra, Sam and Dean walked away and headed back through town to the Impala.

"There are lots of references to water transformation in the lore," Sam said. "Turning to blood, floods... and boiling."

"So, it's the frickin' Apocalypse, the town is lit up with apocalyptic signs, but they're... jokes?"

"You think it's the Trickster?" Sam gulped. "Gabriel, that is."

"Not a chance," Dean said. "Not his M.O. He's not one to leave survivors, you know?"

"So what is it?"

"I don't know. Is My Little Pony one of the Four Horsemen?"

Dean parked in front of a battered motel. The neon sign read 'Two Pines Motel,' and sported two fluorescent pine trees blinking alternately, so it looked like they were swinging in a stiff wind.

"Oh good, there's a fish cleaning station on the premises," Dean said sarcastically.

"We're in prime walleye country," Sam noted. Dean hopped out of the car and headed for the motel lobby.

Two minutes later, Sam was startled by the *thump* of Dean banging on the hood. A key dangled from a fish-shaped key lug in his outstretched hand.

"Let's go."

Sam pulled his duffel out of the trunk and followed Dean into a wood-paneled, simply appointed motel room.

Dean threw himself onto one of the beds.

"So where do we go from here?" he asked.

Sam pulled out a chair and sat down, tugging his boots off and kicking them underneath the wooden table.

"I guess we see if we can find anything on Justin's father. Only real lead we have."

An hour later, the boys were knee-deep in research. Dean was sprawled out on the bed, his laptop on his chest.

"Don Black's DMV records are clean, so are his credit cards—meaning he doesn't have any. Guy is just a poor schlub trying to make a living."

With a couple of simple clicks, Sam had hacked into the local county records.

"Listen to this. From the family court records, Don Black owed $15,000 to his ex-wife in back child support. Yesterday he paid it all off, in cash. How do you explain that? And I took a look at the auto sales in a hundred-mile radius. Seems yesterday he walked into a dealership and bought a Prius, also using cash."

Dean swung his legs onto the floor.

"Huh. Can't say I can picture a demon driving a hybrid," he said. "Okay, he's the World's Number One Earth-Loving Dad. He's not Lucifer. Let's get the hell out of here."

"Can we at least talk to Justin's mom before we leave?" Sam got up, pulled his boots and coat back on and opened the door.

Dean stayed where he was.

"He just paid her fifteen large in cash, you really think she's gonna sell him down the river?" he asked.

"Best shot we've got," Sam responded.

Dean looked at his brother hesitantly. "Where is she?"

"She works at a restaurant down the road." Sam nodded his head toward the Impala, visible through the open door.

Dean dragged himself off the bed. He gave the room a scornful look as he walked outside.

"As long as it gets us out of this motel. Place smells like Ariel took a dump."

A shrill bell announced their arrival at the diner. The small smattering of locals turned Sam and Dean's way, then quickly went back to their lunches. A pretty redhead stood at the pass-through barking orders at an overweight fry cook.

"Tommy, how many times do I have to tell you, medium rare ain't a bloody cow on a bun," she yelled at him.

"Kathy Black?" Dean queried. "Ex-wife of Don Black?"

"Who's asking?" the redhead demanded, her expression stiffening at the mention of Don. Her reaction was enough to confirm her identity.

"Listen, I don't know where he is," she continued, not waiting for a reply, "but if he owes you money I'm not paying it. And I keep a sawed-off under my pillow in case you have any ideas."

"We aren't loan sharks, ma'am," Sam said. "We just wanted to ask you a couple of questions about your husband."

"As he said, *ex*-husband," Kathy replied pointedly.

"Right, ex," Dean said, stepping in. "My partner apologizes. He doesn't know how to talk to women. Do you know where Don might be?"

Kathy frowned, the wrinkles becoming more pronounced on her otherwise attractive face. Years spent trying to wheedle information out of people had taught Dean a couple of things. *Never* ask questions that are going to waste busy people's time, and *never* piss off an ex-wife.

"You cops?"

Sam shook his head. "No. Not cops."

"'Cause he hates cops."

"So do we," Dean said with a Cheshire-Cat smile. "Do you know if there's some place he likes to hang out?"

Kathy's gaze shifted to one of her tables across the diner.

"Listen, I gotta get that guy back there more coffee—"

"Please," Sam interrupted. "We work at the dealership. My partner forgot to get Don's signature on his new car's registration, and our boss is gonna take it out of my ass—"

Kathy waved at Sam to stop talking.

"Fine. Whatever. If he's around, he's usually at Polly's Bar, down round the corner, beige building on the right."

Sam and Dean thanked her and left.

A few minutes later they were outside Polly's Bar, an ugly old establishment squashed between two uglier buildings. Dean pulled open the door and ducked his head as he stepped through the low entrance.

As his eyes adjusted to the dimly lit room, he made out a narrow dingy-looking interior with a small number of patrons crowded into one corner. A high-pitched, fast-talking voice immediately drew his attention. Dean and Sam crossed to the bar, where a Hawaiian-shirted man was holding court with the townies.

"So then the priest says, 'It can't be my credit card, because I answer to a higher power.'" The townies snorted a laugh. "Okay, next round on me." The man gestured around the bar wildly. "For everyone!"

Dean stood watching, Sam beside him, as the guy took in the small collection of half-hearted whoops and claps that followed.

"I gotta go to the head," the man said, peeling off toward the back of the dark room. He entered the hallway, and his head was ratcheted against the wall with a *thwack.* Dean spun him around forcefully, knocking the wind out of the older man, and shoving his forearm under the guy's chin.

Not to flatter himself, but Dean fully expected the guy to wet himself with terror—especially since he was on the way to the bathroom—but the man merely laughed.

"Hey, if it isn't the Winchester boys!" he cried. "Ease up. Certainly took you guys long enough."

THREE

"Shut it, pal. We know what you are, and we know just how to kill you."

It was a less than accurate assessment, but Dean made sure his words overflowed with confidence. No sense letting on that this particular brand of freak had them stumped. *Has to be a freak*, Dean thought. *Only the freaks recognize us.* The pretense was betrayed by Sam's stifled cough. Dean shot him a look—*Shut the hell up*. There was a reason Dean did the poker hustling in the family.

"Well, we *sort of* know what you are. You're a douche, you're causing problems here, and for us violence is usually the best solution."

"Listen guys, I've been waiting more than a while… in a *bar*… for you to get here," Don said with a bit of edge. "I'm not sure a human bladder can take much more pressure. Can this wait till after I hit the pisser?" He shifted his weight awkwardly back and forth between his legs.

Dean shoved the man roughly into a tattered booth tucked into the furthest gloomy back corner of the bar, far from the prying eyes of the watering hole's patrons. *Don't need any of them sticking up for this guy if things go pear-shaped.*

"Not likely, Hawaii Five-Oh. We've got to sort some things out first." Dean cast a sideways glance at his brother. "Sam?"

With a nod, Sam reached into his jacket pocket for the bag of rock salt, but his hand came out empty.

"*Damn* left it in the car," he muttered. Leaving Dean holding Don hostage in the booth, Sam headed back toward the throng of confused folks at the bar, all no doubt wondering what was happening to their free-drinks ticket. He returned with a handful of salt shakers, which he quickly began to twist open.

Should have brought the rock salt shotguns, Dean thought. *Then we wouldn't have to resort to these cheap tricks.* If Don Black was possessed by a demon, he'd be vulnerable to salt, but it'd take more than a sprinkle. Things would have to get messy.

"If you really were expecting us, you know that we've taken down more than our fair share of your kind." Dean's bravado was reaching fever pitch. "Truth is, baby bro here doesn't even need the salt. He uses his kung-fu grip, your ass is smote back to the pit."

It was clear that all three of them knew he was bluffing. Anyone with a passing familiarity with the Apocalypse knew about Sam's demon-blood addiction and where that dark road had led him.

Don chuckled softly.

"You think… you think I'm a *demon*?" With a bemused look, he lifted one of the salt shakers from the table and upended it, spilling its contents into his mouth. After a moment, he nonchalantly spat the salt onto the table. "Bam."

Well, since he's not choking to death on his own boiling entrails, I guess he's not a demon. Dean considered the situation, but didn't see any other alternative. *Might as well ask the bastard.*

"Fine then. I give. What the hell are you?"

"Hell? That's your problem, Dean. Always looking in the wrong direction." Don reached out and grabbed Dean's chin, and before he could object, tilted it upward.

"Whoa, buddy," Dean snapped, "bad touch!"

In an instant, Sam was holding the blade of Ruby's demon-killing knife to Don's throat.

"You guys aren't great listeners. What is a cursed knife gonna do to an *angel*?"

Sam and Dean shared a stunned look. If Don was telling the truth, he had a point. Without an angelic blade, they might as well be throwing peanuts at him.

"An angel?" Sam asked, slowly pulling the knife away from Don's jugular. "What kind of angel goes around boiling little old ladies and setting off apocalyptic omens?"

A jackass angel, Dean thought, *which doesn't exactly narrow it down.*

"I really did think you'd be here a week ago," Don said sheepishly. "I left plenty of harmless clues. I didn't get to the frogs and the boiling and whatnot until I realized you weren't catching on. Isn't one of you supposed to be smart? A doctor or something?" Sam looked away, a little embarrassed.

"Lawyer, actually. Ain't that right, Sammy?" Dean said, slapping his brother on the back with a smirk.

Don seemed to struggle to hold back his laughter.

"Lucifer's vessel on Earth is a *lawyer*? How perfect is *that*?"

"I dropped out of law school," Sam interjected pointedly. "And I'm nobody's vessel."

"That's the spirit, Sam. Not to mention exactly what I brought you here to talk about," Don said a little too excitedly.

"Next time you want to talk, try calling before you hurt any kids," Sam said.

"Nobody got hurt. It was a bunch of frogs. And it's kind of hard to get in touch with you two, what with the mojo carved into your ribs." Don said, referring to the Enochian Sigil, an ancient and complex pattern that the angel Castiel had burned into Sam and Dean's ribcages as protection against both sides in the Apocalypse: the angels and the demons. Without it, Michael and Lucifer would be on them faster than Dean on a bacon cheeseburger.

"Fair enough," Dean relented. "So what now? You stick the rest of the angels on us, we bolt, and we start this dance all over again tomorrow?" Even as the words came out of his mouth, Dean knew the 'bolting' part wouldn't work. If it came to blows, the odds were in the angel's favor. They weren't leaving the bar unless Don wanted them to.

Don sat up straight.

"Not at all. This has nothing to do with them, and everything to do with helping you."

"Only help we need is keeping off angel radar," Dean growled.

Sam's eyes darted over to meet his. Dean knew that meant only one thing: he was about to cause trouble.

"You said you wanted to talk about me... about being Lucifer's vessel." Sam began, and then paused, as though trying to find the words. "Everyone we've talked to, on *both* sides, acts like it's inevitable. That the battle is between Dean and me."

Don nodded gravely.

"But there has to be another way," Sam said. "There always is."

"You're right. Becoming Lucifer's vessel isn't the only way to end the war; it's just the fastest. I can't guarantee you'll love the alternatives, but they *are* out there."

"Sam, don't let this guy get inside your head," Dean said, worried. "We don't know for sure who he is, and even if he *is* an angel... well, their track record ain't so great."

"Look who's talking," Don responded. "At least *I* didn't bring on the End Times. And Dean, let's not forget about your part in this little dance."

This guy's just as much of an asshole as the rest of the angels, Dean thought. Despite their common reputation as agents of God's will, forces of good, and the gold standard for morality, all the angels Dean had met over the last year had been shifty, manipulative dicks. Except Cass, of course. Castiel had rebelled against the rest of the Heavenly Host when the angels conspired to bring about the Apocalypse.

"Why would you help us?" Sam asked. "Why break from the party line?"

"Fellas, I have a vested interest here," Don said in a low whisper. "I've been cooped up for thousands of years, couldn't even get a weekend off to visit your lovely little corner of the world. Now everything's changed. It's all hands on deck for the Apocalypse, and here I am. In the paradise God made for you." He gestured at the bar. "I *love* it here."

Dean stared the angel down.

"So, what? You want us to keep running? Keep the Apocalypse raging until you've filled up on piña coladas?"

"Not in the slightest. I can show you how to defeat Lucifer *without* becoming the Michael Sword." Don's gaze drifted to Sam. "And without Lucifer playing house inside of Sam. It just so happens that I'd get to stay on Earth as well. Win, win, win."

Dean saw Sam's Adam's apple bob up and down as he swallowed hard. He could see the wheels spinning in his brother's head, trying to work out the possibilities here. All told, Sam was in a much worse spot than Dean. Win or lose, Sam had flicked the switch on Judgment Day, and if the battle between the Winchester brothers did come to pass… Well, either the Devil would win, or Sam would be dead.

"We're gonna need more than that," Dean said. "We've got no reason to believe any of this crap."

"Then let me give you the full picture," Don said, anger brimming in his voice. "I've spent the last few thousand years as a warden with a very high-profile prisoner—until the day you boys let him spring the coop." Don leaned in close, his breath washing over Dean's face. Dean flinched. *Guy should lay off the onion rings.*

"I was stuck in *Hell*," Don continued, "guarding the gates like a good soldier while you were off drinking demon blood and betraying your race. I had to watch souls *screaming* with no reprieve while Satan and his pals tortured them." With that, he gave Dean a knowing look.

Dean felt his blood boil.

"That's enough," he growled, struggling to control himself. He had spent some quality time in Hell, and after experiencing the equivalent of thirty years of torture, he had accepted a bargain... Dean had tortured other souls in exchange for being taken off the rack himself. That moment of weakness had broken the first of the sixty-six Seals that had freed Lucifer.

Don looked over at Sam.

"And you just opened the back door for him," he spat.

Sam's fist clenched around the demon-killing knife. The blade pushed into the table's wooden surface, carving out a deep gouge.

"I *suffered* for my work. For my *creator*. But now that Lucifer's free, there's nothing for me to guard. I get called up here, and what do I find out? God's gone. MIA."

"That's not true," Sam said softly, his eyes on Ruby's knife. He had always had more faith than Dean, but that faith was being sorely tested these days. The archangel Raphael had claimed that God was gone, but how were they really to know? How was anyone—even the angels? If God didn't want to be found, he wouldn't be found. That didn't stop Cass from searching for him (*or her*, Dean thought) across the whole damn planet.

"All that time spent in the pit, you hear things," Don continued, ignoring Sam's quiet riposte. "A lot of truly awful things, but every now and then… a secret. Something Lucifer didn't want me to hear. A tiny clue as to how he can be defeated, earned by years of my suffering."

"Can't be true," Dean said with a gravelly edge. "You'd have told the rest of the angel gang and we wouldn't be having this conversation."

"You don't understand," Don scolded. "Do you think, when all is said and done, that Michael will just *kill* Lucifer?"

"Yes," Sam said grimly. For Sam, that was the central dilemma.

"Then you don't know how Michael's mind works. He's going to defeat Lucifer, and then *humiliate* him. He'll invent a new level of suffering even worse than Hell and stick Lucifer in it to wallow, and *who do you think he'll get to guard it?*" Don was seething now, almost spitting as he spoke. "I'm *not* going back to Hell. Not after living up here."

"And you know how to—"

"Kill Lucifer entirely? Remove the need for there to even be a Hell? Yes." Don was suddenly icy calm, which was somehow creepier than his anger. "I'm gonna give you boys a minute to wrap your brains around all this," he added with a broad smile as he stood up. "Even angels have to pee."

* * *

Sam watched Don disappear into the back hallway of the bar, uncertain if he should try to stop him. At this point, it didn't seem like he was going to run off.

"What the hell was that?" Dean asked, his hands at his temples. He didn't handle information dumps well.

"If it's true—"

"Of course it's not true," Dean interrupted. "You think something like that would slip Cass's mind? That Michael isn't even going to off Lucifer?"

"He's our friend, but he's still an angel. He hasn't always been honest with us before." Sam knew that was hard for his brother to hear—Dean had been growing closer and closer to Cass since the angel had rebelled against Heaven.

Dean squinted at Sam, stupefied. "You're not considering this, are you? Some crazy comes up from Hell and has an offer that's too good to be true? This sounding familiar?"

"Is this about Ruby?" Sam asked pointedly. After all of the work the brothers had done to fix things between them, Sam's relationship with Ruby was still a delicate subject. It would be off limits completely, if anything was off limits to Dean.

"This is about us wanting to get off the hook, to throw the yoke off our backs and let somebody else pull the load."

Dean wasn't entirely wrong, but that didn't change the fact that they needed options. Before they met Don, their choices were either to accept Michael and Lucifer, or to let the world fall apart while they looked on.

"It's not just our Apocalypse," Sam said. "If Bobby came to us with another way to end the war, you'd listen."

"Bobby's different. Bobby's human."

"Who's Bobby?" a voice asked from behind them. It was Don, back from the bathroom. Looking refreshed, he held up his hand to the bartender. "A round for me and my two new friends."

The bartender threw a hardened, distrustful glance at Sam and Dean, then started to pour their beers.

"Bobby ain't on your radar, and he's not gonna be," Dean replied.

Sam leaned toward Don cautiously, trying to extend an olive branch.

"Say we believe you. Say we're even willing to help you. What happens next? Why do you need a couple of humans?"

"Because the book was written for humans," Don responded, as if it was obvious.

"The book?" Sam asked, confused. "I thought you heard this from Lucifer directly?"

"That's right. I heard about the *book* from Lucifer."

"And?" Dean asked, annoyed.

"And what?"

"And what is it?" Dean spat out, the words almost falling on top of each other.

"A manual. A book of strategy, if you like, a... a war guide... A cheat sheet for the Apocalypse."

"Written by?" Dean demanded.

Don grabbed a beer from the bartender's outstretched hand.

"God," he answered.

"And you walked away?! I knew y'all were idjits, I just

didn't know the extent." Dean was always relieved to hear Bobby Singer's voice, no matter how annoyed he sounded. He may not be blood, but he was the only family the boys had left.

"Told him we needed some time to think it over," Dean said, shifting his cell phone away from his ear to protect his hearing from the auditory onslaught. Dean was alone in the fish-scented motel room while Sam had gone out for food. Dean found it hard to think on an empty stomach, and there was no way he was gonna share a meal with Don the d-bag angel.

"I bet you did. Did you also tell him to come and bring me some new damn legs?" Bobby responded with his usual rancor. Dean had forgotten momentarily about Bobby's disability. Bobby had been stabbed by Ruby's knife a few months back and become paralyzed, left to live out the Apocalypse in a wheelchair. It was the worst possible fate for a man who prided himself on being self-sufficient.

"I kept you out of it. The less the angels know about you, the better. For all of us," Dean said.

"What, because I'm a slow-moving target now? I can take care of my damned self, Dean." Bobby's voice cracked slightly, betraying the hardship his impairment had caused.

"I know you can, Bobby," Dean said, and then tried to reroute the conversation back into productive territory. "Do you know anything about this book? It's called *The War of the Sons of Light Against the Sons of Darkness.*"

"Everybody's heard of it," Bobby replied, sounding more like his usual self. "It's a segment of the Dead Sea Scrolls, and one of the most widely read apocryphal texts in

Christendom. Trouble is, nobody's read the ending."

"Why's that?"

"Because it don't exist. When the scrolls went up for sale in '54 there was a big to-do. Somebody broke into the Waldorf Astoria, where they were being auctioned, and the next day they couldn't find the last page, what they called the 'War Scroll.' Lore says it was destroyed... That the Devil didn't like what it had to say."

So much for an easy answer, Dean thought, *But at least Don's story checks out.*

"And the bit he said about it being a field guide to the End Times?"

"More like a field guide to gutting the Devil," Bobby said grimly. "It gets pretty specific. Battle formations, a timeline, you name it. But that last page... how to defeat Satan himself? That could change everything."

"Thanks for keeping expectations low, Bobby. So if it's been destroyed, how does Don the angel lead us to it?"

"Should of asked him instead of storming off, dimwit." There was a pause on the other end of the line. "Could be it wasn't destroyed, just hidden. Put someplace safe where Lucifer knew no one would find it."

"So all we have to do is find something hidden by the Devil himself. Easy peasy."

Dean heard the door open behind him, letting a gust of cold air rush in, rustling the drapes and sending a chill down his spine. He turned to see Sam enter the room, a guilty look on his face.

"Bobby, I've gotta go..."

And then Dean saw him. Don the angel, striding in right after Sam.

"Sam, what the hell's going on?" Dean dropped the cell phone to his side, but could still hear Bobby's tinny voice calling out from the speaker.

"Dean, I'm sorry. Really, I am. But you're not the one that's facing an angel firing squad no matter what he does." Sam tried to hold eye contact with Dean, but the older Winchester looked away. He stared instead at Don, who was still wearing that damn Hawaiian shirt.

"What did you say to him?" Dean asked the angel harshly.

"I told him the truth. That you'll understand it all in time." Don's words were the last thing Dean heard before the sudden, precipitous drop.

Sam awoke to the sound of screaming, terrifyingly close. It was accompanied by the thrashing wails of some sort of otherworldly creature. The noise rattled the air around him, and then gave way to a man's shouting. And was that… music? *What the hell happened?* He was totally alone in a dark, curving hallway, both ends of which were obscured by turns. Coming from one direction was the sound of screaming. From the other, silence. *This is how a hunter's instincts can get you in trouble,* Sam thought as he slowly stood, his legs faltering, and walked carefully toward the maelstrom. *Most people would run away from screaming. Thanks for the death wish, Dad.*

As he rounded the corner, he started at the sight before him. His brother, clearly in a similar state of shock, stood in the flickering light of an old-fashioned movie theater. On the silver screen, a massive squid attacked a submarine while sailors threw harpoons at its colossal eye. Sam reached way back into his childhood memories. *The* Nautilus? *Is that* 20,000 Leagues Under the Sea? Sam was stupefied. *What did Don do to us?*

He saw an exit sign and pushed his stupefied older brother toward it. They stumbled outside and squinted as the afternoon sun temporarily blinded them. Blinking, Sam looked up at the impossibly bright sky and saw the silhouette of a massive building. *The Empire State Building,* he thought. A classic cherry-colored car motored past them, in pristine condition. Happy families strode down the sidewalk, wearing outfits straight out of *Back to the Future.* Sam stared at them. *Something's gone really wrong.*

He looked over at Dean, who looked back at him, an I-told-you-so look on his face.

"Dude. I think that dick sent us back to 1954."

FOUR

The time-travelers stood on the sidewalk, completely stunned. A crowd of women in full skirts, hats and gloves, and men in sharp suits and derbies flowed around them. In their Levi's and leather jackets, Dean realized the Winchester boys looked out of place in the smart corporate landscape, to say the least.

That winged chimp really has sent us back to what looks like New York in 1954, he thought, his brain struggling to process. It seemed Don had dropped them smack dab in the middle of Times Square, but there wasn't a camera-wielding tourist anywhere in sight. The place was also suspiciously clean and quiet, no crumpled piles of paper or garbage, and no blaring rap music emanating from any of the stores nearby.

"First, we get our bearings, then I beat your ass," Dean announced.

"I didn't—" Sam began.

"Don't, Sam. Nothing you can possibly say will make up

for you throwing us under the bus, *again*."

"You're not the only one with a stake in this, Dean. That means, sometimes, you follow *my* plan."

Dean scanned the bustling crowd, wary of continuing this discussion in public.

"Alright, smarty-pants. You wanted to do the time warp again, so what's the next move?"

"We get off the street."

On that point, Dean had to agree with his brother. Trying their best to blend into the crowd, they quickly turned and headed north toward Central Park.

Dean deftly grabbed a *New York Herald Tribune* from a green newsstand that squatted on the corner of 47th and Broadway. Some things don't change, no matter what era you are in; sleight of hand is still sleight of hand. Dean peered at the date: June 26th, 1954. He shook his head. That asshole had shot them back almost half a century without even an explanation of where or how to find the War Scroll.

Despite their predicament, Sam was smiling.

"This is amazing," he said.

"What are you, Buddy the Elf, fresh from the North Pole?" Dean chided. "We've been to New York a dozen times."

"Yeah, but how many times have we been to the *fifties*?" Sam retorted.

"The real fun starts in the sixties."

As they crossed a busy intersection, a man in a trench coat clipped Dean's shoulder.

"Hey, watch it buddy," Dean said with automatic vitriol, but when he looked at the guy, for a half-second he thought he saw the face of Castiel. The man looked up in alarm, and Dean realized his mistake. It wasn't Cass, and they didn't know anyone in 1954. There wasn't a friendly face for miles, or decades for that matter.

The boys were no strangers to angelic time jumps—they had been through this before, when Anna tried to kill John and Mary Winchester in 1978, and when Cass took Dean back to 1973. The past wasn't something Dean liked to visit or even remember, and now he was back. Plus, he was super hungry—another drawback to time travel.

Sam looked over his shoulder at the man in the trench coat, and then back at Dean.

"Dude, this isn't the New York we're familiar with. Try to be a little less conspicuous."

As they left Times Square, Sam took one last look. Rather than the giant three-story-high video screens back in the present day, the streets were lined with theaters and coffee shops. The iconic signs that had made the square famous were mazes of neon. A two-story-high Pepsi Cola bottle-cap sign mooned over the square, which was filled not with mid-western tourists in fanny packs, but a vital post-war workforce eager to create the American dream. The fifties saw the beginning of the consumer society that perpetuated after World War II; buying things created a wealthy America, and the indications were all around them. A Chevrolet sign topped a building, under which was a Canadian Club Scotch

Whiskey sign, and below that was the large-toothed smiling face of Ed Sullivan, hanging off the side of the building in front of them.

Sam grabbed Dean's arm.

"We could go see *The Ed Sullivan Show*!"

Dean looked at his brother scornfully.

"Sam, I'm not hanging around here playing *Mad Men* with you. We get the page from those scrolls, and somehow have Don get us back to 2010. Nothing else."

"I just thought we could take in this once-in-a-lifetime opportunity to see living legends… living."

Dean made his way up Broadway, and Sam followed a few steps behind. Dean took a right at 55th Street, and he seemed to know exactly where he was headed as he crossed the street, dodging in between cars. *Good thing there are no jaywalking tickets in the 1950s,* Sam mused.

Dean pushed in the door to the Carnegie Deli and Sam dutifully followed him inside, knowing there was no point in resisting his brother's appetite.

They slid into a booth looking out onto 7th Avenue. Dean didn't need to look at a menu; this was the only place in the whole wide world where Dean's favorite thing diverged from his usual bacon cheeseburger. A waitress appeared at their table in a full pink skirt edged with white bric-a-brac.

"What can I get you gentlemen?" she asked with a heavy New York accent.

Dean smiled for the first time that day.

"I'll have a pastrami on rye, extra mustard, potato salad, and a root beer, please."

Sam shook his head. *Nothing makes Dean happier than a meal.* He looked up from his menu.

"I'll have the turkey Reuben, light on the Russian dressing, and a side of coleslaw," he said. The waitress nodded and scribbled on her pad.

"Comin' right up," she said and smiled as she left to place the order.

Once she was out of earshot, Dean looked expectantly at his brother.

"Alright, captain. What's the plan?"

Sam had been pondering their next move, but hadn't come up with any bright ideas yet. They knew very little about the location of the War Scroll, only what was publicly available on the internet in 2010. What they did know was that a private sale happened at the Waldorf Astoria Hotel on July 1st—in just five days. But how would they even get close to infiltrating that transaction?

"Well, we could try to get jobs at the Waldorf," he said. "We wouldn't call any attention to ourselves if we actually worked there."

Dean shrugged. Getting a real job wasn't their usual process, mostly they just pretended to be FBI agents, or priests, or CDC inspectors. Doing actual work wasn't part of Dean's *modus operandi.* But, considering the circumstances, they didn't have a choice. They didn't know nearly enough about the time period to successfully pass as government officials.

Their sandwiches arrived, five inches of beautiful meat piled onto freshly baked bread. Dean was beside himself with joy.

Minutes later, Dean was finishing up his pickle and the last bite of his sandwich. As they got up to leave, Dean looked at the check and pulled a ten spot out of his pocket. They walked past the young waitress on their way out.

"Thanks," Dean said, giving her a big smile.

She coyly lilted back. "No, thank *you*."

Dean pulled open the door of the deli and looked back to smile smugly at Sam.

"Looks like Betty Draper has a thing for me."

"You're gonna wanna run, Dean," Sam said with an equally smug look.

Dean looked at him questioningly. Then they heard a woman's voice yelling after them.

"Stop those men!"

They looked back at the waitress, who was holding the very modern ten dollar bill Dean had just put down.

Without a second thought, Sam bolted down the street with Dean a step behind him. They dodged through stalled traffic at the intersection, nearly causing a pile-up when the light turned green.

Moments later they were casually sauntering east on 54th Street.

"To the Waldorf?" Dean asked.

"Guess so," Sam replied. He took out his BlackBerry, intending to Google the hotel's location. Instead, he stared at the mess of jumbled pixels on the phone's LCD. Not only would it have no signal in the fifties, the phone's hardware had been damaged. *Either time travel does a job on electronics, or it broke in the fall*, he surmised. He quickly put it back in his pocket, not wanting to draw any more attention to them with his anachronistic device.

"Hey, what time is it?" Dean asked.

"I don't know, my phone's useless," Sam answered.

"Yeah, mine too. Won't turn on."

Sam shielded his eyes and looked up at the sun.

"Maybe an hour till sunset," he said. "On second thought, let's find a place to crash first. I don't know if it was the time travel or the dine-and-dash, but—"

"But little Sammy could use a nap?" Dean quipped.

"Take a look in the mirror," Sam replied. "The bags under your eyes have bags under their eyes."

"And whose fault is that? You think maybe all of your shenanigans are finally taking their toll on me?"

The brothers continued to bicker until they passed a block of pre-war apartments called the Villard Houses. A sign in front advertised a 'vacancy,' which Sam figured was close enough, and they strolled into the building and up to apartment 3E.

An old woman answered the door, and directed them to take a look at the apartment across the hall. It had clearly once been part of a larger penthouse, but had been walled off into a smaller dwelling with a half kitchen, bedroom and adjoining living room. After years of living in dilapidated motels and the backseat of the Impala, the boys weren't picky. With literally no money to their names—at least any they could actually use—Dean asked the landlady if he could give her the rent at the end of the week. She agreed; she just needed their names. They offered up two aliases. Sam was so tired that he couldn't even place which band they said they came from.

Unfortunately for the Winchesters, the one thing the apartment didn't have was a bed.

"Couldn't we have just stayed at the Waldorf?" Dean said grumpily.

"You think they'd let us pay at the end of the week, genius?" Sam replied. Before Dean could respond, Sam went to the bathroom. He climbed into the claw-footed bathtub and rolled his coat underneath his head. It wasn't nearly big enough for him, but he didn't care.

Within a minute, he was asleep.

FIVE

Barney Doyle's back was killing him. Most boys his age were learning to drive, dating girls, and having fun, but that wasn't a possibility for Barney. His mother had been taken ill, forcing the fifteen year-old to find a job and take responsibility for her care.

There weren't any grown men left in the Doyle's Breezy Point, Queens house—just Barney and his mother. His father had passed away three years before, so when his uncle James had said that there was an opening for another security guard at the Waldorf Astoria, Barney's mother believed it was a sign from Heaven. She was Catholic, of course, and she took her brother's news as an answer to her prayers.

Although he normally hated his job, Barney had been looking forward to today. He and his uncle had taken one of the hotel's trucks and were on their way over to Red Hook to pick up a box that had been shipped over from Israel, or someplace equally exotic.

Barney hadn't paid much attention while he was still in school, so he wasn't quite sure where Israel even was. He knew that it was a new country, and was somehow controversial, especially with his mother. Barney wished he had been better about his studies, not that it mattered now. He was stuck in this job and as far as he could see you didn't need much learning to be a security guard.

When James and Barney arrived at the Red Hook Docks, a worker signaled for them to park at dock thirty-six. The truck bumped its way over the pier. They waited. The diesel engine was spewing exhaust almost directly into the cab, but Barney didn't mind. This was a nice change from the boredom of the hotel.

A large burly guy in a white T-shirt banged his fist on the front of the truck.

"You guys from the Waldorf?"

James pulled his heft out of the truck to answer the guy face-to-face.

"Sure are."

"Sign here," the burly guy said as he shoved a clipboard at James. He signed without reading the form.

Handing it back, he asked, "Where is it?"

The burly guy motioned behind him.

"Carton five. Says it's extremely fragile." he replied, then walked away.

Barney leapt out of the truck to help his uncle with the carton. It was about four feet by two feet wide, made of fresh pine. The pungent tar smell tickled Barney's nose as he bent down to inspect the roughly hewn container.

"Stop dicking around and help me get it into the truck," James growled as he attempted to get his short arms around the base. Barney complied, hastily grabbing hold of his end. "Lift up your side more," his uncle said.

"I *am* lifting," Barney replied, watching as his uncle struggled to negotiate the carton over his stomach. His side was already much higher than James's on account of his height, plus he wasn't nearly as tubby.

Holding the container awkwardly between them, they managed to crab walk around to the back of the truck and the closed back doors.

"Jesus, Mary, and Joseph. Why didn't you open the doors beforehand?" James demanded, breathing heavily.

"'Cause you didn't tell me to," Barney said, staring at his uncle.

"Well, put your side down first and open the door."

Barney squatted, holding his side of the carton. As he got it to knee height, his uncle's grip faltered. The shift in weight distribution caused Barney to lose his hold, and the corner of the wooden crate hit the ground with a heavy thud.

Barney looked up in shock as his uncle swore at the top of his lungs. As he made the sign of the cross over his chest, James simultaneously cursed Barney to Hell.

Barney blushed a deep scarlet. "It's fine, Uncle James. Let's check it. I'm sure it's fine."

They pried a corner of the carton up, and Barney saw that the contents were packed densely with hay. James pushed Barney out of the way and with one hand pulled the rest of the top off. Stuffing his pudgy hand into the hay, he revealed a clay pot. It was tall, burnt orange in color, with a good bit of dirt on it. James wiped away more of the hay, and revealed three more jars.

As James inspected the first jar, its cover slid off the top and onto the ground, landing with a heavy *crack*. A strange, putrid smell emanated from the urn, which reminded Barney of the stench when the pilot light on their gas oven went out.

When his uncle opened his mouth, Barney readied himself, sure that his uncle was going to berate him, despite the accident being his fault. However, before James could start yelling, the oddest thing happened—he choked. It was as if he was vomiting in reverse, with oily bursts of black smoke flying into his mouth and down his throat.

Barney gaped as his uncle reached out toward him, and then everything went dark.

Sam and Dean sat on a hard fake leather couch outside the Waldorf's general manager's office. The rickety side table next to Dean was piled with magazines. He slid one off the top and showed it to Sam.

"Yum. Eva Marie Saint." Dean leered at the picture of the young starlet with her blonde hair swept back, very nicely filling out a blue sweater. "From TV stardom to the movie *Waterfront*," Dean said, reading off the cover.

"She's an old woman." Sam said, rolling his eyes at his brother's incredible capacity for horniness.

"Not now she isn't." Dean almost jumped in excitement. "Marilyn, I want to *meet* Marilyn, do you think she stays here?"

"We didn't travel over five decades back in time so you could sleep with a couple of starlets," Sam replied.

Dean furrowed his brow. "It wasn't my idea to travel here, period. Besides, these women are icons, Sam. Completely different. If we have any free time after we nick the War Scroll, I'm going to find Marilyn."

"Okay, Dean." Sam shook his head.

"Sam and Dean Winchester?"

Dean flinched at the sound of his own name before quickly remembering that Sam had given it to the receptionist when they applied. Apparently, being this far removed from their own time meant that caution could be thrown out the window.

The man who had spoken wore a three-piece suit and was holding open a door that lead into an interior office.

"I'm Ernest Harold, General Support Manager at the Waldorf. Please come in." The man graciously swept his hand toward his office.

Sam and Dean settled into a couple of leather chairs on one side of the man's very messy desk.

"Terribly sorry about the clutter," Mr. Harold said, shuffling some papers around. "I have 200 employees to oversee and I can't seem to manage all the paperwork. As you know, this is a prestigious establishment, with a rich history of providing impeccable accommodations to the most discerning travelers, statesmen and royalty throughout the world."

"And Marilyn Monroe," Dean offered.

Mr. Harold frowned. "The privacy of our clients is of the

utmost importance in this position. You will work closely with people that you see on the silver screen every day. We do not allow any... fraternizing with the hotel's guests."

"Of course not." Sam leaned forward. "We completely understand. My brother is a fan, but he's a very *reserved* fan. Aren't you, Dean?"

Dean smiled tightly. "Yes. Haven't fraternized in months, myself."

"Of course. So, tell me a little about yourselves," Mr. Harold said, leaning back in his chair. "Whatever you would like to share."

This struck Dean as sort of funny—*What could they possibly share with this over-stuffy dope?* He decided to be straightforward.

"Sir. Mr. Harold—Ernest. My brother and I are new in town. And, frankly, we don't have any money. But we are hard-working, strong, and charming. We can do anything you need us to."

The dude seemed to be impressed.

"You remind me of someone," he said, peering at Dean. "Have you been to the pictures and seen *On the Waterfront* yet?"

Dean leaned back, smiling. "Classic Brando."

"Classic? He's a very new actor. At least, I believe he is." Ernest looked confused.

Dean stuttered hastily. "I meant to say a new, classic-*looking* actor."

"Ahh, you're right. I do love a good picture." Ernest swept his hair out of his eyes, then turned his attention to Sam. "And you."

"I'll do whatever you need me to do, sir," Sam said.

"Well, you both are fine fellows." Ernest got up and moved around his desk. "But I have only one position available. Congratulations, Mr. Winchester." He stuck his hand out toward Dean.

"Thank you, sir," Dean said with a smile as they shook hands. "You won't regret it."

"I'm sure I won't. Go see Mable in uniforms. She'll set you up. I have paperwork for you to fill out, but we can do that later. I expect you'll make about twenty dollars in tips—"

Dean nodded. "Not bad."

"—a week," Ernest finished.

He shuffled them out the door.

"Go up these stairs and all the way to the end of the hall. And Sam. Might I suggest you get a haircut? This isn't Amsterdam."

For Dean, it was the perfect end to a perfect interview.

"Sorry Sammy, guess you're too European to work this town. Maybe try again in the 1970s."

Sam shrugged. "I'm going to the public library to see what I can find. Besides, I think you're better cut out for this part of the plan. You know, the mindless labor."

Dean nodded proudly and disappeared into a door marked "Uniforms."

Sam's immediate concern was to find someone in the city who could translate the scrolls. Without Bobby as a resource, and with all of their lore books sitting in the Impala's trunk back in 2010, it would be nearly impossible for Sam to do the translating himself. *Not that I'm entirely sure what language they'll be written in.* Thinking things through, he realized that they were going to need some heavy-duty artillery—it was unlikely the scrolls' owner would hand them over without a fight. Anyway, Sam felt naked without a firearm.

While Sam was contemplating that dilemma, Dean appeared in the doorway wearing a burgundy wool bellhop jacket with golden rope tassels hanging from the sides and gleaming brass buttons down the front. A petit fez perched on his head, with a braided, golden chinstrap pinching his scowling face.

Sam smirked.

Dean stepped past him.

"*Don't* say anything."

That afternoon, Dean found himself lugging a seemingly endless stream of leather suitcases up to various different guests' rooms. He quickly bonded with Rick, the African-American elevator operator, and they were soon discussing baseball as Dean rode between floors.

After a particularly heavy set of bags, Dean was not-so-attentively leaning against the lobby's centerpiece—a large, statuesque clock trimmed in gold leaf—when a girl who looked to be in her mid-twenties approached the front desk. She was wearing a royal blue suit with a pencil skirt, and a pillbox hat that matched her canary-yellow shoes. A cabbie brought a suitcase in and dropped it at her feet. She tipped him elegantly and he bowed his head before heading back outside.

"Ms. Julia Wilder checking in, please," she said to the receptionist. Her brunette hair was pulled back, and Dean noticed with surprise a long scar on the side of her neck.

The young woman turned her head toward Dean, looking him up and down. Her glare was so intense that Dean felt as though she'd just given him the third degree without even speaking a word. She turned her head back to the front desk and demurely pulled her hair over the scar. Dean kept staring, transfixed by her lithe but strong legs and her serious demeanor. *She's hot*, he thought. *Maybe I won't have to track down Marilyn after all.*

Dean sidled up to her, completely forgetting he was supposed to be working.

"Hi," he said giving her the full-on hundred-watt Dean Winchester smile.

The girl ignored him. Had she known more about Dean, she wouldn't have bothered.

"You here for business or pleasure?" he asked. "Or just to see the big clock?"

She looked at him. "May I help you?"

"No. But I could help you," Dean whispered. "Maybe I could buy you a drink?"

"I don't think so."

"You here with your husband?" Dean probed.

"I'm not here to socialize. I'm here for an auction."

"Dead Sea Scrolls?" Dean asked without thinking.

She squinted at him.

"No," she said.

"Excuse me, boy," interjected the desk clerk. "Are you going to get the lady's bags?" He eyed Dean with venom.

"Of course." Dean bent down, but before he could grab

the suitcase, Stevie, a smelly kid from New Jersey who wore his bellhop pants a little too tight in Dean's opinion, swiped the bag and placed it on a cart. He wheeled away, Ms. Wilder striding behind him.

Dean stood by the reception desk shell-shocked, though still alert enough to salute when Ms. Wilder turned to take one last look at him before entering the elevator. It was rare for a woman to truly grab his attention as she had. Of course, he'd faked interest plenty of times; it used to be a hobby of his while he and Sam were in between cases. Dean would bet himself just how many minutes it would take him to convince the bartender, waitress, or lonely female patron into his bed. Dean's belt notches were many. But this girl… this girl seemed special.

Not far away, Sam sat in the main branch of the New York Public Library. Rows of shelves lined every inch of the room; thousands upon thousands of books, and not an Internet connection in sight. Sam didn't mind doing the research, but Google had become his crutch, and he felt handicapped without it.

First he pulled a series of books on archeological digs, but found very little information. After trawling through the card catalog, he decided to look at the archived New York newspapers. The scrolls, Sam remembered, had been first discovered in 1947, so there must be at least one article somewhere that could lead them to a contact. After fruitlessly pouring over several months' worth of broadsheets, Sam was flipping through a June 1st *Wall Street*

Journal when he spotted a small ad in the classified section:

Four Dead Sea Scrolls, Biblical Manuscripts. Would
make an ideal gift to an educational or religious
institution.

The ad gave a local number and an address, which Sam
jotted down on a scrap of paper and slipped in his pocket.
That was as solid a lead as he was going to find on the
scrolls themselves—now they just needed a translator. He
wished that Don had briefed them a little more thoroughly
before the unceremonious time-jacking. Sam regretted going
behind Dean's back to talk to the angel, but at the time, there
seemed to be no other choice. The secret fear that Sam had
been carrying around since they got to 1954 was that they
would never find their way back. What if they were unable to
procure the War Scroll—would Don just leave them to rot?

Without occult books to refer to, Sam was limited to
commonly available biblical texts. *I don't even know Don's real
name*, Sam realized. *All I know is his job description: guardian of
Hell's gates.*

Luckily, that was all he needed.

Flipping through an especially old book, Sam found a list
of angel names and one in particular stuck out: Abaddon,
Guardian of the Gates. *Don, Abaddon—has to be the same
guy*, Sam thought. Further down the page, the book traced
Abaddon's motley history. Scholars couldn't seem to decide
on the angel's true nature, some believed that he was among
the most powerful of the Heavenly Host, others claimed he

was fallen and in league with Satan. In fact, in some places, Abaddon was used as an alternate name for Hell, and even the Devil himself. *Great*, Sam thought.

For the moment, Sam decided that he wouldn't share those particular juicy details with Dean. *I'm in enough hot water with him as it is*, he figured. But, to be safe, he discreetly tore the relevant page out of the book and slid it into his pocket, alongside the scrap of paper with the information from the advert. If it turned out that Don had less than angelic intentions, Sam wanted to be ready.

Dean tugged at the chinstrap on his hat. He needed a break. Mercifully, the lobby was quiet and the dickhead front desk guys were engrossed in their work. He made his way downstairs and threaded his way through the halls under the building, finally reaching a set of steel doors. Throwing caution to the wind, he swung them open.

A hotel security guard stood on the other side with his back to Dean, and a box truck idled outside the loading dock. The man was tubby and middle-aged. He turned around slowly, looking as if he'd been caught committing a crime.

Dean politely nodded a greeting. "Guess I'm lost," he said. "Where's the little boys' room?"

Instead of answering out loud, the man simply pointed back the way Dean had come.

"Great," Dean said. He was about to call off his reconnaissance mission, when he saw what the security guard had been hovering over—it was a simple wooden crate, damaged on one end, covered in strange characters. *Probably worth getting a better look at,* Dean decided. "Actually… I think I can hold it," he said. "I'm gonna get some fresh air."

Under the guard's watchful eye, Dean maneuvered his way past the crate and to the edge of the loading dock, but he wasn't able to get a better look at the contents. *Damn security goon and his thighs,* Dean thought. He jumped off the loading dock and walked down the alleyway, rounding the corner onto Park Avenue, then stopped.

Hebrew? Could the lettering have been Hebrew? By pure chance, he may have just come impossibly close to the scrolls, and he couldn't pass up such an opportunity—even if that meant beating the ass of a civilian. He turned around and started back to the loading dock.

James peered inside the truck. Barney's crumpled body was pushed to one side on the floor, his neck twisted at an unnatural angle. The sight of his nephew's corpse prompted no reaction in James. If anything did, it was the smell. *Meat,* James thought. *Still fresh.*

James turned and grabbed a black rubber hose attached to a waterspout. He turned on the water and sprayed down the inside of the truck. The water ran pink as it flowed out and over the bumper. He turned off the hose and pulled Barney's body onto the dock. Then he picked the body up easily with one hand, opened the top of the crate and pushed it inside.

Clunking the crate closed, James wheeled the carton into the back of the Waldorf Astoria.

It's still safe, he thought with pride. *She'll be pleased with me.*

Holding onto his stupid bellhop hat, Dean hurried back down the alleyway. He slid back around the corner just as James disappeared into the hotel. With finesse, he jumped onto the dock and banged through the steel doors.

The security guard and the carton were gone.

After a couple more unproductive hours at the library, Sam decided to stop off at the new apartment; he wanted to call Dean. As he fiddled with the key in the lock, he noticed out of the corner of his eye one of their neighbors walking toward him down the hallway. He half-nodded a greeting as the young woman brushed past him in the narrow corridor, briefly glancing up to admire her petite dark-haired figure as she moved away from him, before carrying on fiddling with the stubborn lock.

Finally there was a click as the key connected with the mechanism and Sam managed to get the door open. By this point his mind had wandered far from the mission at hand to fantasies about living a normal life—one that held room for girls and movie dates and romantic dinners. It all came crashing back as he took in the sight before him. The apartment had been completely ransacked.

Sam wondered how, after being in 1954 for less than twenty-four hours, he and Dean had already made an enemy.

SIX

No sulphur, Sam noted, sniffing the air. *It wasn't a demon.*

He kicked at the shards of glass that littered the scummy tile floor of the apartment's tiny bathroom. The intruder had been thorough, upending or smashing just about every object in the small space that wasn't built into the floor. *They even smashed the toilet*, Sam realized. The bathroom mirror had also been broken, which accounted for all the glass on the floor. *Just what we need*, he thought, *more bad luck.* Sam closed the water valve leading to the sputtering half-toilet.

It wasn't like there was much to steal. They had been whisked through time with only the clothes on their backs and the contents of their pockets. *Who had done this? Were there angels here too?* Sam wondered, a nervous chill running through him.

He felt helpless. Lost in an unfamiliar time and place, with all his usual tools unavailable to him, and the end of the world in sight. *Because of me*, he remembered. *I did this.*

My fear, my weakness, brought on the end for everybody. In these moments, when the guilt overwhelmed him, and images of the billions who would die filled his mind, Sam craved the blood. It didn't make any sense. Demon blood had given him strength, but it had also clouded his judgment. It had made him turn his back on Dean, the only person who could ever truly understand Sam's situation.

It had made him start the Apocalypse.

Despite all of that, Sam craved it for one simple reason: it made him feel powerful. The demon blood unlocked something deep within him, something that had been left there by Azazel, the yellow-eyed demon who had killed their mother, Mary Winchester, and marked Sam as part of his growing army of special, part-demonic children. Sam was the only one left alive. *Was that why I was chosen to be Lucifer's vessel? Because Azazel made me this way? Because I was the most special of the special? Or simply because I survived?*

Sam moved cautiously back to the main room, pushing those uncomfortable thoughts from his mind. The lock on the front door didn't show any signs of being forced, though it had been difficult to open. Sam was definitely paranoid enough to have checked the locks in both the door's handle and the deadbolt when he left a few hours earlier. He scanned the main room of the apartment for other entry points. There was a small, metal-barred window overlooking the street.

Looking down, Sam saw the bustle of a New York street at midday. The window was high enough up that it would take a ladder and some patience to get to it, making it unlikely someone would be able to break in without attracting attention. Not that Sam was sure the good people of New York would bat an eyelash at broad-daylight larceny, but the window's metal bars were still firmly in place.

Attached to the main room was a small kitchenette, much like the ones in motels that the Winchesters had become intimately familiar with over the last few years. *Scratch that*, Sam thought, *I've become familiar with*. Dean never, ever cooked... unless you counted assembling bread and shoplifted deli meat as cooking. Even when they were kids and Dean was ostensibly the caretaker, Sam had had to fend for himself.

Inside the kitchenette was a window, taller than the one in the living room, and covered by a garish red curtain. Pushing the curtain aside, Sam saw the rusted metal of a fire escape. Mystery solved.

Put bars on the inaccessible window, but don't even put a lock on the fire escape? Different time, Sam thought. The question now was the motivation for the break-in. Sam and Dean didn't look rich, or important. *Could someone already know about us? About our mission here?*

Sam briefly considered keeping the burglary to himself and avoiding Dean's inevitable freak-out. The boys had spent a considerable portion of their time together on the run—from law enforcement, vampires, shapeshifters, demons, Hellhounds... and now the forces of Heaven. Knowing they were being followed after less than a day in 1954 wasn't going to go over well.

Sam reached for his BlackBerry, realizing again as he did

so that it wouldn't work. *Living without technology is a bitch. How did Don Draper do it?* But calling Dean wouldn't have been an option anyway, since his BlackBerry wasn't in his pocket.

It was the one thing he had left in the rented apartment, knowing that it would be useless in 1954. *Stupid*, he berated himself. It was a rookie mistake, one his father would never have made. Sam checked his other pockets, finding his wallet intact alongside a pack of gum. Reaching into his jacket pocket, Sam's heart sank. Something else was missing, and it was a much bigger deal than a useless cell phone.

Ruby's knife.

The one weapon the boys had had with them had vanished from the inside pocket of Sam's jacket somewhere between the library and the apartment. It was, as far as Sam and Dean knew, one of a kind.

And now it was gone.

Dean may not have been the smartest Winchester, and he certainly wasn't the one you wanted to help translate an ancient document, but after years of digging through yellowed lore books, he had picked up a few things. He knew, for example, that when he saw crazy-ass lettering, he was better off calling Sam than trying to figure it out himself. Dean figured his value came more from his 'give 'em hell' attitude than from his G.E.D.

The symbols on the side of the crate certainly fell into the 'crazy-ass' category. Was it Hebrew, or something older? *A crate with biblical text on it getting dropped off at the Waldorf? This is almost too easy*, Dean thought. All he had to do was follow it to its destination, grab the scroll, and get clear of the place before any more hot girls saw him in his embarrassing monkey suit.

Trouble was, Dean had already lost the crate. The workman who had delivered it must have slipped into the service elevator while Dean was sorting all of this out in his head.

He hurried along the loading dock to the service elevator's oversized doors. As he reached out to press the 'down' button, assuming that's where the crate was headed, the doors sprang open.

"A lot of guests need their luggage taken to the loading dock?" asked the mustached man who was waiting in the elevator. Dean recognized him as one of the asshole desk clerks from upstairs.

"Uh, yeah, lady wanted to see the…" Dean trailed off, looking around the poorly lit dock for anything that could possibly interest a guest, "the place where we keep the carts." He gestured weakly toward a line of derelict luggage carts parked in the corner.

The clerk stared hard at Dean for an excruciatingly long moment, then cracked a wry smile.

"Kind of an unspoken rule that we wait until our shift's over, buddy," the man said, patting Dean on the back. "If a lady wants to see your, uh, *cart*, she'll still wanna see it after you're done working." He pulled Dean into the elevator by the shoulder, but Dean resisted.

"Maybe give me a minute here?" Dean asked.

"You got a phone call. Your dad."

Dean shrugged the man's hand off his shoulder and forced open the closing elevator doors. John Winchester had been dead for years, or, depending on how you looked at it, was not even born yet.

"My *what?*" Dean demanded, suddenly deadly serious.

"Or brother? Or your cousin? I don't know. Some guy. Sounded kind of annoyed. And annoying, for that matter." The man pulled Dean's hand off the elevator door, which continued to close. "And here's a pro tip. Don't actually try anything on those carts. You'll end up rolling all over the place, the lady will bonk her head, and it'll be all tears and whining for the rest of the night. Trust me."

It wasn't a dignified position to be in, but Sam didn't have a choice. He was on his hands and knees, clawing around the base of the phone booth for dropped change. He had only had a few coins, and Dean was taking his sweet time to get to the phone. *Probably got distracted*, Sam thought. *If he's with a woman...*

"Sam, that you?" a voice sounded through the phone.

"Dean! I've been waiting a—"

"Yeah, 'bout that, couldn't you have waited a little longer to check in on me, Mom? Made me lose a lead on our scrolls."

"I'm not checking in," Sam said, aggravated. "I thought you'd want to know we got robbed."

"We? I didn't get robbed. All I own here is this stupid hat, and I sure as hell still have that."

"Our apartment was broken into—"

"What?"

"They tore the place apart." Sam started to pace with the phone, then realized there was only a foot of space for him to move either way in the booth. He suddenly understood why cordless phones had been invented.

"Calm down, big guy. You sound a little pissed." Dean said, lowering his voice.

"They took… my BlackBerry."

"Yeah, that's rough Sammy," Dean said, obviously faking sympathy. "Seriously though, who the hell cares? Who you planning on texting in 1954?"

"You don't get it," Sam responded. "They took my 2010 phone, full of 2010 technology, meaning we could have a serious *Back to the Future II* situation."

"What, so Biff is going to steal our Delorean?"

"No, we could seriously alter the timeline. Introduce things now that aren't supposed to exist for decades—"

"Am I gonna have to kiss Mom?" Dean said, his smirk evident even over the phone.

"Dean." Sam knew he had to break Dean out of his streak or he was going to be hearing Marty McFly jokes for the rest of the day. "Please."

"Fine. Remember what Cass told me, though—whatever we do, that's what happened. We can't change history, we can just live in it for a bit. We break something, it was always broken, that's how it was—always."

"Cass told you that because he was trying to prove a point. Why would Don send us back if we couldn't change anything?" Sam asked. "If the scroll really was destroyed in 1954, we *are* going to change that."

"Well don't count on the d-bag coming by to clarify any of it."

"There's something else," Sam admitted. "Whoever broke in was thorough. Not just a smash and grab job."

"So they were motivated. Had something particular in mind," Dean said.

"Could someone have overheard us, someone else who wants the scroll?"

Dean exhaled loudly. "This is gonna be harder than I thought."

"In 2010, the last thing I loaded on the phone was the Wikipedia page for the scrolls. Probably no one will ever be able to recover it. But what if they can? What if there is someone out there—"

"Who is a technological genius fifty years ahead of their time, and *also* cares about the scrolls? I don't think so," Dean said.

Sam was silent. He knew he had to tell Dean the rest of the story, but couldn't face letting his brother down. Finally, he gulped down a breath and bit the bullet.

"There's one more thing that's missing. Ruby's knife."

"Damn it, Sam—"

"I know," Sam replied, trying to head off Dean's inevitable tirade.

"You left the knife in the apartment? What were you *thinking*? I thought *I* was supposed to be the dumbass?"

"I didn't leave it. Someone must have taken it off of me."

"What, so now we have ninjas after us?" Dean asked, exasperated.

"There was this girl, in the hallway…" Sam trailed off, letting Dean's imagination fill in the rest.

"That's just perfect. I mean, we've been porked before, but this takes the cake." Dean took a breath. "Sammy? You there?"

"Yeah, Dean. I'm here."

"With or without the knife, we gotta move forward," Dean said, then added in an undertone. "This crate I saw, it had a bunch of markings on it, I think in Hebrew."

"Sounds right."

"My point is, if the package is in Hebrew, imagine what language the scroll itself will be in—"

"You're just thinking of that now?" Sam chided. "According to the books I found, similar texts from that region and time period were written in early Herodian square script, but that's more the symbology than the language. The language would be Aramaic."

"Save it, Dan Brown. My point is, how are we gonna read this thing?"

"I'm working on it," Sam said. "Let's worry about finding the scroll first."

"Good chat, Sam," his brother responded, an edge in his voice. "I'll try to track down the scroll before the Hamburglar catches up with me. Try not to lose your pants."

"Wait," Sam spat out, "when are we meeting up?"

"Meet me back here when my shift ends. Eight o'clock."

Sam heard Dean hang up.

He stepped out of the phone booth and back into the swirling storm of people outside. *I guess Dean can handle himself for a few hours*, Sam thought, turning south, away from the Waldorf and back toward the library.

Two hours later, Sam was no closer to speaking Aramaic. Being in one of the biggest libraries in the world, the texts were certainly available, but the language was far more complex than Sam had imagined. Without help, it could take months to get an accurate translation.

I wonder if Bobby knows Aramaic? It wasn't that crazy a notion, since a large portion of the biblical lore books that Bobby studied were in ancient languages. *Not that we have Bobby here*, Sam thought. For a brief moment, he considered looking up the Singers in the phone book. Bobby was born in the fifties; it was possible that at that very moment an infant Bobby was first learning to scowl.

Sam again wished that he had gotten more information from Don before being sent back. What were they supposed to do once they found the War Scroll? Translate it in the past, or hide it *Bill & Ted*-style for their future selves to find?

The boys didn't often get a chance to plan ahead, so when the opportunity presented itself, Sam decided he was going to take it. He found a phone book in the lobby and used his last ten cents to call the American Bible Society—apparently it was home to the greatest concentration of biblical texts outside of the Vatican. It was as good a place to start as any.

SEVEN

The benefits of Dean's job were manifold. The women he helped to their rooms were uniformly stunning, from which Dean surmised that even in 1954, enough money could buy you beauty. They were also generous. The twenty dollars a week the manager had quoted turned out to be on the very low end. Dean had no idea how much his tips could actually buy, but he imagined it was a lot. He wondered if most people knew such arcane facts—had Dean been out hunting demons on the school day when the kids learned about inflation rates?

The most obvious benefit to the job was access, but that was also the downside. He was tantalizingly close to the scrolls, but he was now under the close supervision of the more dickish of the two desk clerks. After several hours of work, he still hadn't been able to venture down to the vault.

His opportunity came shortly after sunset, when the clerk finally left the front desk. Dean pushed his luggage cart into the elevator and asked Rick to leave it on the top floor, hoping that nobody would come looking for him this time. Slipping into the employees-only corridor that led away from the ornate lobby, Dean marveled at how quickly the hotel went from world-class to low-class. Water stains ran down the cheap wallpaper, bringing to mind the Winchesters' usual stomping grounds. While Dean enjoyed the change of pace that the Waldorf represented, the drab familiarity of the hallway helped put him in hunting mode.

Not taking a chance on the service elevator being in use, Dean took the back stairwell. Calling it dank would be an understatement. The bare-bulb lighting was hardly enough to see by, but probably helped cover up the unfortunate state of the stairs themselves.

Toward the base of the stairwell, he heard a low scraping noise and slowed his pace. It sounded like something was being dragged across unfinished cement.

"My God, I…" intoned a man's voice, before fading to a murmur. Glass clinked against glass, followed by the sound of a bottle slowly pouring out its contents.

Dean padded down a few more steps and craned his head around the corner. He was glad, for once, that Sam wasn't stomping his heavy feet beside him. There were advantages to being the less muscle-bound Winchester. Despite that, the stair he was perched on felt less than stable.

"I didn't mean to do it," the man said, his voice full of quiet desperation. "You know I would never…"

Leaning forward as he listened for a reply, Dean nearly slipped off the crumbling concrete step, and pieces of the slab skittered downward. The voice stopped and moments later Dean heard feet pounding away from him. *Crap*, he swore under his breath, the noise had clearly spooked the man enough to send him running.

Dean slammed his shoulder through the doorway into the sub-basement hallway, sending a radiating pain through his arm that probably wouldn't go away for a week. The man hadn't gotten far, having slipped to the ground less than ten feet from the stairwell.

"Whaddaya doin', trying to… ugh," the man said, gulping down air. "Trying to give me a coronary?"

"Slow your roll, dude," Dean answered as he approached. The man's face was flush and covered in sweat, and Dean recognized him immediately as the guard who had brought the War Scroll crate into the Waldorf earlier. He also recognized the bottle of Wild Turkey that was upended and dripping onto the cement floor. "Hard day, I take it," he said, leaning in to read the man's ID badge. "Mr. McMannon?"

The man shuddered back a sob and lifted the bottle to his lips to swill down what hadn't spilled.

Dean inclined his head at the sorry sight. "Been there."

Was it possible that this mess of a guy was responsible for guarding the vault? If so, it was just a matter of keeping him acquainted with that bottle. Dean had no qualms about robbing a passed-out drunk.

"Hasn't been a great few days for me, either. Hell, hasn't been a great decade," he said.

Lumbering to his feet, McMannon gave Dean a wary look.

"Decade just—" he began, then hiccupped, "started." Clearly, the guard wasn't ready for a heart-to-heart with an intrusive bellhop.

Dean gave him his best car salesman grin.

"How 'bout I get us another bottle?"

James McMannon was in control of himself for the time being. He couldn't exactly recall how he had come to be in the sub-basement, or even what day it was, but at least he felt in control.

He watched the bellhop scurry back up the stairs to get another bottle. Something about the man—was it his smell?—was unsettling. James briefly considered killing him when he returned, but quickly banished the thought. *Why would I do that? Why would I even think it?* It was then that the image popped back into his mind: his nephew, Barney, head hanging like a rag doll's, his eyes totally lifeless.

Where had he seen that? Was it a terrible dream? Deep down, a part of James knew that he had done an unspeakable thing—but that part of his brain was currently drowning in Bourbon. At any rate, it wasn't James that had killed Barney; it was the strange animal living inside him, and that animal seemed to be, for the moment, asleep.

He shook his head to banish the strange thoughts. Now where was that kid with the new bottle of whiskey?

Paranoia was deeply ingrained in the hunter lifestyle, and Sam Winchester had been checking for tails since he was five years old. Walking through the maelstrom of mid-town

Manhattan was proving to be unimaginably difficult for him, especially with the knowledge that he'd been followed once that day already.

Double back, wait a few minutes, then keep moving, Sam repeated to himself over and over. It was his father's mantra, and it was clearly designed for small town America, not the overflowing streets of New York City.

The towering brick building that housed the American Bible Society was located at 57th Street and Park Avenue, a few blocks north of the Waldorf. Sam had resisted the temptation to check in on his brother while walking past, but he was still feeling the frustration of living without a cell phone. He imagined Dean had already made another attempt to get near the scroll, but it would be a few hours before his shift was over and Sam could find out for sure.

Sam's contact was waiting for him in the Society's front lobby. He was a well-built man stuffed into a suit that was too small for him. His thin necktie accentuated the unflattering fit. His arm was in a canvas sling, leading Sam to wonder what sort of trouble the man had gotten himself into.

"Mr. Sawyer?" Sam asked.

The man nodded and gestured toward a set of chairs.

"Please, call me Walter. Have a seat. Can I get you a drink?"

Before Sam could respond, Walter dropped ice cubes into two tumblers and poured amber liquid into each one.

"I regret I couldn't be more helpful on the telephone," Walter said as he handed Sam his drink. "I'm not sure I understand what you're looking for."

"I'm not sure either, not yet. I'm in the process of buying a religious relic, something of family interest—"

"You're Jewish?" Walter interrupted with a slight squint.

"No, it's not… not that, exactly."

Walter knocked back his drink absently, his attention fully on Sam.

"But you mentioned something about Hebrew relics, Old Testament manuscripts." He paused for a moment, his eyes asking the obvious question. "If you don't mind my asking, what's the 'family interest'?"

"In-laws," Sam said with a shrug.

The scholar seemed to accept that, for the moment.

"And once you have acquired the documents, you'll need them interpreted."

"Translated," Sam corrected. "I think biblical interpretation is best left to the individual."

Walter pulled a crooked half-grin. "Fair enough." He brushed a lock of his unkempt brown hair from his forehead. "Does this have something to do with the Dead Sea Scrolls?"

Sam was careful to keep his face neutral. "What do you know about the scrolls?" he asked.

"They're the most important historical discovery of the century," Walter said with precise, almost rehearsed diction, as if he had said it many times, to many people. "Any century, really. Though whether people accept that is a different matter entirely."

"It's not the first apocryphal Old Testament text," Sam replied, studying Walter's reaction.

"Apocryphal. What makes it any less relevant than Genesis or Revelations? Or Matthew, Mark, Luke and John, for that matter?" Walter spat with thinly veiled distaste.

"Have you read them? The scrolls?"

Walter didn't respond immediately, instead he looked into Sam's eyes as if he was passing judgment, determining whether he was worthy of sharing what he knew of the scrolls.

"No."

Sam forced a smile and took a sip from his very strong drink. *Straight whiskey*, he realized. At least it was afternoon. As he set the glass on the nearby end table, he noticed a red blot seeping across Walter's canvas sling.

"Your arm alright?" he asked, indicating the bloody stain.

Walter glanced at it carelessly. "Ah. I should really be more careful on the subway," he said, and stood up. "Let's go to my office and talk about the scrolls."

The sub-basement of the Waldorf Astoria was spinning around Dean Winchester. His head was rested against the cushion of a tall-back chair, his feet propped up on the security desk outside the hotel's vault. His sobriety was long since gone.

"You think you've had a crap week, let me tell you something, James," Dean said, gesturing wildly with an almost-empty bottle of vodka, the only liquor he had managed to swipe from the bar upstairs. "I come from… the future."

For his part, James wasn't listening to a word of Dean's

rant. He was far more than three sheets to the wind, his pudgy cheeks and eyes were both red, his eyelids drooping with exhaustion.

"The friggin' future, man."

James studied his hands intently, as if they were part of somebody else's body.

"We have this thing, the internet, it's like porno city. Anything you want. What are you into, man? Asians? They've got Asians," Dean said with a knowing look. *Boy* did they have Asians.

James's head drooped toward the floor. Dean, realizing that this was his moment, shut up and watched for any sign that James would snap out of it. Instead, he dropped to the floor entirely, his girth hitting the concrete with a slap.

"Gonna feel that tomorrow," Dean said as he moved toward the vault door. In his inebriated state, he stumbled over James's legs and nearly face-planted himself.

The vault was like that of a small bank, with a heavy combination-locked door which no doubt lead into a room full of safety deposit boxes. Dean knew that breaking into the main vault would be relatively straightforward—after all, he had a bit of experience in that regard—but finding the War Scroll inside might prove trickier. He'd seen James bringing the large crate in earlier, but he had no idea how big the scroll itself was, or whether it had been filed into an individually locked safety deposit box.

As he listened to the tumblers on the main door click into place, he heard James twitch on the floor. *Poor bastard*, Dean thought, *seems like he's got enough problems as it is. This ain't gonna help*. Not that Dean knew what James's problem was, since he hadn't been particularly chatty during their marathon drinking session.

After a few minutes, the heavy door swung open. All of Dean's fears about finding the scroll were immediately relieved, as the center of the vault was filled with several large jars. They looked to be thousands of years old, and each was capped with a lid inscribed with symbols. Dean moved quickly toward them. He lifted the lid off the nearest jar, to find, to his surprise, a shape was carved onto the inside of the lid—a rudimentary Devil's Trap. The holy symbol that could contain a demon.

Before Dean could react, a throaty growl sounded behind him.

James McMannon stood outside the vault, totally sober, his eyes jet black. While Dean took a heartbeat to consider how totally screwed he was, James charged.

EIGHT

Despite his considerable heft, James's possessed body moved with the speed and lightness of a man half his weight. His meaty hand grasped Dean's neck as he slid him off his feet and up against the wall of the vault. Dean's feet strained for the solid floor, his toes dangling inches above the cement.

James looked at Dean with a discerning eye, as though he had just discovered a brand-new species of insect. He rolled Dean's head from side to side as Dean gasped for breath.

"Listen buddy," Dean managed to choke out. "I know you're super glad to get into a new meatsuit—though frankly you could have picked someone in better shape. How 'bout you leave the poor shmuck alone?"

James brought Dean's face close to his own and *sniffed* him.

"Whoa, guy, I'm not into the kinky stuff," Dean

squawked, noticing the wild look in the man's eyes. "This is a little too *Mutual of Omaha's Wild Kingdom* for me. How about you let me go?"

With a swoop of his arm, James threw Dean clear out of the vault. He sailed over the ramshackle table outside and hit the concrete wall, head first. He slumped to the ground, consciousness fading quickly. The last thing Dean heard before blackness took him was a howling, ferocious *bark*.

When Dean woke up, the asshole desk clerk was looming above him. Dean turned his head with difficulty. He noticed the vault was closed and James McMannon was nowhere to be seen.

Dean lifted his arm to the desk clerk. "Can I get a little help?"

"You're fired. Return your uniform and get out."

Dean managed to lift himself up on one elbow.

"You mean I don't get to keep this cute little hat?"

The desk clerk sneered, turned, and walked away.

Dean felt the goose egg on the back of his skull. *So much for working from the inside.*

As he got to his feet, Dean had to brace himself against the wall. He stumbled a little—he hadn't been unconscious quite long enough for all that vodka to metabolize.

After returning his bellhop monkey suit, Dean stumbled out onto the dark sidewalk. The sun had set, but when? How long had he been out? His watch had stopped when he came to in 1954, and he hadn't managed to get it going again. He looked both ways, trying to figure out which direction the apartment was. Then he heard the quick clip of shoes on the sidewalk. Two NYPD officers were quickly approaching him, and that couldn't be good news. Dean spun on his heels and tried to cross the street, but the officers quickly grasped both his arms.

"Had a little too much to drink did you, guy?"

Dean looked at them, a tad bleary-eyed.

"Not at all officers. I just woke up. Had the most wonderful night with Marilyn Monroe. She's a hell cat."

"We should let DiMaggio have a bat at your face for that one," said one of the officers, as the other hailed a paddy wagon.

When it arrived, they shoved Dean roughly into the back of the vehicle and sped away.

By the time Sam got to the police station, Dean had been sitting in a cell for a couple of hours. The station chief led Sam down into the holding cells beneath the old building, where he discovered his brother sitting contently on a clean bunk drinking coffee and playing poker with his cell mate, a guy in a rumpled suit who looked like his three-martini lunch had got out of hand. Dean jumped up when he saw Sam.

"You have ten bucks on you?"

"Dean, I can't use any of my money. It's useless."

"Exactly, so give me a ten," Dean whispered, indicating the guy behind him.

Sam dug in his pockets and pulled out a bill. Dean took it and threw it down on the ground between the cots.

"I'll see your five and I'll raise you five," Dean said. He then sat back against the wall.

"Too rich for my blood," the guy said.

"Guess the pot is mine then." Dean pulled a pile of change and bills toward him. "Thanks for a good game."

The guard unlocked the door.

"Thanks Joe, keep up the good work." Dean smiled at Sam as he held up his winnings in 1954 dollar bills.

The boys made their way out of the station.

"Nice going with staying under the radar, Dean."

"I didn't have a choice. I was *this* close to nabbing the scroll. And news flash! McTubby the guard wasn't any regular guard. He was possessed by a demon, and now he's on the loose. And it really doesn't help that you lost Ruby's knife."

They stepped out onto the street.

"Wait, what do you mean he was possessed?"

"You know, black eyes, super-human strength, the whole shebang, right here in 1954."

"What did he want?"

"To eat my liver? How should I know?"

"Well, did he say anything?"

Dean paused, trying to remember. "He didn't so much talk, as… bark."

"What, like a dog?" Sam asked, amused. When Dean's facial expression remained stony, he realized it wasn't a joke. "Wait, really? Like, a demon guard dog?"

"Half dog, half man? Sort of a man-dog. More dog than man. Whatever. It doesn't matter. The most important thing right now is staying out of its way long enough to get the scroll. Getting back to 2010 alive would be a nice perk."

By the time the Winchester brothers made it back to their small apartment, it was almost three in the morning. They spent half an hour comparing notes and going over the events of the last twenty-four hours. Sam told Dean everything he had learned at the library and from Walter, minus the information about Abaddon.

Given all they had discovered, the boys were now faced with a couple of problems. Though they knew when the transaction was going to take place, they didn't know who the actual buyer of the scrolls would be. They knew that a banker had been involved in the sale, but it would take some legwork to find out who that was. Even if they did find him, it would be much easier to take the scrolls *before* the actual transaction, rather than trying to grab them at the Waldorf Astoria, especially now that Dean had lost his job. They also had no weapons, and no idea how to contact Don once they actually had the War Scroll.

The one mercy granted them that night came from an unexpected source. Their next-door neighbors had been going at it with some vigor the whole night, to the point that the wall was shaking. At the height of the banging, a Murphy wall bed sprang loose from the wall where it had been hidden from view.

"The good news," Sam said, "is that the thief didn't find it either." He then claimed the bed and was asleep in minutes.

Dean lay on the worn couch. *Feels like I haven't slept in years.* His thoughts drifted to the leggy brunette in the lobby of the Waldorf Astoria. In 2010, it wasn't unusual to see a woman traveling by herself; in 1954 it was another story. He wondered who she was and where she had come from. There was something about how she carried herself. He was drawn to her confident walk and the way she had looked right at him—almost *into* him. Dean thought that after hunting down the demon-possessed guard, he might hang around and try to run into her again. He fell asleep trying to craft an opening line that would be suitable for the era.

In the morning, Sam and Dean sat on the steps of the New York Public Library sipping cups of coffee. Dean couldn't believe coffee was just five cents, and a whole pizza was seventy-five cents. It was like living in food paradise.

They discussed what their next move was. They decided that Sam would send a telegram to the address on the *Wall Street Journal* classified ad, saying that he was interested in buying the scrolls.

Dean wanted to go back to the Waldorf and find James— it couldn't be a coincidence that demon was hanging around the site of the upcoming auction. But before returning to the hotel, he headed to a secondhand store determined to buy a suit, after which he planned to get a close shave. If he was going back to the Waldorf as a civilian, he didn't want to look out of place.

* * *

Sam found a Western Union and sent a telegram to the party selling the scrolls.

INTERESTED IN BIBLICAL SCROLLS SEEN IN CLSFD AD IN WSJ STOP HAVE FUNDS STOP SERIOUS BUYER STOP PLEASE RESPOND QUICKLY STOP SINGER

In fact, they didn't have any funds, but Sam was going to cross that bridge when he came to it. He thought the little hat tip to Bobby was appropriate, and he wished more than ever that Bobby was there to help them.

Sam told the clerk where he could be reached, and said he would stop back in an hour to see if there was a response. He then made his way to Gimbels.

Browsing the men's section, Sam found a wool suit for twenty-eight dollars. He had the money—Dean's tips and his poker game in the holding cell had netted them about a hundred bucks—and Sam decided the suit was worth it. He wore it out of the store, his regular 2010 clothes stuffed into the Gimbels bag.

Sam noticed a barber shop right outside the department store. Only "a little off the top", turned out to be about four inches. Sam stared at himself in the shop's mirror. *Now that is different*, he thought. The barber smoothed his hair back with a little Murray's Pomade and he was ready to go.

When he stopped back at the Western Union, a telegram was waiting for him.

*SINGER STOP WILL CONSIDER GENEROUS OFFER
STOP MEET AT 21 CLUB AT 11 AM STOP ASK FOR
FELDMAN*

Sam looked up and saw a clock on the outside wall of a nearby a bank; it was 10:30 a.m. He asked a passerby for directions, and then started north up Sixth Avenue; he would get there right on time.

At the 21 Club, Sam admired the lawn jockeys mounted on the porch roof of the street level restaurant below. He had never been here before. Whenever the brothers had been in New York, it had always been on a hunt. They had never really got to enjoy the culture of the city.

Sam entered the dark restaurant. Red leather booths ringed the room and every inch of it was strung, hung or hugged with a toy of some sort. A maître-d' ushered Sam to a table where a young man in a dark-brown suit was already sitting, Sam was sure he couldn't be a day over twenty-five. He wondered how this kid could possibly be in the business of selling ancient biblical texts.

"Mr. Feldman?" Sam asked.

"No, I'm his attaché, Mr. Benjamin Shochat." The man stood up and shook Sam's outstretched hand. "I speak on Mr. Feldman's behalf. You're Mr. Singer, I presume?" The man had a lilting accent that sounded Middle Eastern.

"Yes. Good to meet you," Sam replied. He sat down and motioned for the waiter to bring him a glass of water. "I'm interested in the scrolls and I'd like to bid on them, but I want to see them first." Sam had clocked that the man was empty handed when he walked up to the table. If he could convince Shochat to take him to the Waldorf and show him the scrolls, he was in business.

Mr. Shochat studied Sam's face. "You are working for someone, yes?"

"I'm not at liberty to say just yet," Sam improvised smoothly. "But if I was speaking on behalf of someone else, it would be a very serious buyer with a large amount of capital. This person would like me to examine the merchandise first, however."

"Not possible," the young man responded with a snort. "They are being kept in a vault, under heavy security."

"At the Waldorf Astoria," Sam said with a smile, metaphorically laying his cards on the table.

"How do you know that?" Shochat was clearly ruffled and trying not to show it.

"I know things. I'd like to see the scrolls."

"How do I know you have sufficient funds?"

Sam stood up. "I think I've already proven how serious I am Mr. Shochat. Kindly have Mr. Feldman contact me if he wants to do business."

Shochat was looking increasingly nervous. It was clear he was in over his head, and was afraid that if he didn't act carefully, he was going to let a big fish go.

"Okay, wait," he said hastily. "Please sit." He drank a little from his water glass. "Mr. Feldman has another interested party, and they've made an initial offer of 100,000 US dollars. Are you willing to go higher?"

Sam realized that since he didn't actually have any money

at all, he could say anything he liked. He sat back down at the table.

"If the scrolls are genuine, twice that price would be a bargain," he said blithely.

Shochat leaned back in his chair, clearly impressed. Then Sam remembered that in an era of twenty-eight-dollar suits and seventy-five-cent large pizzas, 200,000 dollars was an enormous amount of money. He waited while Shochat thought it over. *I just need an invite to the auction, that's all.* He and Dean could do the rest themselves.

"I'll get back to you," Shochat said at last and stood up. "I'll speak with Mr. Feldman. I can't negotiate for him."

"Fine," Sam said standing up as well.

The young man set a derby on his head, tipped it in Sam's direction, and left.

Dean stretched comfortably in the large leather barber's chair. He was impressed by the incredibly close shave he'd been given. *Why did men ever give these up?* he wondered.

He had bought a secondhand dark-colored suit, a white shirt, and a black derby. Dean had never been a hat guy, per se, but he liked the feel of the derby. He wondered if he could conceal a weapon of some kind in it.

Out on the street, close shaven and besuited, he felt completely incognito. Now he could slip around the hotel unnoticed, giving him another chance at the scrolls.

A few minutes later, Dean stepped into the opulent lobby of the Waldorf Astoria. No alarms went off. *Disguise is working, I guess,* he mused. Using a key set he had neglected to return the day before, he accessed the back stairwell. Slipping quietly into the sub-basement, he immediately realized his plan wouldn't work.

Apparently, someone had taken his intrusion yesterday very seriously—there were now three guards waiting outside the vault, and all of them were armed. Before they noticed him, Dean slipped through a half-open door to his left.

He found himself inside a dank supply closet, containing a single metal chair with a man slumped in it, his back to Dean. Cautiously, Dean moved toward him.

It's James the security guard, he realized. *Fast asleep—Wait, do demons sleep?* Since he wasn't carrying any weapons, he decided to let the sleeping dog lie. Then he caught sight of the burlap sack in the corner and remembered a handy factoid: During the nasty New York winters, janitors used salt to melt ice on the sidewalks in front of important buildings like the Waldorf Astoria. And it looked like the hotel's salt supply was stored in this very cupboard.

Dean ripped open the corner of a bag and emptied half of it. He'd need to move fast if this was going to work. He hefted the sack in his arms.

"What the St. Mary are you doin'?" James asked, suddenly awake and wiping saliva from the side of his mouth.

Dean hesitated, the bag of salt raised above the guard's head. Making a quick decision, he lowered the bag to his side.

Neither man spoke for several seconds, then Dean cleared his throat.

"Getting salt," he said.

James rubbed his eyes, which were a normal greeny-blue color.

No sign of demonic possession. Nevertheless, Dean knew that the demon could still be inside James, biding its time.

"Do you remember me?" Dean asked.

James leaned forward in the chair, running his hands through his short hair.

"No, buddy. Why would I?"

Looks like he has the world's worst hangover, Dean thought. Oddly, he felt some sympathy for the man.

"It's nothing. Thought maybe you went to my church," he said.

James looked up at Dean, his face blotched and red.

"Take your salt and leave me alone," he said, without a hint of recognition on his face.

He really doesn't recognize me, Dean thought. *Maybe Cujo's moved on?* He did as he was told, hefting the bag of salt and starting toward the door. He considered 'accidentally' dropping the sack into James's lap as he walked past, but he controlled the impulse. There were three guards outside the door, each one capable of putting a bullet in Dean if they realized he was back at the Waldorf.

Slipping back into the stairwell, Dean dumped the sack of salt and considered the situation. If James *was* still possessed, it was one of the strangest demons Dean had ever encountered. The hosts usually retained the memories of the demon, and vice-versa. *Maybe it's not a demon at all. Maybe it's something else—that could explain the barking.*

Back in the lobby, Dean crossed to one of the bars. He

ordered a Seven and Seven and sank into a deep red-velvet club chair.

"May I join you?"

Dean looked up. The girl from the day before stood in front of him. She was dressed in a slim burgundy suit, with a skirt that stopped just below her knees. Not waiting for an answer, she sat down opposite him.

"So, one day you're a bellhop, the next you're at the bar as a guest. That's peculiar," she said, looking him over. Her eyes seemed to tick off each article of clothing Dean was wearing, as well as taking note of his features.

He leaned forward. "It's also peculiar that you noticed," he said.

The girl smiled, but didn't blush.

"How could I forget? It's not often a man offers to buy me a drink within thirty seconds of meeting me."

"Give it a little time. When the sixties hit, girls like you will be—" Dean stopped himself. *Why ruin the swinging sixties for her?* "Anyway, I apologize for being so forward. It's not like me at all."

"You're already lying to me? That's not a great sign."

"Okay, it is exactly like me," Dean said, leaning back in his chair.

"It's okay, it's refreshing. It means you're not that complicated."

"Is that supposed to be a compliment?"

The girl laughed. "Sort of."

Dean lied again. "I didn't catch your name yesterday."

"Julia. Julia Wilder."

She held out her petite gloved hand and Dean shook it politely, grinning at the strange formality of the gesture.

For half a second, he almost told her his real name. "I'm Malcolm. Malcolm Young," he said instead. "Nice to meet you."

"You didn't answer my question, Malcolm. How are you a bellhop one day and a guest the next?"

"Big promotion," Dean said carelessly.

She beckoned over the bartender.

"Scotch, please. One ice cube," she instructed.

Dean raised a brow. That was a stiff drink for such a small woman. As though she could read his thoughts, Julia leaned forward.

"My father and I have lived all over the world. I'm very adept at drinking liquor. It's unusual for a woman, I know."

Dean smiled. "I was actually going to say impressive."

"So Malcolm Young, tell me about yourself."

"Not much to tell, really. I'm in New York on business with my brother."

"What kind of business are you in? Besides carting bags, that is."

Dean adjusted his secondhand suit jacket.

"Family business. Extermination. I was in the bellhop outfit so I could explore the hotel without alerting the guests."

"Are you saying there are bugs in the Waldorf Astoria?"

"You didn't hear it from me." Dean raised his glass. "To being bug free."

Julia Wilder clinked his glass, then, with a lady-like swig, emptied hers. She stood up and smoothed her skirt.

"Very nice meeting you, Mr. Young. Again."

"You're leaving?"

"I have an appointment. Are you going to be in the city much longer?"

"We're waiting for a bid, then we go home," Dean said. It wasn't a total lie.

"Perhaps I'll see you again." She smiled and then walked across the lobby to the guest elevators.

Dean watched her and sighed. *Why do all the cool girls live in the past?*

NINE

Sam stopped by the Western Union, and found another telegram from Mr. Feldman was waiting for him.

JULY 1ST NOON PRESIDENTIAL SUITE WALDORF ASTORIA

Sam had done it, he had gotten them an invite to the auction. Now the challenge was getting hold of the scroll itself. *Could get dangerous, especially if Dean is the one who comes up with the plan.*

The obvious next step—they needed guns. Their usual contacts in New York were for the most part not even born yet, so Sam had to come up with an alternate solution. He decided to make his way to Little Italy. Thanks to his older brother, Sam had seen all the *Godfather* films dozens of times, and figured it couldn't all be fictional. *After all, Mario Puzo knows what he's talking about.*

Leaving Canal Street Station, Sam aimed for some of the smaller side streets of Little Italy. Ten minutes later, he stood in front of a restaurant with a CLOSED sign in the window. Inside, he could see several middle-aged men sat talking around a large table. A similarly weathered-looking man sat out front, picking grape seeds from between his teeth.

"Hi," Sam began hesitantly. "I was hoping to speak to someone, about a… business arrangement." Now that he was standing in front of what could be a real Mafioso, he had no idea what to say.

"Members only," the man said looking up. Sam noticed that one of his eyes was swollen shut.

"That's quite a shiner," he commented.

"Look kid, move along if you know what's good for ya."

Normally, Sam wasn't one to cause a scene. In this case, with the weight of the world resting on his shoulders, he was willing to break with tradition. He took a deep breath and plunged in.

"Listen, guy, I don't have time for subtlety. I need guns. *Lots* of guns." Sam pulled his remaining dollar bills from his pocket and waved the wad at the guy. "I'm willing to pay—"

"Whoa. Put that away." The guy looked both ways along the street. He got up and pushed Sam roughly inside the foyer and against the wall and frisked him. Sam stood completely still. He knew better than to wiggle around when a Goodfella was getting handsy.

"Up there, second floor."

Sam thanked him and headed for the stairs, passing the small cluster of guys who it turned out were playing a poker game in the main room—he made a mental note to tell Dean, in case they needed to replenish their cash reserves.

A small man, about forty years old and wearing a cable-knit sweater, sat at a desk on the second floor landing. Two bigger guys stood by the wall, their hands clasped in front of them. They were clearly packing some sort of weapon.

Sam cleared his throat and explained what he needed: two shotguns, two handguns, and no questions.

The transaction went very smoothly, all things considered. In the end Sam was only able to afford the two shotguns and ammunition, but within a few minutes he was holding a packed duffel and surrendering the last of his cash.

As he was preparing to leave, Sam hesitated.

"Um, actually," he began. "I don't know how I'm going to get these back uptown. See, I gave you all my money, and—"

"Bambi will drive you," the cable-knit guy said. He motioned to the slightly bigger of the two men near the wall. Bambi nodded.

A black 1953 Cadillac idled in the back alley. Bambi held open the trunk while Sam dropped the duffel inside. Then Sam reached to open the back door of the car.

"Upfront," Bambi ordered. "I ain't a chauvinist."

Sam was pretty sure he meant 'chauffeur,' but regardless, he did as he was told, and they were on their way. As they cruised up 5th Avenue, Sam stole a couple of glances at his driver. His mouth looked like it had been cut with a meat cleaver, with pock-marked skin that hung in indefinite wrinkles down his face.

Sam attempted small talk. "So, why do they call you Bambi?"

"'Cause of my doe eyes," Bambi growled and looked at Sam with big droopy, brown eyes. They would have been adorable, if they weren't filled with murder.

"Ahh." Sam realized he was in a car with a complete sociopath. Give him a demon any day.

When they reached the apartment, Sam pulled the duffel bag from the trunk and said goodbye to Bambi. The car departed at speed.

Sam carefully stashed the shotguns in the small apartment, and smiled to himself, pleased with his hiding place. He then decided to see if Dean had made any progress at the Waldorf.

When he arrived at the hotel, he immediately spotted Dean. He was sat at the bar, chatting to the bartender, who clearly thought he was a lunatic.

"Aww, he's great," Dean slurred. "When they play 'Stairway to Heaven' he goes like, *da dah daaaah.*" Dean mimicked an air guitar. "You're going to love them. Led Zeppelin—look out for them."

Sam tapped his brother on the shoulder. Dean turned toward him, bleary-eyed. "Hey bro. How ya doing?"

"Dean, we're in the middle of a job. What are *you* doing?"

"We're in the middle of the century! Sit down, have a drink."

"Not now Dean. Come on man, let's go home."

Dean scowled and slid off his seat. "Okay, fine."

Dean stumbled away from the bar with Sam holding his arm. Then he looked at his brother, suddenly dead sober.

"What took you so long? I've been playing drunk for hours. That girl over there to the left—I had a drink with her. She said she had an appointment and she's been lurking around the lobby ever since."

Sam looked around, but he couldn't see any girl. He wasn't entirely sure that Dean was just *playing* drunk.

"Sam, I think she's here for the auction. For the first hour, I just thought it was my animal magnetism, but I'm starting to think she's onto us."

"You don't say," Sam replied, pulling Dean along by the arm. "By the way," he said, "*I* haven't been sitting around wasting time at a bar. I scored us an invite to the scrolls auction, and the hardware we need to pull it off. Three days from now. Noon. Here."

As the brothers walked out the door, the girl who called herself Julia Wilder followed close behind. She was now wearing a blonde wig and a light-green suit. It was the best disguise she could put together from her suitcase upstairs. Now that she had confirmed that the two young men were working together, she allowed them to escape from her sight and made her way to the lobby phones.

"Columbia 367," she directed. After several seconds, a voice answered the phone. "Hi. It's me. You were right, they're together. Definitely casing the place."

As the other party spoke into her ear, Julia's face fell.

"No, I know. They won't. I won't let them," she said. With that, she hung up and went back to her room.

TEN

In Dean's pretty extensive life experience, there really wasn't very much that could compare to a good bacon cheeseburger. Despite that, the hot dog—with everything—that he devoured as he and Sam marched back to their apartment came close.

Sam was decidedly less enthusiastic about their dinner.

"Nothing like mystery meat you bought from a guy wearing a skirt," he said distastefully, swallowing the last of the bun and flicking ketchup off his fingers onto the sidewalk.

The sun had set behind the towering buildings, casting long inky shadows over the boys' route. But as the city fell into darkness, it seemed to be coming alive.

"Can you imagine the kind of supernatural critters that must be running around these alleys?" Dean asked as they passed a particularly decrepit-looking apartment complex.

"Dad's journal had a lot on New York," Sam replied. "Wouldn't be surprising if there were other hunters working the city—we know there are in the future," he said thinking of General Cox. Sam gave his brother a cautious look, as if he was worried Dean wouldn't like what he was going to say next. "It might be something to consider if we need backup."

"Backup schmackup," Dean responded. "What do we need other hunters for? We've got guns. Plus, you think we'd be able to convince anyone to help us once we start talking about the Apocalypse… and coming from the *future*?"

"Guess you're right."

"Damn straight. We tell anybody what we're doing here, we risk them interfering," Dean said definitively, knowing that *interference* may well be the least of their troubles. That certain people—and/or forces of Hell—would kill or worse in order to stop Sam and Dean was left unspoken. They both knew it, so it bore no repeating.

They walked up the cracked steps of Villard House. The sound of an ancient television set echoed out of the landlady's open door as they passed by.

"Lady's watching the DuMont Network in there," Dean said with a grin.

"The what?" Sam asked, his brow furrowed.

Dean just stared at him, incredulous. He sometimes forgot how young Sam was. Not that Dean himself had been alive to watch the DuMont Network, which, in 1954, was due to be shut down in two years, but he watched enough TV to be familiar with its history.

"*Cavalcade of Stars*? *The Honeymooners*? Not ringing a bell? Seriously?"

"Do you watch those shows before or after *Dr. Sexy,*

M.D.?" Sam asked, derisively.

"I'm off *Dr. Sexy*," Dean said.

"Tell me again about the girl," Sam said, his voice serious.

"Julia."

"She was tailing you?"

Dean slipped the key into the door of their apartment.

"She was definitely interested," he replied.

"Becky Rosen interested, or demon Meg interested?" Sam probed.

"Listen buddy, both of those chiquitas were after you," Dean said, trying to keep the vision of Becky rubbing Sam's chest out of his mind. "So, where are they?" Dean looked around the room. "You lose the guns just like you lost the knife?"

"Dean, it was stolen," Sam retorted. Then, realization dawned on him. "...By a *girl*. Brunette, cute, about five-foot six?"

Dean nodded.

"Could be the same girl that brushed past me in the hall," Sam continued. "Right before I realized the knife was gone." He walked to the Murphy bed, pulled it down, and extracted the gun-filled duffel from the bed's cavity. "As for these, they're safe and sound."

Dean watched Sam wistfully. *The kid really has become a good hunter, despite everything*, he thought. He grabbed the weapon-laden bag and opened it.

"Fifties women, dude," he said as he appraised the contents. "It's like a big riddle, and Betty Draper is the... thing you get for solving a riddle."

"Wait, are you still *into* the girl who you know is *on to* you? We got robbed already, Dean. We don't have time for you to get played."

"Don't start. I know. I'm not hitting on anything that was born before the microwave." Dean hefted one of the shotguns, and expertly tilted the weight of it back and forth to feel its balance.

"I was thinking…" Sam began, then trailed off.

"Spit it out, big guy," Dean said. "Thinking about taking a crap? Thinking of getting us some toothpaste? 'Cause your breath is *ripe*."

"If this wasn't 1954, we'd be loading these with salt, right?" Sam asked, grabbing a few of the shotgun shells. "But here, we're not. Because we're not just fighting demons and ghosts and things that go bump; we're robbing humans. Humans who didn't do anything to us, or to anyone, didn't do *anything* wrong, and we're going to hold guns to their heads? Doesn't it faze you even a little to be the bad guys?"

"We ice Lucifer, nobody's crying over a little bit of armed larceny," Dean retorted.

"So the end justifies the means?" Sam paused. "'Cause it sure didn't when it meant me juicing up on demon blood."

Sam's words drilled into Dean.

"That was different," he growled.

Sam shook his head and started to pace the room, the creaky floorboards giving slightly under his weight.

Dean looked at his brother impatiently. *Why does he always have to make things so complicated?*

"It *was* different," Dean persisted. "Look, I'm willing to

go pretty damned far to get this stupid scroll. Whether that includes killing or maiming some poor bastard who gets in our way, I'm not sure yet. Won't know that till my finger's on the trigger. But Sammy, I sure as hell am not willing to lose my little brother." Dean let out a sigh. "Saving you is the reason we're here."

But Sam's face was resolved.

"Nobody else gets hurt," he said. It wasn't a statement, it was a command. "I have enough blood on me already."

Dean reached into his pocket, felt the wad of bills, and started toward the door.

"Where are you going?" his brother demanded.

"To buy salt," Dean responded, and the door shut on him.

James McMannon stood on the threshold of his sister's brownstone house, bathed in the flashing red and blue of a police cruiser's revolving lights. Peering through the open curtains, he saw his sister. Maria's face was blotted with tears, her left cheek pressed into the thick of an older man's shoulder. *Maybe a neighbor*, James thought, not recognizing the man. *At least she has someone.* If he went inside, they'd ask him to explain something that couldn't be rationally explained, to tell a story that no sane person would believe.

Two uniformed officers were visible as well, both of them wearing the forlorn grimace of men sharing bad tidings. *Your son is dead*, they're saying. *We found his body.* James didn't need to read their lips, all he had to see was his sister's anguished face.

The sight drove James off the stoop and back onto the

narrow sidewalk. He began to shamble slowly northward.

Over the course of the evening, he had managed to piece together his shattered memories of what had happened to Barney—what he had *done* to Barney. He had never felt particularly in control of the direction his life was taking, but this was something different entirely. For a good chunk of the past few days, James hadn't been in control of his hands, his feet, or anything in between. Now he felt like a stranger in his own body, just stopping by until the next occupant moved in. Every few hours, he would simply wake up in a new place, unsure of how he had got there. The memories might eventually return, or they might not. Only one had stuck—

I killed Barney. And people are going to be looking for me. New York was a city with a million small, dim corners to hide in, and his only option was to find one of them and disappear into it. *My sister's son,* he thought, the words burning into his psyche. *The only person she had left.* Facing her was not an option. He had to vanish.

However, as the swirling light from the police cruiser faded into the distance, James found himself doing something peculiar. He was walking back toward Manhattan, toward the first place people would be looking for him—the Waldorf Astoria. A nagging voice in the back of his mind insisted that everything could be worked out, if only he was back at the hotel.

If only he was near the vault.

ELEVEN

Sam left the apartment before the sun had crept above the skyline, knowing it would be hours before Dean woke on his own. They weren't accustomed to staying in one place for this long, and with the auction still two days away, there wasn't a particular need to roll out of bed early. For Dean, that was an overdue invitation to get more than four hours sleep. For Sam, it was an excuse to get some time to himself.

Dean had indeed bought salt for the shotguns, but he had stayed out nearly the whole night finding it. Sam didn't want to know how Dean had spent the rest of his time, considering Dean's tendency to fraternize with less-than-virtuous characters. *I suppose I'm one of them*, Sam realized. *Nothing less virtuous than jump-starting Armageddon.*

After a twenty-minute walk, Sam arrived at the clerk's office for the borough of Manhattan. It was just before eight in the morning, but there was already a line forming at the information desk. A young woman, probably twenty years old and wearing a slightly too-tight sweater, stood behind the desk.

By the time it was Sam's turn, she was starting to sound frazzled.

"Can I help you, sir?" she asked, the tone of her voice indicating that she hoped she couldn't.

"Long morning already?" Sam responded with a smile, thinking that charm would be the best way to pull this off.

"No, sir. Did you have a records request, or is this a social visit?" she said tersely.

Sam was momentarily thrown.

"Uh, yeah. Yeah I do," he stammered, and pulled out his wallet. He flipped through the selection of counterfeit IDs and badges, none of which were appropriate to the era. Settling for the most promising one, Sam flashed it at her briefly, then folded it back into his wallet before she could get a good look.

"Secret Service," he intoned, changing tack to sound more serious.

The girl glanced over her shoulder at a morose-looking man sitting behind a typewriter, toward the back of the cluttered office. *Her boss*, Sam decided. He didn't look any happier to be there than she did.

"Just one moment," she said, getting up to talk to her boss. After a brief back-and-forth, the man came to speak with Sam directly. His narrow tie was knotted too tightly around his neck, making his head look like a bright-red balloon about to pop. *Must be part of the dress code*, Sam thought.

"Can I help you?" the man asked gruffly.

"Hi…" Sam replied, looking down at the man's nametag,

"Mr. Walker. The Secret Service requires a selection of blueprints for the Waldorf Astoria hotel." Sam pulled out the fake ID again, intending to flash it for only a moment, but Walker grabbed the wallet out of his hand.

"Counterfeiters," he barked.

"Uh, excuse me?" Sam responded, his hand reaching protectively for his wallet.

"What does this have to do with counterfeiters?" Walker asked, handing the wallet back to Sam.

"Oh, right. I don't deal with counterfeit money," Sam said, then he lowered his voice. "I protect President..." His mind raced, *Who was the President of the United States in 1954? After Truman, before Kennedy.* "Eisenhower. Sorry, we usually refer to him by his code name." He leaned in, whispering, "It's 'Papa Bear.'"

The girl, who was now standing next to her boss, gave Sam a curious look, but Walker didn't seem to have noticed Sam's lapse.

"That right?" he said.

"He'll be staying at the Waldorf Astoria in a few days. In the Presidential Suite," Sam said.

"I'll be damned. Ike staying right down the street from us!" Walker said, excited.

"Yes," Sam agreed. "It's very exciting for the people of New York. We—my colleagues and I—need to review the plans to look for security weaknesses in the hotel." It was half true. With the plans, Sam was hoping to find an alternative entrance into the suite that wouldn't draw suspicion from the Waldorf's security, who would recognise Dean.

"They ain't got that at the hotel? Seems they probably got a better idea about their plans and such than we would." Walker had a point, of course, but the Waldorf employees would also know that Eisenhower had no plans to visit in the near future. This was the only way.

"Just doing my due diligence," Sam replied.

"Marcia, see if we ain't got that in the records," Walker commanded, sending the girl scurrying away into the back room. "Say, what's old Ike like, anyhow?"

"Oh, he's... great. Just a swell guy. Really... tall."

"Yeah? Got any stories?"

"Of course, but, you know, they're top secret," Sam said, trying to hold his poker face.

"Ah. 'Course." Walker said, disappointed. He looked like he was going to persist when, to Sam's relief, Marcia returned to the desk with the plans.

Finding a corner table in the Records Office reading room, Sam poured over the blueprints, searching for a back door, a nearby service elevator—anything that would make their trip in and out of the Presidential Suite easier. He couldn't help but think about how much simpler this would be in 2010. Electronic records had saved them more times than Sam could count, and symbols that were taking him ages to decipher could have been explained with a ten-second Google search. He'd definitely appreciate that convenience more when—if—they ever got back to the present.

Just as Sam was about to give up, Walker barged into the reading room, another rolled-up set of blueprints under his arm.

"Can't believe I forgot about these," he said, plopping the prints onto the table in front of Sam.

Sam looked at the designs, but wasn't able to make head or tail of it.

"Being as he's the President, it seems appropriate that he use the Presidential Siding," Walker explained.

"The what?" Sam asked.

"Are you kiddin' me?" Walker's face creased. He pointed at a knot of intersecting white lines against the field of blue paper. "You don't know what's under the Waldorf?"

And with that, Sam's plan began to come together.

Dean woke up with a start to the noise of a dump truck reversing down the street outside. The sun blazed in through the small, barred window, brightly illuminating the fact that Sam wasn't in his bed.

"Sam?" Dean called out. "You up?"

When no one responded, he slid off the couch and headed for the shower. *Eight hours of sleep plus time for a hot shower.* Dean hadn't had both in months, probably not since Lucifer had been popped from his cage.

After his shower, he went straight to work disassembling the shotgun shells Sam had bought and refilling them with rock salt. He was nearly finished when the sound of keys rattled in the door's deadbolt.

"Sam, that you?"

"It's me. Don't shoot," came the muffled reply. As the door swung open, Dean's eyes caught on the brown paper bag in Sam's outstretched hand. It bore the unmistakable grease stains that came along with a cheeseburger, and instantly dispelled any hard feelings Dean had left over from the previous night's conversation.

"Fastest way to a man's heart, right?" he said, grabbing the bag and opening it. The smell was amazing, just the thing to remind Dean why life was worth living. "Where you been, anyway?"

Sam sat down next to Dean on the couch and grabbed his own burger from the bag.

"Clerk's office, looking for blueprints," he said.

"And?"

"And the good news is I may have found us an exit. The bad news is there's only one elevator that services the Presidential Suite, and a security desk is right outside it." Sam set his burger down without even taking a bite.

"You not eating that?" Dean asked, mouth full, then registered Sam's annoyance. "What?"

"This would be a lot easier if you hadn't been banned from the hotel," Sam said.

Dean nodded toward the stack of rock salt shells he'd been working on.

"Hey, I've been doin' my part. 'Sides, you're the one that dumped us on the Magic School Bus for this field trip."

Sam didn't protest, but he also didn't jump in to apologize. Dean shrugged. Sam's stubbornness was genetic—their father had it as well, and it was the thing that had driven them apart. Ironically enough, Dean, the boy who worshipped the ground his father walked on, was less like John Winchester than the son who wanted nothing to do with him.

"Look, you wanna do your part, find another way to get into that meeting," Sam said.

"Maybe we need to consider you flying solo," Dean suggested.

"Are you serious?" Sam asked. "A few weeks ago you weren't sure I was even cut out for hunting anymore, now you want me to commit armed robbery by myself?"

"You don't think you can do it?"

"Of course I can do it," Sam answered, agitated. "But is that our best plan? I show up, claiming to have 200,000 dollars in a briefcase, grab the scroll and run?"

"Sounds like a Winchester plan to me," Dean said, licking his fingers clean of burger grease.

"Sounds like a stupid plan."

"Usually it's both."

"Then let's come up with a better one," Sam offered. "From what Walter Sawyer told me, there could be a dozen people and institutions interested in the scrolls, so security is going to be tight. Maybe we can use that to our advantage. Create a diversion."

Dean didn't like where this was headed.

"By diversion, you mean me doing something stupid so you can smash-and-grab the scroll."

"They know you," Sam replied. "The guards upstairs will recognize you, so it won't be hard for you to get a little attention."

"And then they shoot me, you take off with the War Scroll, they shoot you, and our angel buddy can zap our corpses back to 2010," Dean scoffed.

"What if your distraction isn't, you know, violent?" Sam asked.

"Like I ask politely?"

"Like you pretend to be a Fed," Sam said. "Or somebody who doesn't believe the documents are genuine, come to warn the buyers that the seller's a fraud."

"Alright," Dean said, gears clicking into place in his head. "Say that works. I bust up the proceedings, your boy Feldman is distracted, you grab the scroll... What about the demon?"

Sam's face fell. If the demon was acting as a protector of the scroll, there was no telling what it would do.

"Last I saw, that guard seemed back to normal," Dean said. "So it could be in anyone. Assuming it is some kind of protector, he'll be there at the sale."

"And we don't have the knife."

"You mean you *lost* the knife," Dean pointed out.

"If we could get up there early, we could set up a Devil's Trap, lure him into it," Sam said, blowing past Dean's accusation.

"But we can't, so plan B," Dean said.

Sam nodded toward the stack of rock salt shells Dean had spent the morning preparing.

"Salt shells will keep a demon at bay, but how do we get a couple of shotguns upstairs?"

"Easy," Dean said. "We find a case big enough to fit 'em, and you waltz right in carrying it. 200,000 bucks must take up a lot of space."

"Security, Dean. They'll check the case."

As it was still untouched, Dean took another large bite out of Sam's burger, letting the taste linger in his mouth for a bit. He did his best thinking while eating.

"Luggage," he said finally.

"What about it?"

"We wait around the loading dock till it's unattended, which it will be, because those bellhops are frickin' lazy, trust me," Dean answered. "Then we throw the shotguns in a bag headed for the suite. They'll be there waiting for us."

"That's never going to work." Sam let out a sigh.

"Don't see you coming up with a better plan," Dean said angrily, though he knew Sam was right. Getting the guns upstairs was one thing, getting access to them and pulling off the heist was something else entirely.

"We're a little outside our comfort zone, Dean, but we've got to figure this out."

"I know. Stop the Apocalypse, kill the Devil, reunite the Spice Girls, there's a lot on our plate," Dean said, starting to pace the small room. "Maybe we're looking at this wrong. Maybe we go after the scroll once the buyer leaves with it. Jump 'em outside."

"How are we supposed to know who the buyer is?" Sam asked. "We wait outside, they could walk right past us with the scrolls in a briefcase and we'd never know."

Picking up one of the rock salt shells, Dean started to flip the cartridge between his fingers.

"Well, whoever has a frickin' demon following him, screaming bloody murder, that's probably him."

The discussion went round and round, not leading any

place productive for over an hour. Dean wanted nothing more than to get out of the cramped apartment, but this particular dilemma needed all brains on deck. Finally, Sam relented and stepped into the bathroom, giving Dean the perfect opportunity to escape outside for some air. No one wanted to be near the bathroom when Sam was in it.

Seated on the front stoop of the apartment building, Dean watched as a stream of New Yorkers marched past, hurrying away the afternoon. *They don't know what's coming,* he thought, feeling for a moment like Sarah Connor in *T2*, the harbinger of doom nestled amidst the blissfully unaware. *Of course, these people have fifty-six good years left. Not like us.*

Sam joined him after a few minutes, both of them listening intently to the sound of traffic, taking in all of the sights and sounds of the run-down neighborhood.

As if he could read Dean's thoughts, Sam suddenly laughed.

"Admit it," he said. "You miss *Dr. Sexy.*"

TWELVE

Early the next morning, Sam and Dean headed uptown to the Waldorf. Sam had insisted on another walkthrough of the lobby, and if they could get up as far as the Presidential Suite without arousing suspicion, then all the better.

While Dean skulked around the loading dock, Sam headed to the stairwell. He wanted to make sure that the exit strategy he had formulated from the blueprints would hold up in real life.

Slogging his way up the many flights of stairs was the most exercise Sam had done in weeks. Around the twentieth story, ascending to the top began to feel like an impossible task. *It'd be pretty sad to die of a heart attack now*, Sam thought. Whether that would be a good or bad thing for the world was another matter.

In the middle of contemplating that idea, a thunderous *bark* echoed up the stairwell, jolting Sam to attention. A second later, another bark pounded his eardrums, and he gripped his hands against his head tightly. *If that's a dog*, Sam thought, *I don't want to meet its owner.*

With the third bout of vicious howling, Sam realized that the noise was getting closer. It was coming up the stairwell—and fast. *Dean said the demon barked. I don't really want to find out if he's right.* He took the steps two at a time, hoping to outrun whatever hellish beast was downstairs. *Hellish beast*, Sam thought. *It sounds exactly how I always imagined a Hellhound to sound.*

Satan's guard dogs, Hellhounds were the invisible beasts responsible for keeping up the nasty end of Hell's bargains. If the demon that Dean met was somehow a Hellhound, or something like it, they were in even more trouble than they had thought.

The sound of water dripping was driving Dean crazy. Somewhere, some jackass hadn't tightened a valve, or a nut, or whatever it was that kept water from leaking, and now it was ruining both Dean's day and his nice new suit jacket.

He had been forced to hide in a storage locker when a truckload of perishables was delivered to the loading dock, only to have the kitchen staff take their lunch break right outside. It wasn't the most undignified place Dean had ever hidden, but it was up there.

"Have I told you what happened at the Yankees' game?" a muffled voice said outside the locker. For a moment, Dean pictured himself holding a baseball bat and using it to punish the kitchen workers for the twenty minutes of dull-as-shit conversation he'd been forced to endure. *I bet Sam's having fun*, he thought bitterly.

The metal edge of the stair rushed at Sam's face, catching him between the ear and eyebrow and momentarily blurring his vision. He had tripped while running up the flight of stairs, and from the sound of it, the Hellhound—or whatever it was—was only seconds behind him. Pushing himself upright, Sam risked a glance down the cavernous opening in the middle of the stairwell. It led all the way to the ground floor, maybe even underground.

Nothing.

Hellhounds are invisible, Sam reminded himself. *Keep running.*

Lactic acid burned in his calves as he sprinted upward. Ahead of him, the door to the fortieth floor was only meters away. A terrible growling reverberated through the stairwell. Any moment Sam expected to feel the dig of teeth clamping onto his leg, but the sensation never came.

He darted into the hallway of the fortieth floor, slamming the door shut behind him. He scanned the space around him, but didn't see anything that could be used to barricade the door. He did, however, hear something. The familiar electric buzz of a vending machine was coming from a nearby room. Bolting inside, Sam quickly locked the door. He found himself in what looked like a staff break room.

The snack machine weighed far more than Sam expected it to, and as he attempted to slide it along the floor it tipped over on its side. The laminate flooring shook with the massive crash, and Sam flinched. *Everyone on this floor must have heard that.* On the plus side, the machine was much easier to move now it was on its side. Sam slid it toward the door, effectively blocking it.

Bags of pretzels hung haphazardly inside the vending machine, with big chunks of Kosher salt on them. Sam kicked through the glass and pulled out as many bags of pretzels as he could. He crushed them in his hands and poured the contents across the vending machine. Whether that was enough salt to keep a demon or Hellhound at bay, Sam wasn't sure.

He took a few moments to catch his breath, his ragged gasps for oxygen overpowering any noise from beyond the door. Leaning against the downed vending machine, he held in his breath for five seconds, allowing him to hear a raspy intake of air from the other side of the door. Some of the pretzel crumbs retreated under the door with the beast's inhale.

It's sniffing me out, Sam realized. *It knows I'm here.* But the door never rattled and the beast never brayed. Instead, Sam heard the hollow clomping of feet on metal stairs. The creature was moving on.

Sam waited a couple more minutes, then pushed the vending machine away from the door. He stepped over his makeshift salt and pretzel line and sighed. *That was close.*

"You must of been hungry," a voice said from down the hall. Sam looked up to see an elderly woman standing there, wearing a plaid bathrobe and holding an empty ice bucket with both hands. She nodded toward the pile of snacks that had spilled out of the machine, and the accompanying broken glass.

Sam shrugged. "It stole my quarter."

For Dean, sweet relief came in the form of a hotel supervisor, who marched down to the loading dock and admonished the kitchen staff for letting the perishables sit for so long without refrigeration. Dean was spared. As they exited, a burly-sounding line cook with a Jersey accent said something about a package being moved through the kitchen, but Dean couldn't hear the full exchange. The one phrase he definitely heard was "big-ass jars." *They must have been moving the scrolls upstairs*, Dean thought. *Hope Sammy hasn't run into any trouble.*

Wringing the moisture out of his jacket, Dean exited the loading dock and headed back toward the Park Avenue entrance where he was supposed to meet Sam.

Oddly, Sam wasn't waiting. Being the more punctual of the two of them, it wasn't like Sam to miss a *rendez vous*. Taking a chance on not being recognized again, Dean smiled at the hotel doorman and strode boldly into the lobby. The dick desk clerk was on duty, so Dean joined a large crowd that was milling near the lounge's piano. Sam wasn't in the lobby, but the stairwell he'd taken would spit him out right in front of the crowd. A red-haired man was playing the piano with some proficiency, although Dean didn't recognize the song.

Trying to blend into the group, Dean watched as a woman approached the pianist. She patted him kindly on the shoulder, whispered in his ear… and with the practiced skill of a professional, lifted the wallet from his jacket pocket.

She moved off quickly, but Dean was only seconds behind her. As she made her way toward the elevators, Dean grabbed her by the arm and spun her to face him.

"Should have friggin' guessed," he said.

The woman was Julia.

"Ah, how nice to see you again, Mister… I'm sorry, I've forgotten your name," she said formally.

"Don't sweat it, it wasn't my real name anyway," Dean responded bitterly. "Let's go have a chat with the nice piano man." He tugged at her arm, pulling her back toward the lobby. But she resisted, digging her heels into the floor.

"I'm sorry, but I really have to get back to my room," she said.

"We're not done talking yet," Dean threatened.

"Let go of my arm."

"*Give the ginger back his wallet,*" Dean hissed, nodding toward the guy at the piano. Julia began to visibly struggle against Dean's grip, attracting the attention of several other guests.

"Is there a problem, here?" a man asked, looking concerned.

With forced theatricality, Julia squeezed out a tear.

"This man has me confused with someone else," she said with a sob.

Dean realized he had no choice but to let her go, and released his grip on her arm. She immediately hurried toward the elevator. Dean made to follow her, but was blocked by the hairy forearm of the dick desk clerk.

"You've been banned from the building," he said. Then yelled, "Security!"

Julia stepped into the elevator and spoke quietly to the operator. Dean grabbed his opportunity, jamming his hand against the closing doors, halting them before she could disappear.

"What do you want with us?" he demanded. But before he could continue, he was pulled away by a trio of burly hotel employees and dragged roughly outside. He'd never been so quickly and efficiently bounced from an establishment before, and it seemed strange that it wasn't for drunkenness.

Sam was waiting outside, eyes wide and with a fire in them that Dean hadn't seen in weeks.

"What's the haps? Where you been?" Dean asked, but Sam ignored his question.

"We need to leave. Now," he said.

"So, is it a Hellhound, or a dude?" Dean asked, nursing a beer. "I'm lost."

"I don't know. It sure as hell sounded hellish, but I didn't actually *see* anything."

"Yeah, 'cause you were hiding in the snack room."

They had spent the rest of the day and into the evening trying to figure out exactly what the new developments meant for their plan. Dean had insisted that they hole up in a nearby dive bar, despite Sam's protests. With the deal taking place the next day, they hardly had time to drink, but that had never stopped Dean before.

"You couldn't have peeked out for a second?" Dean persisted.

His brother rolled his eyes, fed up with the circular conversation.

"I never saw the one that gutted you, either."

"'Cause that's fair," Dean muttered. "But you didn't see its, like, hoof-marks—"

"It's a dog, not a horse."

"Whatever, but you didn't see—"

"*I didn't see anything*," Sam shot back impatiently.

Their waitress came by with another pitcher of beer, but Sam shook his head at her. He then waited until she was out of earshot before continuing.

"So we have a demon, possibly a Hellhound, a scroll that could kill the Devil, no workable plan for how to get it, and apparently a pickpocket who has her eye on you."

"Yeah, we're doing pretty well, all told," Dean said with a smirk. He pushed back his chair. "Time for bed."

Sam followed his brother out of the bar and into the cool night, torn between needing his bed and wanting to better figure out their strategy for the next day. They had walked several blocks toward their apartment before he spoke up again.

"It's my life on the line. I'm not sure we should be winging this."

"We'll do our best, Sammy. That's all we can do."

Just before midnight, James McMannon found himself standing in the hallway outside the Presidential Suite, walking the distance between the elevator, the stairwell and the suite's door with an even cadence. He couldn't particularly remember why he had chosen this hallway to walk in, or what he had been doing before he got here, but he knew that what he was doing was important. *Someone has to be here*, he thought.

Inside the Presidential Suite, something was giving off an incredible aroma. Like nothing James had ever smelled before. It made him feel very protective, as if it was his own child beyond that door.

Child. Nephew. Barney. Dead.

The words made James furious, but he couldn't remember why. *Did something happen to Barney?*

No matter. James had to concentrate on whatever was inside the suite. The smell.

If anyone tries to take it away, I'll kill them.

THIRTEEN

Sam looks goofy in his suit, Dean thought with a chuckle. It was the morning of their big day, and Sam was doing his best to look respectable, but as usual the formal clothing just didn't look right on his tall frame. They'd been over their plan several times already, but Sam demanded they run through it again. It still wasn't much, but Dean had come up with a new idea overnight that might get them out alive. Whether or not they got the scroll was another matter.

Once Dean had suited up, the two of them made their way uptown to the Waldorf. They were about an hour early, which gave them time to move cautiously. Getting caught with a duffel bag full of shotguns and shells probably wouldn't go over too well with the NYPD, even in the fifties. They'd bought a briefcase at a pawnshop for Sam to carry into the meeting, but with no way to procure the necessary funds, it was packed with old newspapers to give it some weight, and secured with an impressive-looking lock.

Their entire plan hinged on Security not kicking Sam out for being broke before the auction had even begun.

Setting down the duffel on the street outside the Waldorf, Dean looked up at the building's façade and smiled. What he saw there put his part of the plan in motion. *Jesus,* he mused, *this could actually work.*

The elevator rattled disconcertingly as it made its way up to the Presidential Suite. Sam tried to ignore it. He already felt like his stomach was in his throat, what was a little bit of motion sickness compared to the prospect of armed robbery?

Standing outside the elevator were two Waldorf security guards and a uniformed police officer. The cop looked annoyed to be there, probably thinking that no one would care enough about some old pieces of parchment to cause any trouble. Boy was he wrong.

"I'm here for the auction," Sam said, aware that he was stating the obvious. The entire floor looked to be shut down for the event. A desk had been set up perpendicular to the elevators, effectively barricading one entire side of the corridor. The uniformed officer sat behind the desk.

"Your name?" he asked dully.

"Bob Singer," Sam replied. "Maybe under Robert." The policeman looked up at him with exasperation. "But you probably could have guessed that."

"Yeah," the cop said. "Thanks."

Sam took a step toward the suite and felt a hand on his shoulder. It was one of the two Waldorf employees—the grungier of the two; the guy looked like he hadn't slept in a week. Before Sam could say anything, the man narrowed his eyes and sniffed the air. *Like a dog*, Sam thought. *That's creepy.*

"James, what the hell?" the other employee said, breaking the tension.

"He smells like death," James said, his nose furrowing. As Sam girded himself for what seemed like an inevitable brawl, James cracked a smile, then started patting Sam down, looking for a concealed weapon. *Yeah, still creepy*, Sam thought.

Without meeting James's gaze, he turned and grabbed the door handle to the Presidential Suite. *Guess Dean's man-dog theory was right.* Not that it made any sense.

"Your briefcase, sir?" the other guy said.

"What about it?" Sam responded.

"We do not require the combination, sir, but we do require that you leave it outside of the suite. The Waldorf Astoria will take full responsibility for its contents during the auction.

Perfect, Sam thought. *As long as they don't get curious, I'm home free.* He handed the briefcase off to the policeman at the desk and entered the suite. Paintings cluttered the walls of the entranceway, which was by itself fancier than any place Sam had ever stayed. It was a good thing he'd studied the blueprints of the place, or he'd have been too much in awe to keep his focus. To the right, a hallway led to the master bedroom—*The bedroom where Kennedy will someday sleep, and Obama*, Sam thought. To the left, an archway led into a small dining area, the table set with silver utensils and fine crystal.

The suite had its own kitchen, and Sam spent a moment picturing Bill Clinton raiding the fridge in the middle of the night looking for spare ribs.

Across from Sam, past a small couch and chaise longue, was the main room of the suite. A cluster of people stood inside, chatting softly under the light of a chandelier. *Nicer surroundings than our usual jobs,* Sam thought. The only person in the group he recognized was Benjamin Shochat, Mr. Feldman's aide. As he entered the main room, Sam noticed the collection of ornate clay jars on the center table.

"Welcome, Mr. Singer," Shochat said with a wry grin. "So glad you could attend. Let me introduce you to my employer." He waved his hand toward an elderly gentleman who was hunched protectively over the jars. The man looked at least eighty years old, but as he looked up at Sam, his eyes betrayed his still-sharp wit. His olive brow was deeply creased, a telltale sign of a stressful life. The complete absence of laugh lines further proved Sam's assumption—this guy meant business.

"Mr. Singer, this is Mr. Feldman. The owner of the scrolls," Shochat introduced him.

"Hello, Mr. Singer," Feldman said, his voice like gravel. "You have me very curious. Benjamin told me you were a young man, but I hadn't fathomed the, well... *extent* of your youth." He gestured toward the other potential buyers, all of them middle-aged. "I thought this to be an old man's game."

"I'm, uh, flattered, Mr. Feldman. But I'm merely a representative," Sam responded.

The old man pursed his lips, considering that.

"As long as they have the money, anyone is welcome here," he stated.

Sam took that as his cue to mingle. He approached a nervous-looking man, whose red hair seemed to glow in the chandelier-light.

"Mr. Singer—" Sam began, but he was cut off abruptly.

"I know your name," the man blurted excitedly. "You just said it. Why wouldn't I have heard it?"

"Uh, sorry, just being polite." Sam wasn't going to make any new friends in this room, that much was clear.

"Aren't you going to ask my name?" the red-haired man demanded.

"Wasn't planning on it," Sam replied, his attention now fixed on a table of hors d'oeuvres. He clocked a plate of deviled eggs, but was blocked by the red-haired man's hand.

"Eli Thurman," he said, and Sam found himself forced into a long and awkward conversation about what he felt the Dead Sea Scrolls meant for modern theologians. As the discussion twisted around topics Sam barely understood and certainly didn't care about, he had to bite his tongue to stop himself from bringing up the Apocalypse. "Hey Eli, did you know I unleashed Satan?" he wanted to say. The socially-awkward yet talkative man would probably drop dead on the spot.

Twenty minutes of boredom later, Shochat brought the room to attention with a clink of his wine glass.

"Our last guest is arriving now, so we'll be starting the sale."

After all of the surprises the last week had brought, Sam

was too worn out to act shocked. Instead, he just looked the newest arrival in the eye and extended a hand.

"Hi, Walter. Wasn't expecting to see you here."

Dean appreciated irony the most when it involved smashing public property. Yesterday, dripping water had nearly ruined his jacket, and now, the water that sprayed out of the broken Park Avenue fire hydrant would save his ass. The first phase of Dean's plan was complete, and all it took was a wrench and the chutzpah to cause a ruckus in front of all of New York.

Scores of people assembled to watch the plume of water soak the sidewalk, Park Avenue, and a good portion of the Waldorf façade. One of those people, exactly according to plan, was the dick receptionist. A pleasant side effect of Dean's mischief was the squeals of hoity-toity women trying to exit the Waldorf without getting wet. *Ain't happening, ladies.*

Amidst the chaos, Dean was able to slip into the loading dock and enter the service elevator, the duffel bag of shotguns slung over his shoulder. The next portion of his plan could very well be the stupidest thing Dean had ever tried, but there was no knowing for sure unless he did it.

The elevator's dial pushed up to the forty-seventh floor. He'd have to hoof it from there. Exiting the elevator, Dean quickly found the roof-access stairwell and made his way back out into sunlight.

"That you, Johnny?" a voice demanded from across the roof. Most likely the person Dean was looking for.

"It's, uh, Tony. Johnny's... sick," Dean said, hoping that

would at least prevent the man from calling Security. There was a long pause and Dean took the opportunity to unzip the duffel, readying himself for a fight.

"Well, you here to help or what?" the man called.

Dean took the unexpected charity fate had given him. He zipped the bag back up and hoisted it onto his shoulder. Quickly bypassing a large power converter box, he got a glimpse of his target—a mustached man of Italian heritage who could have easily been cast as the third Mario brother. He was seated precariously on the building's ledge, nonchalantly eating a Reuben sandwich.

"You the window washer?" Dean asked.

"No, I just come up here for the fresh mountain air," the guy said dryly, kicking at the large squeegee lying on the roof next to him. "Now get strapped in, I'll lower you down with the rest of the guys."

As Dean stepped closer, he got a look over the edge and into the deep canyon that was 50th Street.

"Yeah, I'll just str…" he trailed off, looking at the mechanism in question. "Son of a bitch," he said, eyeing a mangled knot in the system of ropes, levers and pulleys anchored to the hotel's roof. *I'm supposed to go over the edge of the building strapped to that?*

"What's the problem," the man said. It wasn't really a question. The prevailing implication was that Dean was a sissy, and that a real man wouldn't doubt the efficacy of the system. A slice of corned beef worked its way out of the window washer's sandwich, falling over the ledge and down into the abyss of New York City. The man leant further over the edge and called out, "Sorry 'bout that, Lenny."

Several waves of vertigo washed over Dean, one after another, stopping him from moving any closer to the ledge. Dean hated flying, and standing at the edge of a 500-foot chasm was twice as bad.

Okay, maybe this isn't gonna work.

FOURTEEN

Guess I'll have to find another translator, Sam thought. *Something tells me that Walter won't appreciate having a shotgun stuck in his face.* Five minutes into the sale, Walter had only made a single low-ball bid—whether that was due to strategy or limited funds, Sam couldn't be sure. Of course, Sam didn't have any money, either.

Of the half-dozen interested parties, only three of them were truly serious about buying the scrolls. Eli Thurman, Sam's alter ego, Robert Singer, and a Midwestern man who had introduced himself simply as "Gerald."

Eli had initially offered 100,000 dollars, which everyone knew was too low a price. Gerald quickly countered with 115,000 dollars, which Sam raised by another 10,000 dollars. In the early phase of the sale, Sam concentrated on Shochat, who was moving deliberately around the room, looking out the windows, checking the side rooms, and not-too-subtly fingering the safety on the gun in his pants pocket.

As the bids grew higher, the three less-serious buyers dropped out entirely. Gerald and Eli were the most active in the auction, with Sam chiming in every now and then to keep things interesting. It began to feel like the sale might finish without incident when the sound of a commotion interrupted the proceedings. A large mass thumped against the door, then slid slowly down it.

Sam was the first on his feet, but Shochat pushed him back down to the couch.

"Go, Benjamin," Mr. Feldman said calmly. Shochat followed the order, heading slowly toward the suite's entrance, his pistol raised.

Sam quickly realized that his brother could be the cause of the noise. It wasn't what they had planned, but it might be Dean's plan B. Sam leaned his weight onto the balls of his feet, ready to spring for the clay jars.

"Who's there?" Shochat's voice demanded. He was now out of Sam's line of sight.

The room was silent as everyone waited for a response, but there was no answer.

Come on, Dean, don't get yourself shot.

On cue, Sam heard the door swing open. Two heartbeats later, a gunshot rang out, sending Sam leaping to his feet.

"Stop!" Mr. Feldman cried, putting himself between Sam and the jars.

Sam had enough inertia to plow the older man through the window, but he wasn't going for the jars. He was going for the entrance lounge, where hopefully Dean wasn't lying dead on the floor. His haste caused him to crash directly into Shochat, as he stumbled back into the room, clutching his bloody hand.

"Dean?" Sam called out, pushing Shochat aside.

"'Fraid not, sweetie," a melodious voice replied. A young woman charged into the room, a black pistol in her hand. She was beautiful, and vaguely familiar. *That must be the girl*, Sam realized, *Julia*.

Across the room, Walter swallowed hard. "Dear, what did I tell you about collateral damage?" he said.

Julia rolled her eyes.

"Keep it to a minimum. I know, Dad."

Up on the roof, Dean was experiencing full-blown panic. There was no way he'd be able to go through with the plan. *Rappelling down the side of a skyscraper strapped to a leather harness is not a friggin' option. Sam is just going to have to say "yes" to Satan and fight the good fight.*

"You've gotta calm yourself down, buddy," the window washer said encouragingly. "You get nerves on this job, you're gonna end up schmeared on a taxi like cream cheese."

"What's your name again?" Dean asked.

"Marco," the man replied.

"Listen Marco, I need you to *shut the hell up* for a second."

In all of their years hunting, Dean had never been this crippled by fear. *Well, except for the ghost sickness*, he remembered, *but that wasn't my fault.*

Sam is down there, counting on you. Man the hell up.

"Okay," Dean said, mustering all of his courage. "This is gonna come as a shock, but I'm new at this."

"You don't say," Marco replied, raising an eyebrow.

"So if you could lose the d-bag attitude for a second and help me get this harness on—"

"D-bag? Like a duffel?"

"It's something your kids are gonna call you behind your back," Dean said under his breath, picking up the extra leather harness.

"What's in your d-bag, by the way?"

"Excuse me?"

Marco pointed at Dean's weapon-filled duffel bag, which was still slung over his shoulder.

"Lunch."

"Better eat it now. Leave it up here and it'll be gone as soon as one of these guys comes up to piss."

"Guess I'll have to take it with me then," Dean said.

With Marco's help, he was soon strapped in and standing at the building's precipice. Five other window washers were already suspended from the roof, working twenty flights above the roar of traffic below. The flood of taxis on 50th Street looked the size of Hot Wheels, which didn't help Dean's vertigo in the slightest.

Dangling one foot over the ledge, he tried to count the floors down to the Presidential Suite. *Thirty-fifth floor*, he told himself. *Twelve floors straight down. I can do this. Sam wouldn't even think twice, and he's a salad-eating nancy.* With one last tug on the strap, he began to lower himself down the building's façade.

"Hey, you forgetting something?" Marco called. In his outstretched hand he held a leather belt fitted with spray bottles and a squeegee. "Gotta say, Tony, even for a beginner, you suck at this."

Taking the tool belt, Dean began his descent.

Walter and Julia weren't wasting any time. They'd corralled Mr. Feldman, Shochat and the prospective buyers in a corner of the Presidential Suite, all of their faces wet with tears from the pepper spray Julia had used on the guards outside. No one had been killed, which was a relief, but Sam knew that could change in an instant if someone didn't cooperate.

Blood from Shochat's gunshot wound dripped onto Sam's shoes. With Julia and Walter distracted by their examination of the clay jars, Sam pulled down one of the ornate curtains and ripped it into long strips, giving them to Benjamin to wrap around his hand.

"What do you think you're doing?" Julia yelled.

"Keeping him from bleeding to death," Sam replied angrily.

Before Julia could react, Walter interceded.

"It's okay, Jules. We don't want anybody to get hurt."

Julia scoffed. She was clearly bad cop to Walter's good cop.

"It's too late for that," Mr. Feldman said mournfully. His eyes weren't on his assistant, but rather on the tallest jar, which Walter was carefully wrenching open. Sam noticed that he had dispensed with his sling.

"You think we *want* to do this?" Julia spat at Feldman. "This is for your own damn good."

Sam caught a glimpse of the Devil's Trap inscribed on the

top of the lid as Walter set it back on the table.

"You don't want to be opening that here, Walter," he said.

"I know what I'm doing, Sam."

"Sam?" Shochat questioned, looking puzzled. "I thought your name was Robert?"

"It's Sam to my friends," he said, with a hard look at Walter. "And people I thought were my friends."

Walter looked away. Reaching into the open jar, he grasped at the contents. Sam flinched, the millennia-old scrolls would be impossibly delicate.

"Walter..." Sam said, again trying to warn him. But before he could continue Julia thrust her gun into his face.

"You want to let him concentrate," she said through gritted teeth. "If this goes wrong, people are going to get thrown out the window."

You have no idea, Sam thought.

Walter pulled a petrified-looking black object out of the jar with some difficulty. It clearly wasn't a scroll, but rather some sort of stopper—an additional moisture barrier put in place to protect the fragile parchment, Sam guessed. Walter studied it closely, then set it aside, once more reaching into the jar. This time, his eyes lit up like a kid at Christmas. *He must have struck parchment*, Sam figured.

Outside the suite, something scraped heavily against the door.

"What was that?" Julia demanded.

"You tell me," her father replied without looking up from his work. "You were supposed to handle them." As he lifted the first scroll out of the jar, his joyous look faded. "Not the right one," he muttered.

"Keep looking. I've got this," Julia said, moving toward the door.

Sam took the opportunity to step out of the corner and over to Walter.

"You don't have to do this," he said softly. "You want to read the scrolls, wait for them to show up in a museum."

"That's not how it works, Sam," the man replied. "The document I'm looking for is never going to be in a museum. If the wrong people get their hands on it..." He looked pointedly at red-headed Eli. "Well, that would be bad."

Sam began to wonder exactly what Walter's endgame was. Would he disappear with the scroll, abandoning his life in New York?

Julia returned from the door, pistol again trained on Sam and the others.

"It's nothing," she said. "One of the guards twitching in his sleep. Now let's get out of here."

"This is it," Walter said, hefting a second piece of parchment.

The War Scroll.

That's not good, Sam thought. *They're after the same page that we are. Chances are, they're not going to just hand it over once they hear our story.*

James McMannon woke with a start. His head was ringing, his body was slumped against an overturned desk and his eyes were seared by pepper spray. *Where am I?* he wondered, before recognizing the slightly blurred but distinct carpeting of the Waldorf Astoria underneath him.

Memories flooded back all at once; the girl pistol-whipping him, his nephew, the strange fixation he'd had with that smell... *That smell...* It suddenly filled his nostrils, and everything else faded away. He had to get to that smell. Someone was trying to take it away from him, and that must not be allowed.

"What the hell are you doing?" Sam yelled, getting dangerously close to the barrel of Julia's handgun.

"Back up, or I swear to God I'll put a hole in your face," she shouted back.

Walter took the scroll and put it into his metal briefcase. In his haste to get it squared away, he fumbled the large clay jar, sending it crashing to the floor. As it shattered, everyone instinctively took a step back. Priceless history was buried in the mess of clay fragments, and no one wanted to be the one to step on it.

A look of immense regret washed over Walter's face, then was replaced by abject horror. For an instant, an impossibly bright light spilled out of the jar's broken remains.

That can't be good, Sam thought.

As the sound of the crash subsided, it was replaced by a furious scraping from the entrance lounge. As before, it set the whole room on edge. This time, however, the tumult didn't subside after a few seconds. Instead, it got louder and louder and was punctuated by the sound of something heavy hitting wood, as if an increasingly agitated animal was outside and wanted in. *Like a dog*, Sam thought. *Perfect.*

"Jules?" Walter said.

She raised her pistol to cover the entrance.

"Nothing out there we can't handle," she said confidently.

This would be a good time to interrupt, Dean.

With Julia's attention on the entrance lounge, Sam crouched and began to pick through the clay shards. As he flipped one over in his hands, he found a rough pattern engraved on what must have been the jar's interior surface. *A sigil*, he realized. Angelic magic. *And now it's broken.* Whatever had been contained by it was now free.

The scraping stopped, the sudden and profound silence perhaps even more disturbing than the grating noise of claws on wood. Sam's foot brushed away clay fragments, freeing a path between him and the entrance. Before he could move, Eli's hand gripped his shoulder. The man's eyes were as wide as saucers, betraying his desperation. He didn't want Sam to leave them.

Then the world seemed to fracture. Wind exploded into the room, swirling the curtains and kicking up dust from the splintered jar. A cluster of glass slivers blew past Sam's head, others lodged painfully in his back and neck. Knocked forward by the blast, it was impossible to keep his balance. Sam landed with a thud in the pile of parchment and clay, immediately rolling off to protect what was left of the scrolls.

As he sat up, he saw the oddest sight—Dean, hanging by a thread outside the suite's now-empty window frame, a rock salt shotgun hefted offensively through the opening. He had come through on his part of the plan, although he was a little behind schedule.

"Sorry 'bout that. Windows are mirrored." Despite the needling pain from the glass and rock salt, Sam was incredibly grateful his brother had shown up when he had. But the sense of relief was short-lived.

In the entrance lounge, the door pounded off its hinges, catching Julia off-guard and smashing her against the wall. Walter, briefcase in hand, spun and ran back into the main room, but he couldn't outrun the beast outside, which quickly overtook him. Claws dug into his leg, pulling him backwards.

From the main room, all Sam could see was Walter's face as he disappeared out the door.

"Little help here?" Dean called out, still hanging outside the window. Sam moved to the hole, but instead of dragging Dean in, he pulled the shotgun out of his brother's hand and rushed after Walter.

When he reached the entrance lounge, Sam stopped in his tracks. Walter was pinned to the ground not by a Hellhound, but by the ill-kempt security guard, James. His unnaturally long nails were digging like claws into the biblical scholar's leg, leaving jagged gashes behind.

Sam leveled the shotgun and let loose a rock salt shell. The spread hit James square in the chest, hammering him into the far wall. But before Walter could move, the security guard was back on him, his eyes pitch black. Sam's finger pulled back on the trigger once more, but nothing happened.

Damn it. Out of shells.

"Help me!" Walter cried as James took another swipe at

him, gouging at his face. The demon then used his grip to lift Walter and slam him into the nearby sofa. Blood splattered across the cream wallpaper and a portrait of Harry Truman that hung nearby.

James then dived at the metal briefcase that had been hidden under Walter's body. As he scratched at the lock, Julia scrambled up behind him, her pistol raised.

The shot nearly deafened Sam, who was mere feet from the business end of the handgun as it fired. The bullet tore into James's back, exiting through his right shoulder and leaving a trail of gore across the couch. His limp body slumped over the briefcase, but Sam knew it wouldn't stay down for long.

It took a lot more than that to kill a demon.

"Hey. Ass-hat."

Sam turned to see his brother clambering over the jagged glass left in the window frame. Dean lobbed a set of shells toward Sam, who caught them deftly and began loading.

"Drop your weapons!" a voice shouted forcefully from the hallway. Sam looked up to see a brace of rifles pointed at him, a pair of burly police officers holding them. They were addressing both Sam and Julia, who was still holding her pistol as she tended to her father.

Sam was faced with about a dozen choices. Surrender, run, fight, try to talk... but he chose none of them. Instead he froze in place, fearfully eyeing James's now-stirring body. Julia, on the other hand, spun around immediately and put the policemen in her sights. Like it or not, they were going to assume that Sam was working with her. That left him no option—he had to run.

As the officers opened fire, he dived for cover. Thankfully, their aim was wide, shattering the wood frame of the archway between the lounge and the main room instead of Sam's head.

"Sam!" Dean yelled, his voice worried. He was struggling to unhook himself from his harness. He had his switchblade out and was sawing roughly at the fraying straps.

The sound of gunfire had pushed the rest of the room's occupants further into the corner—except one. Shochat cinched the wrappings on his hand tight and moved toward the broken jar at the chamber's center. Scooping as many of the fragments as he could into his good hand, he deposited them gently in his jacket pocket. Behind him, Eli was squealing helplessly.

Sam heard the sound of Julia's pistol firing several times, then she stumbled into the main room. Walter's briefcase was firmly in her grasp as she headed for the window—and Dean.

"Will that hold two?" she demanded.

"What the eff, lady?" Dean snapped back, stepping away from her.

Seconds later, James barreled into the room, his face twisted into a canine snarl.

Behind him, the police officers stared in awe at the mortally wounded man bounding across the room. Their rifles dropped to their sides as James hurled himself into Julia, who in turn fell into Dean. The trio stumbled, off-balance, then toppled out of the open window.

FIFTEEN

Friggin' demons! Dean's thoughts screamed as the cold New York breeze rushed through his hair. With Julia gripped tightly to his side, he swung nearly fifteen feet out of the window before gravity whipped them back against the Waldorf's stone façade.

Under the combined weight of two people, Dean's harness was near its breaking point. That he had started to saw through it a minute earlier certainly wasn't helping. As they impacted the granite wall, Dean could feel Julia's grip loosen. *Given the circumstances, it wouldn't be the end of the world if she fell*, he reflected. Non-crazy ladies don't bum-rush you next to an open window on the thirty-fifth floor.

Out of the corner of his eye, Dean spotted James clinging to a small outcropping. *Guy must be built*, he thought. *I sure as hell couldn't hold on to that tiny ledge.* That thought was short-lived, however, as James spun toward the suspended couple and flung himself at them. He was risking a long drop if he missed, which was a good possibility considering the strong winds.

He didn't miss. Julia's grip slackened even further as James impacted her. The two of them flailed desperately, further straining the integrity of Dean's harness.

"Pull me up!" Dean shouted at the open window above them. A second later, a policeman's head popped out, but he didn't grab the rope. Instead, twelve stories above him, Dean clocked Marco watching in shock from the roof. "Marco! Pull!"

Then Dean's attention was drawn to the demon clawing its way upward, toward the object Julia was still clutching in one hand—the metal briefcase.

"He's after the case! Drop it!" Dean urged, but Julia ignored him. Instead, she kicked at James, trying to dislodge him. The frayed rope connected to Dean's harness began to twist apart, the strands snapping one by one.

"Drop it or we all die!" he yelled. Julia locked eyes with Dean, and he could see how torn she was. *Guess that scroll's just as important to them as it is to us.*

"You can't read it if you're a corpse!" Dean asserted desperately.

Reluctantly, she held the case away from her body, as if she was about to let it drop. James dug his fingers into Dean's legs, using them to push off toward the briefcase.

That guy's suicidal, Dean thought. *Oh wait—demon.*

James thrashed through the air, grabbing the case tight and wrenching it out of Julia's hand.

Both demon and briefcase plummeted toward the city street below.

Dean looked down at Julia, who was still barely clinging to his harness. Even with both hands free, she wouldn't last much longer.

"You're a crazy bitch, you know that?" he declared.

No one had noticed Eli's exit. As the big guy's partner dangled out of the window with the lady and the briefcase, Eli had taken the opportunity to leave the premises. He prided himself on recognizing opportunities as they presented themselves, and the opportunity to survive was an enticing one.

Upon exiting the Waldorf Astoria, Eli was thrust into a large crowd that had gathered around the security guard's fallen body. The taxi cab the guy had landed on was totaled, its engine compartment several inches shorter than it had been a minute earlier. The sight of his body was sickening. It was as if he'd been hit by a freight train—every part of him smashed into an unrecognizable mess. Fully half of the assembled people couldn't take their eyes off the gruesome display, while the other half gawked at the theatrics taking place 300 feet above, where the two idiots still swung perilously.

What no one seemed to notice was the steel briefcase that had landed a dozen yards from the demolished taxi.

What a day the Lord has made, Eli mused, as he casually picked up the briefcase and disappeared into the bustle of New York City.

Inside the Presidential Suite, chaos reigned. Sam had nearly jumped out of the window after his brother, but was quickly restrained by the two policemen. The room was in shambles, with broken clay, glass and furniture littering the floor. Mr. Feldman tried to relate what had happened to the officers as they cleared the adjacent rooms, but none of them could explain how the security guard had come back to life after apparently being fatally shot. It was nearly a minute before anyone else realized that Dean and Julia were still hanging outside the window.

"Everyone get back," the older policeman ordered. "We have this under control." The officer leaned his head out of the window and tried half-heartedly to grab the taut rope that they were dangling from.

I have to get to the roof, Sam realized. *If they pull him in here, we're going to be stuck in prison until the Apocalypse.*

As the other policeman was occupied with trying to radio a dispatcher, Sam's opportunity to escape had arrived. Leaving the main room, Sam saw Walter crawling toward the exit. He considered what Walter had said about the War Scroll: *If the wrong people get their hands on it... Well, that would be bad.* What were the chances that Sam and Walter were on the same side? Despite strong impulses to the contrary, Sam decided not to abandon the guy. Slinging a hand under the injured man's arm, Sam quickly had him out of the suite and to the bank of elevators.

"Thank you..." Walter managed to gasp, his breath ragged.

"Don't." Sam didn't want gratitude from the man until he had decided what to do with him. Entering the elevator, he pressed the button for the forty-seventh floor.

"Down," Walter wheezed. "We need to get to the street."

"Your daughter is hanging by a thread, Walter. You're just going to abandon her?"

"She is? She's alive?"

"Not if we don't pull her up to the roof quick."

They exited the elevator and worked their way up the service stairwell as fast as Walter's damaged legs allowed. On the roof, they found a stocky, swarthy man already trying to reel in Dean and Julia.

"What in God's creation is going on down there?" the man asked, nodding at Walter's torn-up legs.

Sam searched for the words to explain what had just happened. As usual, the exploits of the Winchester brothers were beyond rationalization.

"Communists," he said decisively. It was the best he could do.

"Help me lift them up."

By that point, the rest of the window washers strapped to the side of the Waldorf Astoria had stopped working and directed their full attention to Dean and Julia. Dean had started to wall-walk horizontally away from the open window of the Presidential Suite. Sam noted at least three sets of uniformed arms reaching out of the window, indicating that backup had arrived. *Won't be long before they think to come up here*, he surmised.

The mechanism for raising the suspended window washers was little more than a hand crank attached to the system of pulleys and levers. The man leaned into the crank with all his weight, but couldn't get it to turn. Sam moved to help him, adding his strength to the guy's considerable heft. Between the two of them, they got the crank to turn, but very slowly. It would take at least ten minutes to pull Dean and Julia up at that rate.

"Little help Walter?" Sam asked, but he could see Walter was in no shape to exert himself. His skin was pale from the blood loss. All of his energy was dedicated just to remaining upright.

"This gear ain't designed for two," the Italian stated.

Glancing around the roof, Sam tried to come up with another option. If he could tell which room Dean was outside of now, he could break the window and pull him inside. Of course, the police were just as likely to come up with that plan, and they were a lot closer to Dean.

"How long's the rope?" Sam asked as mental gears clicked into place.

"Long."

"Long enough to lower them to the ground?" The man mulled that for a beat, examining the thick coil of rope. "Should be."

Sam wasn't reassured but he knew they didn't have another choice. He nodded and the two of them began rapidly unspooling the line. At ground level, a cluster of police cruisers had assembled at the 50th Street entrance.

Either way, up or down, I'm handing Dean over to the cops. Better that than waiting for him to fall, Sam thought, continuing to turn the crank.

When roughly half the line had been let out, a shotgun blast echoed between the buildings. Sam peered over the edge and saw Dean scrambling through an open window—presumably one he had just broken with the other shotgun in his duffel.

"Change of plans," Sam called out to Walter, who was leaning woozily against the railing. "We're going to the subway."

Dean had chosen the window at random. That the room belonged to an attractive Asian woman was mere happy coincidence. That she was drying off after a shower had to be, in Dean's opinion, God's cosmic reward to him for saving Julia's life. *If there is a God*, the logical half of Dean's brain chimed in. *All signs point to absentee Father.*

Unfortunately, the situation demanded that Dean hurry along. Though if cell phone numbers had existed in 1954, he certainly would have left his.

Dean decided that the stairwell was less of a risk than the elevator. Skipping two steps at a time, he practically galloped down the stairs, his duffel jostling on his back. Julia kept up the pace despite everything her body had just been put through. When they reached the bottom floor, Dean knew they'd have to switch stairwells—and that meant going through the lobby.

"Do you know where you're going?" Julia demanded.

Dean's snort was his only response.

"Because if you don't, I'd just as soon go my own way."

"You and me both, sugar. But if you want to get out of here a free woman, the only way is my way." That seemed to shut her up, for the time being. "From the look of things, you royally jacked our plan back there."

"Likewise."

"Hey! I saved your ass. Without me, you'd be just another spot of bird poop to clean off the sidewalk."

Julia opened her mouth to respond, but no words came out.

"Yeah, that's right. What have you done for me, 'sides throwing me out of a window? I knew you were trouble the minute I saw you."

"You wanted to sleep with me the minute you saw me," Julia shot back.

"But I didn't. *Because you looked like trouble.*" They had arrived at the bottom floor, where a myriad voices were audible outside the stairwell door.

"Quiet."

Julia scowled. "You're the one who's ranting," she hissed.

Timing their dash perfectly, Dean and Julia were able to slip into the Park Avenue lobby unnoticed. Most everyone had hurried outside after hearing that a man had jumped. Dean held open the door to the garage-access stairwell—but Julia was no longer behind him. Scouring the lobby, he clocked her walking toward the main entrance.

"You trying to get yourself arrested?" Dean asked as he caught up with her.

She turned to face him, now ice cold.

"I need what's in that briefcase. You have no idea how important it is."

"You've got it all backwards. *I* need that scroll. *You* don't know how important it is. But *neither* of us is gonna go out there after it."

"You can't stop me."

Dean leaned in intimately close. "If you're going to go out there, at least tell me you still have your gun."

Julia reached down to her waist, but the pistol wasn't there. She looked mournfully out on to the street where it had fallen.

"Thought so. Let's get one thing straight—I'm not helping you get away. You know things about the scroll, and I need to know those things too. You're my *prisoner*."

Slapping the side of his duffel, Dean smirked.

"Now unless you want to get an ass full of rock salt, how about you follow me?"

The Presidential Siding was a custom-built underground train station, constructed to allow Presidents, dignitaries and celebrities direct access to the Waldorf Astoria. Their train cars could pull directly up to the hotel, bypassing the need to secure Grand Central Terminal, or sit in New York traffic. Most of the time, the rail siding sat unused, which made it perfect for their getaway.

By the time Sam and Walter made it to the rail platform, Dean and Julia were already there. Sam wasn't overjoyed to see Julia again after her actions upstairs, but watching the tender moment she shared with her father helped take the edge off the hostility.

"You okay, Dean?" Sam asked.

"I will be, soon as we get out of here."

Walter steadied himself against the platform wall.

"I'm almost afraid to ask, but are we meant to cross this?" He pointed at the vast expanse of tracks in front of them. Since they were underground, with almost no lighting, the tracks seemed to extend forever. A steady stream of trains was moving in and out of the area. The mayhem of Grand Central Terminal was just audible over the din of the engines.

"That's the idea," Sam answered. "Before anybody thinks to look down here."

Julia's eyes caught on her father's pant leg, which was dripping with blood.

"He can't dodge a train like that," she said.

Dean pumped his shotgun with conviction. He threw the duffel at Sam.

"He doesn't have to dodge one. He's got to catch one," he said.

The group made their way across the tracks in silence, none of them comfortable with their new-found fellowship. Sam noticed that Dean kept his shotgun leveled at Julia the whole time, which was probably a smart move. Even if they were playing for the same team, Julia had been a little too gung-ho during her aborted heist. He also still wondered if she had been the one to swipe the knife.

With some difficulty, they were able to hoist Walter onto the back of a south-bound train. For the first time in hours, Sam relaxed. They had completely failed in their mission, but somehow, they had survived. Seated across from him, Dean looked glum.

"What is it?" Sam asked.

Rubbing the train's shoddy upholstery with distaste, Dean sighed.

"I miss the Impala."

SIXTEEN

James McMannon felt as if a heavy burden was lifting off his back. A white light appeared before him, and he wanted to go toward it.

There was an eruption of noise.

The light disappeared. James forced his eyes open. In front of him, he could see a wavering group of people—they looked like they were in an enormous, swirling heat devil—as if they were caught in the hot air that rose off the black streets of the city in the middle of summer.

He heard a voice in his left ear.

"Hey. Stay still, the ambulance is coming."

James thought he was answering to the voice, but he realized that all he could hear was ringing. Then he saw that white light again. He got up, at least he thought he did, and walked toward its beckoning glimmer.

At that moment, everything that James McMannon had every thought, felt, or loved left his body.

All that was left was the animal.

In all of Hank Caprezie's years on the force, he had never seen a man fall thirty floors and live, but here he was. And he was one of the family, a security guard.

"Are you sure you're okay?" Hank peered into the guy's eyes. "You need to go to the hospital, stay still."

Without responding, the man slid himself off the crushed taxi. Standing in the middle of the crowd, he looked around, as though searching for something. His neck was at an unnatural angle, which he corrected by grasping it on both sides and twisting his head back into place. When he turned back to Hank, his eyes were pitch black. Hank took an involuntary step back.

"Hey man, I really think you should stay!" Hank called.

The guy didn't listen. Instead, he walked toward the throng of people and disappeared.

I'm going to have a hell of a time explaining this to the captain, Hank thought.

Dean spent the train ride trying to interrogate Walter and Julia. Unfortunately for him, they weren't talking. It was clear they knew much more about the scrolls than Walter had let on in his meeting with Sam, but their motivations were still hazy. *Do they want to protect the scrolls, or destroy them?* Dean wondered. It was possible that they were all on the same side, working toward the exact same goal, but without more information from Walter and Julia, Dean had no way of knowing.

When the group got off the train in lower Manhattan, the bleeding from Walter's leg had slowed, but he was still in need of a doctor's care. They looked at one another. They didn't have the scrolls, nor any idea how to find them. They had reached an impasse.

Sam looked at Dean, his feelings obvious. *It's time to go.*

Just like that, the Winchesters turned and started walking uptown.

"You're just going to leave us here?" Julia cried. "I thought I was your prisoner?"

Dean turned on his heel. "I release you. And from what I can tell, sweet cheeks, you'll do fine on your own. Both of you."

"You're going to need us," Julia called as Walter faltered a step. Sam's face registered a slight flash of sympathy. What Julia really meant, of course, was that she needed them. *Are we really going to leave a bleeding old man on the street, especially if his daughter might be in possession of our stolen knife?*

Dean punched him in the shoulder. "Let's get going."

Apparently, they were.

That evening, Sam and Dean checked into a dive hotel on the Lower East Side. With all the chaos they had caused at the Waldorf that day, it was too much of a risk to go back to the apartment, even if they had used aliases. They bought a pizza and took it back to their room. Despite their exhaustion, they still had to eat, and neither of them was in the mood for the human interaction a restaurant visit would require.

Sam wondered how much Walter and Julia really knew.

It seemed likely now that they had been the ones to ransack the Villard House apartment, and Walter had spoken at length about the scrolls at the Bible Society. But did they know the true significance of the War Scroll? Could they possibly comprehend how important it was for Sam and Dean to take possession of it?

Neither of them knew any of the answers. All they knew was that in the morning, they'd come up with a new plan. Until then, they'd eat pizza and bask in the hopelessness of their cause.

Long past nightfall, Dean stepped out onto the building's front stoop. Sam was already there, staring quietly at the black sky.

"Can't see stars for shit here," Dean said.

Sam's lips curled into a half-smile—the one he reserved for Dean's attempts to cheer him up.

"I hadn't noticed."

"Good work today, Sammy."

"Good work? We got hosed, Dean. We had to run away with our tails between our legs, and now we don't even have a clue where the scroll is. For all we know, it really was destroyed."

"You kept it together in there. Me, I wouldn't have taken well to Julia barging in like that."

Sam nodded. Then, after a moment's silence, said, "Dean... is that a shotgun down your pants?"

Seemingly out of nowhere, Dean produced the shotgun, then hid it once more down the back of his jeans.

"After everything, I wanted to keep it handy. But I don't want to get arrested for firearm possession after what we got away with today."

"Actually, I think the only real crime was destruction of property," Sam said, thinking back.

"Plus breaking and entering."

"And resisting arrest."

"And assault with a deadly weapon."

Sam's brow furrowed in confusion. "When was that? I didn't shoot anybody that wasn't a demon."

Dean smirked. "I shot you."

That was enough to get a small laugh out of Sam.

"Sorry about that, by the way."

Sam reached for his neck, where tiny bits of glass and rock salt were no doubt still embedded.

"No, Dean, I'm the one who should be sorry."

"Hey now, let's not start with this. One 'I'm sorry' is the daily limit."

"I'm serious. I'm sorry I brought us here. We didn't know what we were getting into, and now..."

"Now we're stuck, is that what you're getting at?"

"Maybe. What if Don leaves us here to rot, chasing after a scroll that doesn't exist?"

"No angel douche is gonna leave me stranded with the Cleavers. We'll find a way, Sam. I promise you that."

They sat quietly for a minute, then Sam said hesitantly, "Am I a coward?"

Dean didn't know how to respond to that. In the end he just said, "No."

"I mean, if it was you. If you knew the fight could be won, and all it took was your life—"

"That's not all it takes, Sam."

Sam nodded, but Dean could tell he wasn't satisfied.

"That's *not* all it takes. You saying 'yes' to Lucifer isn't just about giving up your life, it's about giving up everything. Letting the angels have their way with the Earth, with what's rightfully ours. Sam, if I could say 'yes' to Michael and end this here and now, I would in an instant, but we both know it ain't that simple."

"I didn't mean saying 'yes.' I meant..."

"What? Out with it."

"I don't know. Nevermind."

"You're tired. We both are. Get some rest, it'll make more sense in the morning."

When Dean reached the door, he looked back at his brother, still seated on the front steps. In so many ways, Sam would forever be the little boy that Dean had spent his entire youth protecting. A familiar fear raced through his mind. The same fear that had plagued him for months. More than anything else, Dean feared that Sam wasn't strong enough.

He feared that, when the time came, Sam *would* say "Yes."

SEVENTEEN

Sam didn't want to dream. He cherished the opportunity to sleep—it was the dreams that were the problem. After what he'd seen and experienced as a hunter, any therapist would expect his slumbering visions to be horrific—monsters, demons, death and dismemberment—but any of those things would be welcome in place of what he *did* dream about. Family. His brother, his father, even his mother, who had died before he could walk. They were the figures that filled his dreams, living happy lives, untouched by the dark plans of Azazel, Lilith, and Lucifer.

Untouched by Sam's own actions. Breaking the Final Seal. The Apocalypse. The End of Everything. For months on end, the dreams were the same. The Winchester family sitting around a dinner table telling mundane stories about their small problems. *Normal problems.* Dean was younger, maybe seventeen years old, not yet the independent adult man he was in 2010. John was a mechanic, working long hours, but relishing every moment of it. Mary was... alive. What else mattered? Almost everything was exactly how Sam had imagined it as a child, while sitting alone in dank motel rooms waiting for John to come back from a hunt.

The only difference? Sam wasn't there. Their perfect life was only possible because *he* didn't exist. No Sam meant no yellow-eyed demon coming in the night, no fire destroying the house, no death sentence for Mary. No need for John's twenty-year path to revenge. No meeting Jessica, no reason for her to become Azazel's next victim. Sam couldn't close his eyes without seeing it. Somewhere out there, Jessica could have been happy and *alive* without him.

Sam didn't want to dream. Simple unconsciousness suited him much better.

In the morning, Sam and Dean gathered what little stuff they had with them and headed out. They decided that Sam would try to get back into the American Bible Society to see if he could find any information in Walter's office. Meanwhile Dean was going to try to track down James the demon security guard. If he really was a 'guard dog,' he might lead them straight to the scrolls.

Sneaking into the American Bible Society was relatively straightforward. The rear entrance was locked, but Sam used one of his credit cards and picked it with ease. *That's an advantage of working in 1954*, Sam thought. *They're not as paranoid about security.* He briefly considered the possibility that the police hadn't yet been to Walter's workplace, but that was unlikely. Mr. Feldman knew Walter's real name—

indeed it was probably his distinction in the field that had convinced Mr. Feldman to let him bid in the first place.

Entering the busy maze of small passageways at the back of the building, it was nearly impossible to avoid encountering people. Luckily, every scholar he passed had their nose in a book.

Still, got to move fast.

Reaching Walter's office, Sam found the place in chaos. Books littered the floor, a massive shelf was upended and resting at an angle across Walter's desk, and his typewriter had been smashed to pieces.

Sam swung the door closed, hoping that no one would be curious enough to come looking through the ransacked room.

From behind a bookcase, he heard a voice.

"Don't come any closer!"

Walter peeked over the edge of the fallen furniture.

"Sam?"

"What are you doing here?" Sam asked.

"It's my office," Walter said, emerging and looking around. "Or at least it *was* my office."

Sam noticed that he had clean pants on but was still struggling to put weight on his right leg particularly.

"Who did this?" Sam asked. "Cops?"

Walter shook his head. "The police came and went yesterday afternoon, according to one of my colleagues. This must have happened during the night."

"So you made some friends yesterday," Sam said.

"It would seem so." Walter opened the notebook that he was holding. "Anyway, I couldn't sleep last night. I've been here since four. I keep seeing that... thing."

"James—the security guard?"

"That thing wasn't a person. Doesn't deserve to be called a person's name. What about you? What are you doing here?"

Sam perched on the edge of the ruined desk.

"What do you know about demonology, Walter?"

The scholar swallowed, grimacing.

"It's part of the Christian faith."

"And?"

"And I've read the Bible. I've read all the apocryphal texts. I know what they say about demons, I just—"

"Didn't think you'd ever see one?" Sam offered.

Walter avoided Sam's gaze. "My colleagues call this sort of talk 'occult'—'hidden,' out of the ordinary man's view. How is it that you know so much about it, Sam?"

"You could say I'm a bit of a scholar, like you. I just go about my research a little differently. More 'hands on.'"

"So how does one kill a demon?" Walter asked.

Sam remembered Ruby's knife, which was the quickest way of dispatching a demon. *Has Julia got it?* he wondered again. If Sam told Walter the knife's purpose, it was possible he and Julia would go after James without Sam and Dean's help. It seemed sensible to keep some information hidden.

Don't give Walter too much rope. Or he could strangle you with it.

"There are ways," Sam finally replied.

Nodding, Walter flipped his sketch over so Sam could see it. In broad gray strokes, Walter had laid out the basic shape of a hellish-looking canine creature, its snarling teeth dripping with blood. It uncannily resembled the mental picture Sam had of a Hellhound.

"Not drawing a kids' book, huh?"

"For a second, while it was attacking me, I could swear it..." Walter stopped, collecting his thoughts. "I could swear it changed. Became something else." He tapped the drawing with the pencil. "This."

Now it was Sam who was confused.

"What do you mean, like a shifter?" He caught himself, remembering that Walter wouldn't have a clue that shapeshifters existed. "I mean, did it physically change shape? Grow fur?"

"I'm not sure. I was distracted by all the scratching and biting."

Sam took the notebook from Walter, squinting closely at the hellish image.

"I take it that's not the typical demon's M.O.?" Walter asked.

"No. Not at all." What the hell kind of creature was this—could it be a Hellhound?

"You recognize it?"

Images of Lilith's white eyes flitted through Sam's memory.

"Kind of," Sam said. "Do any of your books ever mention Hellhounds?"

Walter shook his head, no.

It wasn't surprising, given the mythological nature of the beasts. Their connection to Christian theology was tenuous at best.

"You've run into one before?" Walter asked.

"We've run into a lot of things."

As Sam pondered the possibilities, he realized a particularly dire one. In 1954, Lilith was still alive, probably roaming the earth, eating babies, as was her wont. Could she, or the yellow-eyed demon for that matter, be involved with this strange creature? Sam decided it was worth giving Walter a few more scraps of information.

"Hellhounds are brutal, fearless creatures. They're Hell's enforcers."

"What, like, if you make a deal with the Devil?" Walter joked.

"Yes. Exactly."

Walter blanched. "Oh."

"The last time we saw one, it was obeying a very powerful demon named Lilith. She's actually the reason we're in this situation—" Sam stopped when he saw the strange look on Walter's face. "What's wrong?"

"Lilith?"

"Yeah."

"The demon Lilith, the *first* demon, Lilith."

"Yeah."

"You've met her?" Walter asked, his voice excited.

"I *killed* her," Sam answered. *Well, more or less.*

For a second Walter was silent. Then he rubbed his hands over his notebook as he began to speak, half to himself, as though talking through a math problem.

"There's lore about Lilith, you know. That she has a demonic dog as a companion." Walter eyed Sam. "I may have never seen a demon, but I know my Bible, and it seems like that could be what nearly took my leg off yesterday."

"It may have a dog's bite, but it looked like a regular guy," Sam said.

"Young man, we are talking about thousands of years of human history. Where Lucifer, demons and angels all inhabited the same dark universe. I would think those entities could think up whatever they damn well wanted to."

Sam nodded, he knew that all too well.

"Do you know what it says? The War of the Sons?" Sam pressed.

"If I did, I wouldn't need to steal it."

"How do you know it's important enough to steal without knowing what it says?" Sam persisted. "I mean, why were you after the War Scroll specifically, and not the rest of the set?"

"The rest of the Dead Sea Scrolls are phenomenally important, just not in the same way," Walter said, bypassing Sam's first question.

"Walter, you and I went through something yesterday that would send most people running for the hills, but here we both are. It seems as if we might be after the same thing. Either we can share information, or—"

"Live together, die alone?" Walter interrupted. "We don't trust you. Julia nor me."

"Well, no offense Walter, but we trust you two even less, and for better reasons," Sam said. "So what do you know about the scrolls?"

Walter sighed. He seemed to contemplate his next

sentence very carefully. "I know the War Scroll is important, because... because I've been waiting for it my entire life."

"What, like you were destined to find it?"

"*I* don't have a destiny," Walter said. "All I had was a mother, who told me a story when I was little, the same one every night. A story about the day that good would finally triumph over evil, and how if I was lucky, I'd get to see that day." Sam leaned forward, intrigued. "And if I was very, very lucky, I'd get to be a part of that battle."

Sam's jaw clenched. "Doesn't sound that lucky to me."

"The War Scroll is how good triumphs in that final battle. It's a set of instructions, written thousands of years ago, by incredibly devout Jews during Roman rule in Judea. The Essenes spent their days in solitude, transcribing the Word of God. Some believe they were His prophets."

"And you believe it?" Sam asked.

"I never knew my mother to lie to me."

Sam knew all about destiny, and about the weight of a parent's expectations. It seemed as if Walter had allowed himself to be pushed down the path his mother had planned for him.

"Walter, I think we can help each other," Sam said softly. "Why don't you gather your stuff and come with me?"

"Right, my things…" Walter absently drummed his fingers on the notebook with the sort of deep deliberation that Sam didn't see very often. Not from Dean, anyway.

"Wait," Walter said suddenly, his eyes wide. He hastily pushed aside a pile of dusty tomes, revealing a much larger work underneath. It was roughly ten inches by twelve, set in a thick leather cover. As Walter flipped the yellowed pages, Sam could see they were filled with Enochian, the language of the angels. "Pages are missing," Walter said, in despair. "Without them, I won't be able to translate the scroll."

"If the pages are gone, we'll just have to—"

"No," Walter said, voice filled with new hope, "I don't think they would have found it."

He led Sam through a small door in the back of the office.

"It's in the toilet?" Sam said, seeing the tiny private bathroom.

Walter smiled broadly as he fumbled through a rack of magazines. Hidden amongst them was another ancient volume, with the thickness of a dictionary. If its cover once held a title, it had long since faded.

"You keep *that* in the pisser?"

EIGHTEEN

Slipping into one of his most-often used aliases, an FBI agent, Dean visited the 51st Precinct and got James's last known address. *His sister's house in Queens. Great.*

Dean hopped onto the subway and made the twenty-minute journey to the outer borough.

Burnt-out candles covered the front steps of the McMannon residence. Dean wondered if the vigil was for James, or if there was something else going on that he didn't yet understand.

Knocking on the front door, Dean again pulled out his FBI badge. The woman who eventually opened the door looked battered and used up, her days-old makeup was smeared down her face. She had clearly spent the night weeping.

"Sorry to disturb you, ma'am," Dean said kindly. "I'm Agent Page with the Federal Bureau of Investigation."

The woman wiped a little mascara from the corner of her eye. "You'd better come in."

The woman led him inside, where he found Julia sat on the living room couch, smiling like a wolf.

The woman introduced herself as Mrs. Doyle. "And this is Miss Sands," she added, nodding at Julia. "The police sent her to visit me and check on my well-being. But I expect you'd know all about that."

"I'm not sure, Madam," Dean said, raising an eyebrow at Julia. "It seems strange that they would send such a *young* lady to do such an important job."

"Oh, I know," Mrs. Doyle said. "But she has been very kind."

Julia glared at Dean. Ignoring her, Dean looked around the dark and pokey interior of Mrs. Doyle's home—it was stuffed floor-to-ceiling with religious icons. The deep irony struck Dean immediately. The world could be cruel.

Dean took a seat opposite Julia. She had beaten him here. Somehow. Dean didn't like how the day was going.

"Can I offer you a cup of tea?" Mrs. Doyle said, shuffling in from the kitchen.

Dean smiled politely and took the saucer and cup from her.

"Would you mind telling me when you last saw James McMannon?"

"I've already told the detectives everything I know," she mumbled in reply. "He left with Barney to go to work, and neither of them came home that night."

"Barney?" Dean asked.

"…My son."

"Of course," Dean replied gently, feeling for the woman.

He was certain her son was already dead. "But James reported for work the next day?"

Mrs. Doyle broke eye contact with Dean, and began turning a Saint Christopher medallion over in her hands. "Yes."

Julia shot Dean a suspicious look. "Madam, have you been in contact with James?" Dean asked.

"No."

"The only way we can find your son is if we know everything," Dean persisted gently.

Mrs. Doyle recoiled in horror, her lip quivering intensely. She looked like she was on the verge of total emotional collapse.

"But..."

"What?" Dean asked.

"How could you not know? The detectives, they found..." she trailed off, tears spilling freely down her face. "They found his body."

Smooth, Dean. Although Sam was the more emotionally sensitive of the Winchester brothers, Dean's heart wasn't made of stone. Mrs. Doyle had lost everything she had, and it was already too late for Dean to help her. After the gunshot wound and the fall that James had sustained, his host wouldn't survive once the demon left his body. To all intents and purposes, James was just as dead as Barney.

"I'm very sorry, Mrs. Doyle," Dean said sincerely. "Of course, had I known..."

"You wouldn't be wasting your time talking to me," the woman finished.

"That's not true," Dean said. "I've still got some questions about James."

Mrs. Doyle's face went even whiter, but she nodded okay.

"He ever come home acting strangely? Like he was drunk, or not himself?"

"No."

"He hang out with any shady characters? People that weren't so... wholesome?" he asked, pointing at the largest crucifix in the room.

"He's a good man."

"You don't think it's possible he's involved with this?"

"He's a victim. I know it. Both of them are."

"Did James go to church with you, Mrs. Doyle?"

She nodded, hesitantly.

"But not every week," Dean stated flatly.

"Some Sundays he'd have work."

Julia leaned in and grasped the woman's shaking hands.

"It's terrible this has happened to your family, Mrs. Doyle. But if James was here this morning, then you need to tell the agent."

Where's she getting that from? Dean wondered. Was he missing something obvious here?

Mrs. Doyle faltered under Julia's scrutiny.

"He didn't do anything wrong, I just know it. Please don't hurt him."

I'll be damned, Dean thought. *Julia's good for something after all.*

"Was he here? Did he say anything?" Julia continued her grilling.

"No. He didn't say much at all... That was the strange part. He came in, looking a real mess, went upstairs. I heard him shuffling around. Then he came back down and did something, I don't know, not like him."

"What?" Dean asked.

"He asked if I knew how to get to the train station. But that's not how he said it. It was like he didn't know the word he was looking for."

"And why is that strange?" Julia queried, moving forward in her seat.

"Well, because he worked at Grand Central Station for fifteen years as a desk clerk. How could he not know where it was?"

Julia and Dean exchanged glances. That was strange indeed.

"That was before you heard from the detective?" Julia asked.

Mrs. Doyle nodded sadly. "I don't know where he's going. I just don't want him to get hurt." She looked at Dean desperately. "Promise me you won't hurt him."

"We just want to bring your brother back. That's all." *If only that were true.*

Dean followed Julia out of the dimly lit house and into the bright morning sun in a somber mood. Whatever the demon's interest in the scroll, it was clear he was willing to kill.

"How the hell did you get here before me?" he demanded as soon as they were out of earshot of the house. "And what *the hell* are you doing?"

Julia accelerated her pace, leaving Dean struggling to keep up.

"Hey! I'm talking to you," Dean said, grabbing her elbow.

"What's wrong with you?" Julia asked spinning around angrily. "You stop us from getting the scrolls, then you come barging in on my interview. You're like a bull dressed in heels in a china shop. Skidding around, and breaking everything in its wake."

"You'd never find me in heels." Dean said, scowling. Then he smiled. "Listen, it's clear we're both after the same thing. And even though you're obnoxious, it seems to me we'd be better off working together."

"I get the jump on you one time and you want to team up?"

"I don't need your help. I just don't want to have to kill you."

"Why should I team up with you? I'm always ahead of you, Dean Winchester." Julia smiled, holding up Dean's wallet. "And here I've been writing my love letters to Malcolm Young…"

Dean felt his jacket for his wallet.

"You've got to be kidding me," he gasped. "Impressive. Not very many women can dip like that."

"I'm not most women. That FBI shield is a piece of crap, by the way, totally unrealistic." Julia stopped in front of the steps leading up to the raised subway platform.

"So what do you say? Partners?" Even as he said the words, Dean knew he was going to have trouble convincing Sam. Even though his brother was always the more trusting of the two, knowing Sam, he wouldn't want other people to get hurt finding their way out of this mess.

Julia surveyed Dean. "I guess. For now." She turned and took the stairs two at a time.

"Hey, how did you know?" Dean asked, following her.

"Know what?"

"That James had been there."

"Are you kidding? The whole place smelled like wet dog."

Dean pushed coins into the payphone on the subway platform. He waited for the operator and then asked for the Turtle Bay hotel, room thirty-three. Dean listened as the desk clerk rang up to the third floor. In that era, it seemed some hotels only had one telephone per level. Through the receiver, Dean heard his brother's heavy footfall as he approached.

"Dean? What's going on?"

"Meet me at Grand Central. The guard dog is taking a train today. Don't know where or what time."

"When are you going to get there?" Sam asked.

"Soon as I can. I'm at 111th street in Queens. Oh, and Sam? I might have company."

"Um… I was going to say the same thing," Sam admitted. "Walter was at his office. He has a book, and some ideas about what is possessing James."

"Fair enough. Julia got to James's sister before I did. Anyway, we'll meet you at Grand Central."

Sam hung up and retreated back to the room where Walter was rewrapping his injured leg with clean gauze.

"We've got to meet Julia and Dean at Grand Central."

Walter looked up, surprised. "Grand Central? Is that where the scrolls are?"

"Seems guard dog James is taking a train ride. We need to follow him, he's our only lead."

"Well then, let's go."

Sam stuffed the shotguns into the bottom of the duffel bag and put his and Dean's 2010 clothes on top. They'd used the clothes to conceal the shape of the weapons in the bag on their way to the Waldorf, which turned out to be fortuitous, since they hadn't been able to return to their apartment. Walter had taken a small suitcase from his office. It was empty, but could hold the scrolls when and if they found them.

"How much money do you have?" Sam asked.

"Not much. Three dollars." Walter said, looking through his worn leather wallet.

Sam looked at the window and the fire escape beyond it. They were going to have to hoof it out the back. There was no telling who was watching the hotel. Plus, Sam didn't want to pay for two nights. He opened up the creaky, dust-laden window. Down below, a large dumpster was about twenty feet too far away from them. It was going to be difficult getting an old man with a leg injury out of the window.

"I can make it," Walter reassured Sam.

The two men scrambled down the fire escape to the platform that hung about twenty-five feet in the air. Sam was six-foot four—that meant he still had to drop nineteen feet to the ground. He hit the uneven pavement hard.

"You okay?" Walter called.

Sam gave him a thumbs up, and then rolled the dumpster underneath the fire escape. Walter slowly let himself down, dropping with a thud. Sam pulled him off the dumpster and they hurried to the sidewalk.

NINETEEN

Julia and Dean sat in silence on the train. She had grabbed a newspaper that had been left on the seat and behaved as though she was engrossed in its contents. Dean watched her with curiosity out of the corner of his eye. Here was a woman who was just as comfortable holding a gun in people's faces and just as good at getting information out of them as he was. Dean shuddered a bit—*She's just like me, but hotter.*

Not being someone to let a tender moment go undisturbed, Dean leaned over her shoulder.

"What you reading?"

"*The Times.* Do you mind?" Julia turned the page and tried to ignore him.

He scooted closer, and she moved away.

"Aw, come on, don't be like that," Dean whispered. "I'm reading too."

Julia peeled off a page of the paper and passed it to him.

"You gave me the comics."

Julia's small heart-shaped face beamed.

"Kids like the comics."

Some twenty minutes later, the conductor announced that they were pulling into Grand Central Terminal.

Dean and Julia alighted from the train and quickly found Sam and Walter waiting for them underneath the large concourse sign. They all eyed each other suspiciously.

"So, now what?" Sam asked.

"We know he's getting on a train," Dean said, "we just don't know which one." Hundreds of people were rushing to make afternoon trains back to the suburbs, clogging the station's hallways. There were dozens of possible destinations, and none of them seemed more likely than any other.

"Okay, well let's just think a moment," Julia said as she studied the departure board. "James is after the scrolls, right? But why?"

"Your dad and I were asking ourselves that," Sam said, and Julia shot a look at her father. "James isn't possessed by a typical demon," Sam continued, "but something more like a guard dog."

"Okay, but the question is why?" Walter said.

"Someone put the guard-dog demon in with the scrolls. I saw a symbol on one of the jars, something we see quite often." Sam meant the Devil's Trap he had seen on the inside of the lid on one of the jars. "The symbol traps a demon inside it, and we can only assume that James accidentally released the demon and it possessed him. And it seems that it will go to every length to protect the scroll."

"Dad, did you know this?" Julia looked at her father with a glint of anger in her eyes. "Did you know they were cursed?"

"I didn't know for sure," Walter admitted.

Julia turned away from her father, clearly miffed that he hadn't told her about the hidden danger.

"Was there anyone at the auction that you recognized, Julia?" Sam asked, trying to anticipate where James could be going.

"Well, there was one guy, but everything was moving so quickly."

"Who?" Walter asked.

Julia searched in her purse and pulled out a billfold.

"The guy in the piano bar."

Dean stared at her incredulously. "The guy whose wallet you lifted was at the auction? Why didn't you tell us before now?"

Julia shrugged. "I lift a lot of wallets."

Dean took the wallet. Inside was a California license.

"Eli Thurman, Berkeley address."

"Wait, Eli the red-head?" Sam asked. "He disappeared right after the case fell. Slipped out while the cops were going after you guys."

"That's as good a guess as we can make," Dean said. "We in agreement?"

Walter nodded, then, after a pause, Julia agreed.

"Good," Dean said. "'Cause if we weren't, I was going to ditch your asses. Let's find that train."

The four stepped up to the ticket counter and asked

which train was leaving for California. The ticket clerk looked over his schedule.

"Not to California direct. Goes to Albany, Detroit, then Chicago. Then there is a Chicago-San Fran, the Overland Route."

"Good enough. Four tickets, please." Sam gestured for Julia to pay.

"I don't have enough money for that," Julia whispered.

"One hundred dollars and two cents," the ticket guy said as he eyed the strange quartet. "You'll have to re-ticket in Chicago."

Dean drew his face close to Julia's.

"Between all of those wallets, you don't have a hundred bucks?"

"My father and I live off of these!" Julia hissed. When Dean didn't relent, she stuffed her hand into her purse. "Fine. Give me a second."

Instead of cash, she pulled out a locker key. She walked over to a bank of steel lockers running alongside one of the station walls. Popping open a locker, Julia took out a large leather suitcase. She popped the clasps on the case and took a pair of socks from inside. She then returned to the group carrying the case. She pulled out a wad of cash from the socks and handed it to her father.

"That's living in style," Dean whispered to Sam.

"Two tickets in a sleeper car," Walter said to the clerk. He took some of the bills and shoved them over the ticket counter, then looked at Dean and Sam. "You boys find your own way."

The brothers were speechless. *These dicks don't understand who they're dealing with*, Dean thought. Walter took the tickets and led Julia away by the arm. Dean and Sam managed to lock step with them.

"You like jumping on moving trains," Walter growled. "Here's another opportunity."

On the train platform, Julia pointed out Eli Thurman's red hair. He was holding a large leather suitcase, which was wide enough to house at least four of the jars. James the security guard wasn't far behind—he was skulking around a steel pillar, keeping out of sight of Eli.

He looked as if he'd been dragged through Hell and back. *I know how that is, buddy*, Dean thought.

The plan was that Walter and Julia would check into their sleeper car and keep an eye on Eli. Sam and Dean were instructed to jump down to the other side of the tracks and, once the train pulled out, they could run alongside and jump on board, ticket free. The only thing they had to do was keep moving if they saw a ticket guy, because he would ask for their names and car number.

When the porters weren't looking, Sam and Dean walked to the end of the train and dropped down from the platform onto the rails. The platform was about chin high, giving them lots of cover to sneak around to the other side of the caboose.

"Not quite first class accommodations," Dean said as he moved along the other side of the train, trying to pick a good area where they would have enough time to run and enough train to catch once it started to pull out.

"What do you think they make of us?" Sam asked as he and Dean walked through the filthy underbelly of the tracks.

"I don't know. You're the one that made friends with Wally the Wonder Professor."

"He's a scholar, Dean. He understands the Bible, he can read Aramaic or whatever those scrolls are written in. Once we get that scroll he's going to be useful."

"Have you thought that these are regular people— well, sort of? They don't handle the idea of possession, Satan and Armageddon well. You didn't tell them about Armageddon did you?" Dean turned around, his eyes boring into his brother.

Sam moved past him, clipping him with the duffle bag.

"No, I didn't Dean. Jeez." Sam kept walking into the tunnel. Dean sighed, and followed him into the darkness.

Even though Leanne Keeny was almost a full head taller, she still struggled to follow Rose McGraw's quick step to the penthouse. Rose's large bottom swung from side to side, a movement that would have made any sailor think of home. Leanne on the other hand was lithe and leggy, a farm girl who had escaped to the big city. Getting a maid position at the Waldorf was a big thing, and her first real job besides castrating horses on her parents' farm.

Leanne tried to concentrate as Rose explained that the Waldorf Astoria expects every employee to respect each guest's privacy. Rose leaned closer, her onion breath making Leanne cringe. Rose said conspiratorially that once Joe DiMaggio was here with another woman, not Marilyn, but Leanne didn't hear it from her. Rose wiggled her red eyebrows to further emphasize how confidential that information was.

At the penthouse door, Rose dug into her apron pocket and pulled out the maid's skeleton key. She knocked, and then slipped the key into the latch.

The place was a mess, the shootout at the auction the day before had left everything in a shambles. Tufts of fluff dotted all the silk couches, there was blood on the Oriental rug and strange scratches on the floor, furniture was turned over—it was a war zone. Rose clucked her tongue, she needed to go get Maintenance. She told Leanne to get started cleaning up the pieces of glass. She would be back in a couple of minutes.

Leanne looked around the room. Then she pulled a waste bin from the maid's cart, and got down on her hands and knees with a dustpan and brush. As she swept up the shards of glass, she noticed they weren't actually glass but clay. Leanne pushed them into the basket. As she shifted her weight, she noticed in the other room that a jar had rolled underneath the bed, half obscured by the ruffled bedspread.

Leanne pulled the jar from its hiding place and carried it into the main room. She peaked outside to make sure Rose wasn't coming down the hallway, then set the jar on the table. It was tall and oblong, and the same dusty color as all the pieces that littered the floor. Leanne thought that surely the owner would be happy that one of the jars wasn't broken.

Then curiosity got the better of her. She dug her nails into the seam of the jar. At first, the lid wouldn't give, it was stuck by some sort of tar-like substance. Finally, it twisted a bit and Leanne managed to separate it from the jar. Beneath it was a horsehair stopper formed with more tar. Leanne looked around for something to pry the stopper off. She spotted a letter opener on the floor and shoved that between the seal and the lip. A whooshing sound escaped from the jar.

Leanne was knocked to the floor, her legs splayed akimbo, as a dark, thick smoke poured out of the jar, taking shape on the floor. It grew larger and broader, almost to full human size. Leanne tried to pull herself up, but the black smoke enveloped her ankles—it felt like her legs were caught in two tons of wet cement.

The last thing Leanne remembered was the acrid smoke shooting up into her mouth and forcing itself down her throat.

Ten minutes later, when Rose returned to the room with Sal the maintenance guy, Leanne was nowhere to be found.

"Children these days. You just can't trust them. Leaving the job on the first day. My stars," Rose sighed.

Sal nodded his head in agreement and they went about their business cleaning up the Presidential Suite.

At first Anthony didn't notice the leggy blonde girl as she rushed into the Roman Art wing of the Metropolitan Museum of Art. The museum got hundreds of visitors a day, and he thought she was just in a rush to meet up with the group of elementary school children who were wandering around on a class field trip. It wasn't until he heard the sound of glass breaking that he decided to step into the hall and take a look around.

The girl stood in the middle of the hall. At her feet lay the remains of a glass case that housed several Roman jars from about 70 AD, if Anthony recalled correctly. As he watched, she pushed another glass case over and grabbed the pottery jars one by one, smashing them to the ground.

A column of smoke began to rise from each of the smashed jars. Anthony's first thought was to find a fire extinguisher, but then the woman moved to another case and did the same thing.

"Hey lady, you can't do that!" Anthony labored toward her, reaching for his gun. "Stop it or I'll shoot."

The woman didn't seem to hear him. She turned on her heel and pulled at a long case displaying a half-dozen small silver boxes. The case toppled and broke. Puffs of smoke rose from the boxes.

Anthony aimed his pistol at her. "I mean it ma'am. Don't touch another case!"

The woman turned toward him. Her eyes were pure black.

"Jesus, Mary, and Joseph!" Anthony exclaimed fearfully as he instinctively squeezed the trigger. The shot hit her in the shoulder. Children screamed and ran out of the room. But the bullet hole didn't even slow her down. She pulled over another case, and more smoke filled the air. Columns of greasy vapor drifted down the hall where the cases had been smashed, seeming to rise and move with a will of their own.

Anthony stepped closer. A pillar of smoke billowed up in front of him. That was the last thing he remembered.

* * *

Dean noticed the train moved faster than he thought it would.

"Come on, Sam," Dean shouted as he pulled himself onto one of the ladders that hung from the side of the cars. He held out his hand to his brother. Sam pursed his lips as he huffed alongside the tracks. He took off the duffle bag and threw it at Dean.

"Come on, tough guy. You're running like a seventy year old."

Sam kicked his ass into high gear and thrust his hand toward Dean. His brother pulled him onto the steel grating between the two cars. Safely on the platform, Sam doubled over, trying to catch his breath.

"It's hard to run in these pants," he gasped.

"Sure it is Sammy." Dean brushed the tunnel soot off Sam's shoulders. "Let's find Dad and Sis."

Mary Anne Struthers couldn't believe her eyes. She was sitting on her fire escape facing north, with the Hudson River and New Jersey to her right, trying to get cool in the midday heat. That was when she saw a group of people on the overpass of the tunnel above the train tracks. About twenty of them were standing there, some even looked like children. As the 4:40 train left Grand Central Station headed toward Albany, every single one of the people stepped off the bridge and disappeared below. Mary Anne wiped her brow, thinking she must have imagined it or it was some kind of mirage. But as the train pulled further north she saw the same people swarm down its sides and into the caboose.

Strange, she thought. Then she shrugged.

She felt for the bottle of cold beer by her foot and continued to watch the world go by.

TWENTY

Dean and Sam found Walter and Julia's car. Julia opened the door, and Dean noticed she must have decided now was a good time to freshen up because she had styled her hair and put on a fresh blouse and skirt. The brothers squeezed into the sleeper cabin. It had two pull-down beds, one on each side of the roughly six foot-square space. Velvet jumper seats ran parallel on either side of the car. Walter was sitting down, studying the book that he and Sam had retrieved from the Bible Society.

"So what's next, sports fans?" Dean said. "We just going to sit around here and do our summer reading list? 'Cause I'm still trying to finish *James and the Giant Peach*."

"Sit down. I've found a couple of citations that might relate to what I think is possessing James." Walter looked at Dean and Sam over a pair of smudged reading glasses. "And yes, in lore they are very often found with Lilith. But not only Lilith, there are other demons which are identified with them as well."

"Like who?"

"Like Satan's wives, Eisheth and Agrat Bat-mahlat."

"Wait, Satan's wives?" Dean didn't like the sound of that at all.

Sam blanched. "So we're dealing with pre-biblical scrolls, which most likely have pre-biblical demons like Lilith protecting them? That could be a bloodbath."

"What do you mean?" Julia gripped her hands together.

"It means that everyone on this train could be in danger," Sam explained. "It's impossible to get everyone off. We're going to have to demon-proof the entire train."

"How?"

"Okay, well, we can trap them or we can kill them with a knife—that we no longer have."

"Can a demon jump from body to body? I don't want to be possessed by a demon." Julia's voice caught in her throat as she continued, "If you guys spend so much time around demons how come you don't get possessed?"

In unison, Sam and Dean loosened their ties and pulled at their collars, revealing their protection tattoos. Julia blushed as she looked at Dean's.

"Oh. I see. Okay then. So what's our next step?" she asked.

The boys formulated the plan. First they would need to get Eli into a safe place. Then they would have to set it up so that as James followed Eli, they could trap him in a Devil's Trap. The unfortunate thing was James, the real James, was probably toast. The guard dog was having a field day, probably pissing all over everything. There was no way the man's body was going to come out unscathed, especially after the gunshots and that fall he took. After that they were going to have to relieve Eli of the scrolls. And they had to do that carefully, because no one knew what else was lurking in the jars. Then there was Eli. They didn't know anything about him. The safest thing now was to just assume he was human, he would bleed like everyone else.

"So what do we do first?" Julia asked.

"I think dinner," Dean said with a smile.

"Really?" Sam asked.

"I reckon the dining car is going to be our best bet for the showdown—set up salt and Devil's Traps. Later tonight, when it's closed down, we draw Eli in there. James stays out, we rough up Eli, take his milk money and run."

"I'll stay here. There are still a hundred questions I have. I'll order in." Walter made himself comfortable.

"I'll go." Sam said.

"Why don't you stay here with Walter. Or start marking up the other end of the train, away from us?" Dean motioned with his eyes toward Julia, who was paying no attention to him.

Sam shook his head. "Fine."

Dean grinned at Julia. "I guess it's just you and me."

She looked at him. "I think you need to wash your face first." She motioned toward the small bathroom.

Dean opened the door and, looking in the mirror, noticed a large smudge of soot on his cheek. He rubbed it off with some spit and his fingers.

"Good as new. Let's go sweetheart." Dean opened up the cabin door. "Food's on you, money bags."

Sam handed Dean a half-dozen red wax pencils out of the duffel bag. "Mark as you go."

Posing as a young couple in love, Julia took Dean's arm as they negotiated the narrow hallways to the dining car. At each door leading to a new car, Julia would keep look out while Dean pulled up the carpet. On the bare floor he drew a Devil's Trap, and then laid the carpet back over it.

"What about the windows?" Julia asked.

"Hopefully we're only dealing with one. But if there are more demons coming, we'll have to salt the windows and any other way they could get in."

The dining car was functionally opulent, with white linen tablecloths, plush springy red-velvet seats and flowers in crystal bud vases on each table. A maître d' led them to a table. Dean pulled out Julia's chair for her.

"I didn't know you could be such a gentleman."

"It's a working dinner, sugar nips, don't get any ideas." Dean squinted at her. "Plus, there's our guy now."

Eli Thurman was reading a newspaper while shoveling beef bourguignon into his mouth. The case—presumably containing the scrolls—was placed firmly between his knees. Dean looked around, and noticed that on the other side of the door, at the far end of the car, James was pacing past the window, glancing in frequently to check on Eli.

"Wow, that guy is hardcore."

"Hard what?"

"Never mind."

"So can I ask you a question?" Julia smiled at Dean.

"Sure."

"Who are you guys, really?"

Dean looked into Julia's eyes. He instinctively knew better than to trust her. But something pulled at him from inside, he felt some sort of connection to her. He resisted.

"I'll lay it out straight. We are exterminators of a sort. And I am in the family business. But what I do and how I do it, it's best if you don't know."

"But you know about demons, inscriptions within ancient pre-biblical urns. You mentioned a knife that can kill demons. And it's not the first time you've run into whatever almost killed my father," Julia said carefully. "It seems to me that there is much more to you than meets the eye."

"There's always much more than meets the eye—but we haven't known each other for that long," Dean said with a wink.

"So, my life is in your hands and I'm just going to have to trust you?"

"Basically." Dean looked down at the menu. "No burger?"

"I'm serious. I want to know who you are."

Dean closed his menu in a huff.

"Okay, listen lady, I know you've been playing it pretty cool up till now, but I don't trust you or your dad. I don't know what your bag is and I don't want to know. But in my experience a gun-toting pretty face only leads to one thing. Trouble. So I'm steering clear of you. We're here to get the scroll and get back home. We can pretend this is all for one and one for all musketeers crap, but when the time comes I'm going to do my job, just make sure you do yours."

Julia didn't blink, she didn't even blush.

"You think I'm pretty?"

TWENTY-ONE

Sam took a couple of wax pencils and decided to start from the back of the train. As people slept in their seats in the economy cars, Sam quietly moved through, marking all the doors with Devil's Traps. He had to move quickly, Devil's Traps took a while to draw and it was a long train.

Sam finally reached the storage cars, and made his way to the caboose. On the ceiling as well as on the floor, he carefully drew a Devil's Trap. His back was to the door when a man in a uniform opened it and stepped in.

"Hey, what are you doing in here?"

Sam spun around. "Oh sorry, I was trying to find my bag. I forgot to bring my shaving kit to my cabin."

"Well, let me help. You take that side, I'll look on this side," the guy said as he waddled toward Sam. "What's the name on the suitcase?"

"Ahh, George. George Michael."

"What do you do George?"

Sam tried to seem anxious about finding his suitcase.

"Oh, you know." Sam was drawing a blank. "I'm a song and dance man."

"Really? Because I would have said you were a liar!"

The uniformed man dived at Sam just as he ducked and rolled out of his way, knocking a pile of steamer trunks over. The man's eyes flashed black as he flung himself over the trunks. Sam didn't have a weapon—he had stupidly left the salt-packed shotguns in Walter and Julia's cabin—and he doubted that there was any salt hanging around the storage car. Sam kicked the demon in the face, then swung at him with a heavy-handled suitcase. The large man fell face first, giving Sam an opportunity to move toward the door, past the Devil's Traps.

The guy leapt to his feet with surprising grace, and threw himself at Sam, landing rather nicely in the middle of the hastily drawn symbol on the floor.

"Get me out of here," he growled.

"Sorry, guy. You need to answer some questions first."

"Go to Hell."

"Really, that's all you got? How many more of you are there?"

"You'll never possess the scroll. It doesn't belong to you."

"What do you know about it?"

With that the demon took out a pistol.

"Don't!"

Sam lunged at him, but the demon put the barrel to his head and pulled the trigger. Sam lay on top of the brain and blood spattered corpse. Black smoke screamed out of his mouth, and gathered as a dark cloud on the ceiling. With a whoosh it flew out an air vent.

Crushed and frustrated, Sam pulled himself up and retreated back to the cabin.

Walter was finishing a ham sandwich.

"Good lord, what happened to you?"

"Guy, or demon rather, just blew a man's brains out. Where's Dean and Julia?"

"Still eating."

"We have to tell them. Let's go. Grab your books too."

Walter hurriedly picked up his jacket. Sam grabbed his duffle bag and handed Walter a shotgun.

"Do you know how to use one of these things?"

"Of course. I fought in both wars."

Sam had forgotten that this was an era where generations of people had lived through two world wars. It seemed strange to think that the third war would be Armageddon itself.

Sam and Walter made their way to the dining car.

Eli dabbed at the corners of his mouth and set the napkin onto his plate. He then grabbed for the case that housed the scrolls.

Dean looked at Julia. "You're on."

Julia glanced at Eli, and drained her martini glass. She approached Eli's table.

"May I join you?"

Eli didn't look up as he pushed out his chair. "I'm sorry, I'm leav—" His eyes met Julia's large baby blues.

"Oh please, do have one drink with me. It's so dull traveling alone. Don't you think?"

"I thought you were with that fellow over there?" Eli looked up, but Dean was nowhere to be found.

"Oh that plebian, not at all. He invited himself to sit with me. All the while, I was hoping to join *you* for dinner."

"Me?"

It was clear that Eli did not remember Julia. The refined woman wearing a blouse and a nice-fitting red suit looked quite different from the gun-toting, jeans-wearing, 1950s Lara Croft who had stormed the Waldorf's Presidential Suite.

As Julia continued to chat up Eli, Dean met Sam and Walter in the hallway in the next car.

"Another demon," Sam reported.

"Damnit. From where?"

"I don't know. The one in the caboose was a security guard. Strange thing was his uniform said he was from the Metropolitan Museum of Art."

"Let's get everyone out of the dining car and get this freaking scroll from Howdy Doody. 'Cause I want to get back home," Dean said.

Julia was still talking to Eli when the boys and Walter walked into the dining car. Even though Eli was only giving one-word answers to Julia's questions, he was clearly enthralled. Walter sat at the table right behind Eli.

Sam quietly ushered the other diners out of the car. After flashing a police badge, he said he was train security and there had been a series of thefts. Everyone was asked to go back to their cabins and seats and check all their belongings.

Dean asked all the waiters, most of whom were African-American, to go back to the kitchen car. This was official train business, he explained, and they needed to use the dining car.

None of them moved. "What kind of official train business? We weren't told of anything," a lithe black guy said to Dean, "and they always tell us if it has to do with service."

Dean noticed that James had disappeared from the doorway. *That's not good*, he thought. He turned to the waiter.

"Can you get me all the salt you have in the kitchen?"

"Salt? Sir, I'm truly sorry, but I can't—"

"Listen, dude, I get it, you're just trying to keep your job. But right now there is a distinct possibility that a whole host of very ancient and pissed off demons are on this train. And I need that salt."

"Demons? Why didn't you say?" The guy pulled a small green cloth bag out from the collar of his shirt. "Chicken bones, feather, little dust. Demons don't scare me none."

"Hoodoo?" Dean asked.

"Born and raised and taught by my momma."

"Great. Then please get me all the salt you have, and start making lines at the doors and windows."

"You got it. Name's Ray."

"Nice to meet you. Dean." Dean shook Ray's outstretched hand. A couple of other guys followed Ray out of the dining car to the kitchen.

Julia looked down at her watch. "Well, look at the time. We really do need to retire. We reach Chicago quite early tomorrow, don't we?"

Eli noticed the car was now empty of diners, save for two big guys and the old man seated behind him. Finally, he took a good look at Sam. Recognition dawned on his face. Eli got up and moved to pick up his case.

"I'll take that," Walter said, pulling the case from underneath Eli's chair.

"That's mine. You can't have it. I remember you—you were at the auction too." Eli looked around the room. "You all were."

Dean trained a shotgun on Eli.

"Yes, and you took something that we need."

Walter backed up behind Sam and Dean as Julia stepped away. Eli visibly started to panic.

"You don't understand—I need those."

"Yeah, buddy, so do we. Sort of like the entire planet hangs in the balance."

An enormous crash echoed from the dining car ceiling.

"What was that?" Eli shrieked. Small flakes of paint floated down from the gilded ceiling.

"They're on the roof," Sam cried. "Walter, Julia, make these signs everywhere!" Sam threw them wax pencils.

"You," Dean indicated Eli. "Stay where you are."

Eli shuddered as he watched Walter attempt to open the locked case. A series of bumps and thumps emanated from above.

"What's going on?" Eli demanded, sounding scared.

"I'll tell you what's going on," Dean snapped. "The contents of your little suitcase there comes with a whole mess of angry demons that are bound to protect it. During your *Thomas Crown* moment they were released, and now they're after whomever has the scrolls. So bite it, buddy. Right now we're saving your sorry ass."

Dean hastily drew a Devil's Trap on the ceiling, then another right next to it.

Ray and the other waiters returned from the kitchen car.

"Hey man," Ray said warily, "I don't want to be the bearer of bad news, but it's looking bad out there. Like a damn demon hoe-down."

"Just my type of gig." Dean handed Ray a wax pencil. "Don't need to be da Vinci."

The banging sound from above stopped.

"Where'd they go?" Julia asked, peeking out of the window.

"They're trying to find another way in," Dean said.

"Will they?" she asked.

"Hopefully not, but if you see one, use this." Dean handed her a shotgun filled with salt shells. "I have a feeling you can handle it."

Dean then grabbed his brother and they moved to a corner to confer.

"So what's the plan?" Sam asked.

"They're here for the scrolls right? But we don't know which one—are they protecting all of them, or only one?"

"I would guess that if Lilith has anything to do with the demon possessing James, then it has to be our scroll. The War Scroll. If you were Lucifer, wouldn't you want to protect the battle plan to defeat you?"

"Right, but… musty old ancient bitch demon, how does she know what we give her?"

Sam and Dean set about tearing up linen tablecloths.

"Hey Ray, are there any canisters in the kitchen, like for flour or something?" Dean asked.

"Absolutely. But I don't think I want to go out there." Ray motioned toward the door scrawled with the Devil's Trap. "They sound like some bad-ass demons."

"I'll go with you."

Dean grabbed the shotgun back from Julia.

"You know, you could have brought along your own firearm, if you're so women's lib."

"What?" Julia asked, puzzled by the modern reference.

Dean aimed the shotgun at the sky as Ray opened the door and they crossed the rattling platform to the kitchen car.

Dean kicked open the door, the stainless steel glinted from the fluorescent lights. He stepped in further.

Ray gasped. The chef, a pudgy man with floppy ears, was splayed out on the floor, his heart split in two by a meat cleaver. The sous-chef had fallen at his side, with a soup ladle impaled through his eye.

"Bernie and Ralph didn't deserve that," Ray muttered.

"Let's get that flour." Dean stepped over the bodies to the baking area. He grabbed four steel flour canisters and handed them to Ray.

"Well, well," a voice said. "I was hoping to meet the son of the mother slain, the vessel of goodness and light."

Dean spun around to face a young girl in a Waldorf Astoria maid's uniform. With her blouse half-unbuttoned, her skirt cinched up, and her lips blood-red, she was clearly a full-on, fully sexed-up demoness.

"Who the hell are you?" Dean's shotgun was aimed right at her heart.

"Exactly. I do love scholars. I'm Eisheth, sister to Lilith."

"Lilith has family?"

"Sister by marriage. I'm one of Lucifer's wives and so is she."

"So you're like Mormon demons? Kinky."

Eisheth's eyes flashed red.

"I wouldn't make it mad," Ray whispered.

Dean moved toward Eisheth. "Well, listen, this was really fun and all, but we better be getting back." He trained the gun on the demoness and stepped toward her, Ray close behind him. "Just a little warning, the salt in here is going to burn a lot, like a bad herpes outbreak. They have that back where you're from?"

"You remind me of the town leper," Eisheth growled.

"Yeah, I get that a lot."

They circled one another until Dean and Ray could backpeddle out of the kitchen toward the dining car.

Ray opened the door and backed out first.

There was a low growl. Dean turned his head to see James perched above them on the scaffolding between the train cars. Before Dean could get off a shot, James jumped at Ray.

Ray hit the deck of the car and almost rolled off. Dean shot James in the shoulder, making the animal even madder. He turned and lunged at Dean.

From inside the dining car Sam had his shotgun trained on the back of James's head. Dean gave a nod and ducked as Sam took the shot. The window shattered.

James's body fell forward, lifeless. The demon inside shot up into the air and out of sight.

Dean spun around just in time to catch Eisheth dragging Ray back into the kitchen.

"Leave him alone, he didn't do anything. We're the ones with the scrolls."

"I've always liked a proper sacrifice," Eisheth hissed. She produced a long blade, picked Ray up by the neck and in one swift movement sliced him from groin to throat.

"No!" Dean got off another shot as Eisheth flung Ray aside and raced toward him.

Dean dived back into the dining car. Two of the waiters pushed a wooden table up against the door's broken window. Eisheth pounded on the other side of the barrier.

Dean pushed his back against the wall—that wasn't a fair way for Ray to go.

"I found out who we're dealing with," he said.

"Who?" Julia came forward.

Eli sat quivering in a corner.

"Bitch named Eisheth. Know anything about her, doc?" Dean looked at Walter.

"Yes, she's one of Satan's wives. She doesn't come up very much."

"Yeah, because she's playing second fiddle to Lilith."

Sam looked to see if Eli had any inkling as to what they were talking about. From the look on his face, it seemed like he did.

Sam leaned over Eli. "What do you know about the scrolls?" he shouted into the little guy's face. "You're not telling us something. Why did you want them so badly?"

Eli scrambled to the other side of a table.

"They're precious. You wouldn't understand. The scrolls were written by the Essenes, devout followers of Judaism. They are pre-biblical."

"Tell us something we don't know."

Just then, the train lurched. Everyone fell forward.

"What is that bitch doing now?" Dean got up and pushed his head out of the window. Eisheth was underneath the train. Sparks flew as a piece of the undercarriage rolled down the incline of the train tracks.

"Hope we didn't need that." Dean trained his shotgun at Eisheth. The shots went wide.

"So now what do we do?" Walter had spread the War Scroll over a couple of tables.

"You put that in here." Dean threw him the metal container.

"But this isn't sterile. This is centuries-old parchment, it can't be exposed to foreign substances."

"Well it's a foreign scroll in a foreign land. *Put it in there.*"

Walter gently wrapped the scroll in a tablecloth and put it in the canister.

"Now give it to Sam."

"You don't understand—" Walter faltered.

"Old man, do you want to get out of here alive or not? Give it to Sam!"

Sam took the canister and placed it in the duffle bag that hung from his shoulder.

"Julia, take the scroll jar and stuff it with strips of

tablecloth. We're going to make a little ancient trade. Who wants to play bargain with a demoness?"

No one raised their hands.

"Okay then, guess I have to have a little *tête-à-tête* with this bitch myself. Sam?" Dean beckoned to his brother.

They huddled together. It was a bad situation and the fact that they were on a moving train just added to their problems.

"This is what I figure," Dean said. "We need to get the passengers away from her. And *we* need to get away from her. I say we play a little Great Train Robbery and detach the cars."

"What about Eli?"

"We have the scroll, right? Just let him go."

Five minutes later, Sam had scaled the train through the back door of the dining car. The roof of the car was rain slicked, and a wind blew off the Great Lakes on his left. He made his way over the top of the dining car toward the bar. Sam had to move quickly in order to get over to the passenger car and detach it from the train.

TWENTY-TWO

Dean cocked his shotgun as he stepped out of the dining car. Julia followed him holding the jar containing the pieces of tablecloth. She salted the door behind her and went after Dean.

"Hey second string!" Dean called into the night air. He and Julia stepped into the next car. A long wooden bar extended down one side.

"Wow, swanky. Hey Lilith's handmaid, where you at?"

Eisheth appeared between them and the dining car. *Great.* Now Dean was going to have to make a deal with Eisheth *and* get around her before Sam detached the car from the train.

Two more demons popped up from behind the bar.

"Drink?" Dean asked as he moved toward them.

"Who is she?" Eisheth pointed at Julia.

"My little sister. She comes with me everywhere. Always tagging along. Sort of like you and Lilith."

"That whore? I was shut away for thousands of years while she got to play out in the world."

"Oh come on, she's family, you gotta love your sister. Well, maybe not. I mean she did get to shack up with Lucifer way more often than you did. Do you think they have a china pattern?"

"Retribution comes to those who wait."

"I think it's 'good things,' but whatever. So Eisheth, how about we make a deal? I give you the scroll, and you go on your merry way. And while you're at it, you can let these poor people who your friends are knocking around in go. They can just jump out of them and leave them in peace."

"War doesn't leave anyone unscathed."

"Semantics, Eisheth. About the scroll."

"Is that it?"

Julia placed the ancient jar on the bar.

A possessed bartender reached for it, black eyes flashing.

"Leave it!" Eisheth eyed the guy. "It's not yours to defile. It's my responsibility."

"So this is all about responsibility? Fantastic. I admire that in a demon. You take your job seriously. I get it. Now we're just going to scoot on out of here."

"Wait! I want to see it," Eisheth hissed.

Dean hoped that Sam was just about done playing model train because things were getting bad down here.

Sam was in fact hanging onto the side of the train, in between the bar car and the passenger car. He was struggling with the hitching mechanism when he realized the steel levers that hooked the train cars together required a key. He scaled the ladder once again.

Sam sprinted across the tops of the cars. He looked into the distance. It was dark, no lights—he couldn't see anything speeding toward him as he ran. One tree branch or tunnel would do him in. Could he die in the past? He was pretty sure he could.

Sam jumped down to the platform of the engine. He tried the door, but the lever wouldn't budge. Sam banged on the door until the engineer emerged out of the darkness. He was a tall guy in striped overalls. *Just like you would expect.* Sam motioned for him to let him in.

"Who are you?" the engineer asked as he pushed open the door a crack.

Sam played dumb. "I seem to have lost my way."

In a flash, he shoved himself through the opening and gave the engineer a smack to the nose with his elbow. The man fell to the ground.

"Where's your hitching key?" Sam demanded.

The prone engineer pointed to a long steel rod hanging on the wall.

"When you feel the train get lighter you push this thing full throttle, okay?" The man nodded.

Sam leapt out of the car and scaled the ladder once again.

Dean heard Sam run across the roof for the second time in five minutes. *He must be close.*

"Why do you want to see it?" Dean challenged. "What's on it that's so important."

Eisheth's eyes flashed red again.

"You know what I think?" Dean continued. "I think you're torn, because you promised your husband that you would protect this thing for him. But at the same time you know what it says. It's how to kill him, isn't it?"

Dean saw Julia glance at him out of the corner of his eye. Her look said, *Surely this isn't the best way to negotiate with a demon?*

Ignoring her, Dean carried on goading Eisheth.

"You know what else I think? I think that you're pissed Lucifer gave you the babysitting job, and now you just might want to read that little battle plan for yourself. You know, take your husband's job, sort of like a senate seat."

Eisheth lunged at Dean. He knocked her back with the butt of his shotgun.

"No touching."

Eisheth lunged at him again, just as the train sped up dramatically. Through the window he could see the passenger part of the train start to pull away. The split-second distraction enabled Dean to push Julia toward the dining car.

Eisheth spun around and attacked Dean. He fell to the ground, face first. The shotgun skittered away from his reach.

Julia darted forward and picked it up, blasting Eisheth in the shoulder and knocking her off Dean. The two bartenders came after Julia, but in a surprising move she coupled a round-house kick with a flash of a blade.

The gashes to the demons' bodies flared orange and they dropped to the ground. *Ruby's knife!*

"What the —! Julia run!" Dean screamed as he rolled over and kicked Eisheth in the chest, sending her flying across the bar.

Dean turned toward the door. Sam was waving urgently. He was now in the process of unhitching the bar car.

Dean leapt to his feet and got halfway out onto the platform, but Eisheth was close behind. She grabbed him and pulled him to the ground in the doorway. Below him, Dean could see the levers clicking as the car struggled to detach. Sam was pushing heavily on the lever.

"Time to go, Dean."

Eisheth got her hands around Dean's throat. He struggled to breathe.

"Wow, 3,000 years in a jar hasn't done anything for your dental hygiene," he croaked.

Dean managed to get his knees up and reverse donkey-kick Eisheth back into the bar car.

"Now!" Sam screamed.

Julia opened fire on Eisheth. The salt bullets penetrated her body, each shot pushing her further back into the bar car.

Dean rolled backward into the dining car just as the bar car split off. The rest of the train hurtled down the tracks.

Eisheth was left standing in the bar car, cursing.

TWENTY-THREE

The bar car plummeted into the darkness of the night. Sam and Dean shut the door behind them. They had gotten rid of Eisheth for now, but she would be after them as soon as she realized that the scroll had been switched.

Inside the dining car, Julia tried to avoid Dean's gaze. He walked up to her and roughly grabbed her arm.

"What *the hell* was that?" he demanded.

"Get your hands off her!" Walter protested.

"Wait your turn, old man, you're in on this too. You have our knife! Do you know how useful that could have been the last couple of days? We're fighting demons, and it's the only thing that kills them. *Hello*, fighting demons." Dean motioned to the carnage around him. "Not to mention the fact that you *did* steal it from us. Do you have anything to say for yourself?"

Julia looked up at Dean. "I'm sorry. We needed to find out who you were. And I took it. I didn't know what it was for, until today."

"Which begs the question: Who are you?" Dean stood beside Sam glaring at Walter and Julia.

Walter stepped forward. "We're hunters. Just like you."

"And you were going to tell us this when?" Sam asked.

"Doesn't anyone care that there were demons on this train!" Eli wailed in panic from his corner.

Dean, Sam, Julia, and Walter turned toward him in unison and shouted, "SHUT UP!"

Julia tried to speak soothingly to Dean. "I know you feel betrayed, but we were trying to protect ourselves just as much as you were. I didn't steal it in order to put you at a disadvantage."

"You sure about that?" Dean spat.

"Here." Julia held out the knife. "I know I can't make up for it." She pulled out Sam's BlackBerry and held it gingerly. "I took this as well, but I don't know what it's for."

Sam grabbed it from her, and concealed it inside his jacket.

"You have a lot of explaining to do, young lady," Dean said.

"Right, well, maybe," Walter conceded reluctantly, "but right now we need to get as much track in between us and that demon as possible."

Dean scowled at Julia. Besides his hunter instincts, which told him never to trust her again, Dean felt a knot of discomfort in his stomach. His feelings were hurt.

Dean sublimated his anger and hurt while they looked at the rail line map of the Water Level Route. It ran from New York City to Albany along the Great Lakes to Chicago. They were just about at Albany.

"We need to get a move on," Dean said as he grabbed a shotgun and headed for the engine car.

Sam and Dean made their way over the platform between the cars.

"Go easy on the guy, I already clocked him once," Sam said as he knocked on the car's door. No answer. Dean took the butt of the shotgun and slammed it against the wood.

The engineer immediately opened the door.

"Okay, okay." He backed up from the doorway with his hands up. "I haven't done nothin'. I'm driving her as fast as I can."

"And you're going to keep driving it all the way through Albany. Don't stop until we're outside of Chicago. You got that?"

"I'll have to call ahead and get them to change the tracks. What do I tell them?" the engineer stuttered.

"Tell them Eisenhower is on board. Top secret mission and there's no stopping," Dean said.

"Really?"

"Yup."

"Wow, okay. Yes sir. Right outside Chicago it is."

Dean nodded and they headed back to the dining car.

"Do you have the feeling that people really are more innocent in the fifties?" Dean asked.

Everyone in the dining car looked a little the worse for wear. Julia sat with her legs up on a chair. Dean immediately noticed their slender shape, and the way her ankles tapered down to her feet. Walter mumbled to himself while sat at a table. Eli was a mess. But the waiters seemed to have taken everything, even the gruesome death of one of their own, in their stride.

"Everyone get some rest. We're skipping Albany and going straight for Chicago. Good burger town," Dean announced.

Everyone grabbed extra tablecloths and lay down on the floor or on tables pushed together. They had over 500 miles to sleep through.

Dean and Sam sat in the corner holding shotguns while everyone else slept.

"I don't trust them," Dean said quietly. "Even if they are hunters. Where do they get off stealing things like that?"

Sam shot Dean a look. *Was he whining?*

"We always steal things."

"I know, but we need them. And, like, I would never steal from another hunter."

"Yeah, but it's not like we know hundreds of other hunters, either."

"Whose side are you on?" Dean demanded.

"I'm on your side, Dean. Why are you PMSing?"

"I'm not PMSing. You are."

Sam thought it best to change the subject. "So what do you want to do?"

Dean peered at Walter and Julia's sleeping figures in the darkness.

"We have the scroll. First light we get the hell out of here."

Sam shrugged. They would find a way to translate the last pages of the scroll somehow. If not, they could always have Abbandon do it for them. He was the one that had told them all about the scroll in the first place, so surely he could read it.

Sam watched as lights from tiny towns flickered across the dining car's blood-red rug. For a moment, in all this craziness, he missed Ruby. It was an awful thing to feel, since she had betrayed Sam into thinking she was on their side. She had fed him her own blood, which made Sam incomprehensibly more powerful than he ever thought was possible for a human being. But, then again, he wasn't really a human being in some senses. *Would a human being drink demon blood?* Sam doubted it.

"What do you think is on the scroll?" Dean asked.

"I don't know. Hopefully a step-by-step recipe, like a brownie mix. Something that tells us what Lucifer's weaknesses are. There has to be another way."

Sam hoped that was true.

At first light the train was on the edges of Gary, Indiana. The morning was grey, low clouds hung over the lake, threatening summer thunderstorms. Dean woke up first, nudged Sam, and they got to their feet quietly. In the half-light Dean could see Julia and Walter covered with tablecloths, still sleeping.

Dean and Sam crept out of the dining car. Sam had the scroll secure in the duffle bag hung over his shoulder. Up ahead, the train tracks took a lazy swing to the left—the train would slow enough for the brothers to leap off. They climbed down the ladder on the side of the kitchen car and waited as the train slowed. Sam took the first jump. He rolled down a six-foot incline into a soft green field. Dean then jumped after him. He hit the incline at the wrong angle and tumbled ass over elbows to the bottom.

"I miss my Impala," he said, dusting his suit off.

The train disappeared into the distance. Julia, Walter, and Eli would all find their way. The most important thing was they had the scroll. Now all they had to do was find a way home—back to 2010.

The boys walked alongside the train tracks. In front of them the town of Gary was beginning to come to life. Small trails of smoke rose from the stacks looming above the steel mills.

"You know who grew up in Gary?" Dean said.

"Who?" Sam asked, looking at his brother—he had a feeling this was going to be bad.

It was. Dean did his best moonwalk, crotch pull and fake head dip.

"Michael Jackson."

"Highly disturbing, Dean." Sam increased his pace.

They reached a dirt road that headed west.

"You're no fun," Dean said. "Let's get to town, get a car and figure out where the hell we're going."

They climbed up a small incline to the road.

"Nice morning," a voice called breezily.

Both brothers swung around. Standing on the other side of the road were Walter and Julia. Julia walked with a sexy swagger toward Dean.

"Shame on you for not waking us first. We wouldn't want

you to leave without saying goodbye." She gave him a push and her tone switched from playful to angry. "Who the hell do you think you are?"

Dean and Sam exchanged looks. Loaded question.

"That scroll is just as much ours as it is yours. You're not taking it from us."

"Listen lady," Dean said, "I get it, you're tough. But we've come a long way for this scroll. A lot further than you have. So you and Daddy Warbucks just go on back to New York. We have stuff to do."

Sam and Dean continued to walk toward town. Julia raced to keep up with them, while Walter struggled with his bad leg.

"I didn't risk my behind so you could take it from us," Julia cried.

"Your behind?" Dean smirked. "That's exhibit A that you're over your head."

He and Sam continued walking.

"Take one more step and I blow your balls off."

They paused, and turned around slowly. Julia was aiming a pistol at them.

"This isn't full of rock salt either."

"Aww, man," Dean whined, "are you really going to do this? Where'd you get that?"

"It's the engineer's. Now let's all get to town and have a nice long talk, shall we?"

TWENTY-FOUR

The ragtag group walked in silence. Dean was clearly pissed. Sam was trying to figure out if there was any other way to get Walter to translate the last pages of the scroll.

Julia glared at the nape of Dean's neck.

He turned around.

"You're burning a hole in my head, sweet-stuff. Look somewhere else."

Julia shot Dean a look of distaste.

On the outskirts of Gary they spotted a lone diner on a corner. It was oblong, all glass windows and steel. The rest of the area was basically empty gravel lots.

They headed for the diner. Inside, a Formica countertop ran the length of the narrow restaurant. Each table had an individual jukebox and a window view. Sam could see two waitresses, both of whom wore yellow dresses with frilly white aprons.

Three steel workers made a rowdy group, cracking jokes

at a corner table. Clearly they had just come off the night shift at one of the mills.

Walter and Julia slid onto the benches at one of the tables, while Sam and Dean headed for the men's room.

"I've had enough of the goon suits. Now that we're back in the real America, I'm putting my jeans on," Dean said as he unbuttoned.

"Good thinkin' Palin," Sam said as he too began to undress.

Walter and Julia were speaking in hushed tones when Dean and Sam reappeared. They broke off as the brothers approached. Four cups of coffee steamed in front of them. Dean sat down next to Julia and leaned across her, essentially putting his armpit in her face.

"Excuse me, got to get the sugar." Dean grabbed at the sugar shaker. Julia bristled.

"Okay. First things first," Walter said, "you don't leave without us. We all worked to get the scroll. None of us can lay claim over the others."

Dean huffed. "Walter, we came a long way for this—"

"So did we," Julia insisted.

Just then a heavy-set woman with a large beehive hairdo sashayed up. She slid menus onto the table.

"Hi there. I'm Marge. I own this place. Let me know if you need anyth—"

She trailed off as her eye lit on something outside the diner. Dean followed her gaze out of the window and clocked the deserted lot across the street. Picking their way over the gravel were Eisheth and her cronies, among them several people in Metropolitan Museum of Art uniforms.

"Incoming," Dean said quietly. He got up and pulled a shotgun from Sam's duffel bag.

"Young man, shotguns are not allowed in my restaurant," Marge chided.

"Listen Marge," Dean said firmly, "out there is a group of very dangerous people. So I apologize if your place gets a little messy."

The steel workers in the corner got up to leave.

"I wouldn't go out there if I were you," Dean warned them, glancing over his shoulder. He had the shotgun trained on Eisheth.

"Buddy, what the hell you doing with that rifle?" one of the steel workers demanded.

"Believe me, it's safer in here," Dean said.

Julia pushed Walter toward the kitchen. "Dad, get the salt."

A waitress walked out with a couple of plates of eggs. Catching sight of the shotgun, she promptly spun on her heel and headed back into the kitchen.

"Barricade any doors in the back too," Dean called after Walter.

Ignoring Dean's warning, the steel workers walked out of the door onto the sidewalk. Not two seconds later they were attacked by Eisheth's group.

A little girl in a Catholic school uniform approached the first steel worker. She kneed him in the groin. When he stumbled and fell to the ground, she smiled sweetly, then slit his throat with a jagged rock.

The other two men tried to run. A uniformed Met worker shot out his hand and grabbed one of them by the throat. The demon's strength meant the guy was choked to death in seconds. The third man managed to escape.

Eisheth stood on the sidewalk, looking up at Sam and Dean. The thin strip of macadam that served as the parking lot was the only thing that separated them from her. That and the salt that Walter and Julia were spreading on the window sills.

"Game plan?" Sam asked.

Dean stared out at the waiting group of demons.

"We can stand and fight or make a run for it. Either option is probably a death wish. Though not for you—they'll keep you alive."

Sam looked solemn. He knew it was true. The demons wouldn't hurt a hair on his head. For the rest of them, however, it was a different story.

Eisheth made the first move, but was thwarted by the Devil's Trap Julia had hastily drawn in front of the glass doors.

"Aww, why don't you come out and play Sammy?" she called plaintively. "I mean, we're practically family. I never thought I would get to meet you—my husband's favorite vessel."

Julia looked at Sam with suspicion. "What does she mean by that?"

"Why, you don't know? Sammy here has been chosen—"

Dean blasted Eisheth with a salt shotgun, sending her sailing through the air. She landed on her back, but it didn't seem to faze her one bit.

"You can't stay in there forever," she said levelly.

She gave a signal and the demons attacked. The first wave came from a handful of demons crawling up onto the roof.

"Can they get through that?" Walter asked.

The creaking sound of ripping metal from above signified that indeed the demons could.

"What the hell is going on—they better not be taking off my roof!" Marge went behind the counter and pulled out her own shotgun. She let a couple of rounds loose at the ceiling, right below where the demons were trying to break in. "Damn, I just put a hole in my own roof."

The first demon that dropped down into the diner was a woman of about Julia's age. Her eyes flashed black as she sped toward Walter. Julia drop-kicked her, then tried to shoot her with her pistol. But the demon was too fast. She knocked Julia's pistol away, and pounced on her. Julia twisted, grabbed the demon's neck, and with a mighty kick threw her over her head.

The demon landed flat on her back. Julia crawled over to her pistol just as the demon attacked again. Julia turned and shot the woman. Black smoke poured out of her mouth and her body crumpled to the ground.

"Watch out!" Dean called to her. He spun and started unloading more rock salt bullets at the ceiling as another two demons dropped down onto the counter top. One kicked over the metal cake stand that displayed a cherry pie.

"Hey man, show some respect to the pies," Dean shouted.

He shot the guy in the shoulder. Black smoke shot up and

out of his mouth, disappearing into an air vent.

Outside, the rest of the demons looked like they were itching to join the fight.

Julia spun and drop-kicked another demon.

"How are we going to get out of here?" she cried.

They all heard the rumble at the same time. The cab of a large diesel eighteen-wheeler was barreling over the gravel lot toward the diner. Five demons were dispatched as the grill of the truck ran them over.

"Get out of the way!" Dean yelled.

The truck cab hit the front part of the diner. It tore open like tin foil. Inside the cab was the third steel worker.

"I know trouble when I see it. Get in!" he called.

Sam continued to shoot at Eisheth.

"Not the last you've seen of me, baby doll," Eisheth purred.

Walter, Julia, Sam, and Dean scrambled onto the front of the cab.

"Not so fast." Marge shot out her hand and grabbed Walter's foot. Her eyes flashed black. "Someone needs to stay here and help me clean up this mess."

Walter struggled to hold on to the truck's hood.

The steel worker looked at his side mirror.

"We gotta roll. More are comin' our way."

Marge slashed and pulled on Walter's ankle as Julia tugged at her father's wrists. Meanwhile, Sam and Dean kept Eisheth and the others at bay.

"Dean, help!" Julia cried.

Dean twisted and shot Marge between the eyes. She

rolled off the front of the cab and dropped to the ground. Black smoke poured out of her mouth.

"Go, go, go!" Sam shouted.

The driver punched the cab into reverse and swung wide, running over a couple more demons. As they perched on each side of the cab, Sam and Dean shot at the demons. The truck barreled off. Julia pulled her father into the cab.

"Thank you so much!" Julia exclaimed, wiping the sweat from her brow.

"My pleasure." The steel worked introduced himself. "Name's Mike. It looked like you needed some help. Once I saw what those things did to Benny and Jim, I knew I had to do something. I just gotta return this cab to the mill by nighttime."

"No problem. Can you take us past Chicago?" Dean called.

The truck sped down the streets of Gary and then swung onto a two lane interstate highway.

With the horizon clear of demons, Sam and Dean ducked inside the cab.

"How do you think she found us?" Julia asked. "Wasn't James supposed to be her bloodhound?"

"Dumb luck," Dean said. "We should have headed the other way. She won't find us again. We're going to be long gone." He was sure of it.

Mike let them off 200 miles west of Chicago, just before Davenport. Walter, Julia, Sam, and Dean got off at an unmarked exit ramp. They thanked Mike for saving their lives.

"So now what?" Julia asked.

Dean noticed that Julia had ripped her skirt and her blouse had lost buttons.

"You need to get yourself some demon-fighting clothes," he commented. "Those things aren't going to cut it anymore."

The four of them walked up the road in the twilight. Soon they came upon a friendly looking motel where each room was an individual little house. A small café was attached to the office.

"I think I'm going to check in, then go to bed," Walter said wearily.

"Me too," Sam said. "Dean?"

"Going to stay up for a bit. Sort of jacked up."

Dean headed toward the café.

"I'll join you," Julia said.

"Why don't you freshen up first, sweetheart." Dean suggested with a hint of spite.

Julia nodded and headed toward the motel office.

Dean and Sam stood in the gravel parking lot watching Walter and Julia.

"Ditching them went well." Dean looked at his brother. "Now what?"

Sam shrugged. "Let's sleep on it. Next thing we need to do is get the hell back home."

"Any suggestions? Because I'm getting sort of tired of Pleasantville."

"Let's go back to Waubay, South Dakota, and hope Don has enough wherewithal to pick us up from there. I'll go check us in."

Dean noticed Julia standing in the doorway of her cottage. Moments later, Sam reappeared with two keys and threw one to Dean. He ducked inside his cabin.

Half an hour later, Dean lay on his bed. Sam had decided to grab some food after all. Dean was bored. There wasn't a TV in the room, the only entertainment offered was a selection of black and white pamphlets explaining the local tourist attractions.

"Oh good, a milking museum," Dean said to himself.

There was a soft knock on the door.

"It's open, Sam."

Julia appeared in the doorway. She had changed into a sweater and jeans and a pair of hiking boots. Dean wondered where she'd managed to find clean clothes.

"May I come in?"

Dean sat up. "Sure, yeah."

Julia shut the door, and leaned against it.

"Need some company?" She smiled.

"Not usually."

"That was some fight back there," she said, and sat down beside him on the bed.

Dean shrugged. "I have a feeling you've seen it all before. So tell me, what do you and your father really specialize in? It has to be something scholarly. I know—lying and stealing, maybe even some money laundering thrown in for good measure. Anything to survive—right?"

"I have a feeling you and your brother do the same."

"Maybe, but you're as fake as silicone, baby. And I hate silicone. Ruins the moment, you know."

Julia let out a small laugh.

"Sometimes I have no idea what you're talking about."

She crept her hand closer to his. Dean looked down.

"Sweetheart, I'm tired. Anyway we can put this off until... say never?" Dean looked her in the eyes.

Julia didn't seem to be putting on a front now. It had been a long time since Dean had spent this much time with a woman. The Apocalypse, Sam, Lucifer, it had all worn him down. He was on autopilot. Dean wondered whether he would wake up some day and his entire life would have been one bad dream.

"Maybe you like me so much because you know we are both always pretending to be someone else. I see myself in you." Julia breathed shallowly. "Maybe you see yourself in me."

"Wow, there are so many different ways I could take that." Dean smiled. "But sorry, I don't get close to people. Not in my line of work."

"Me neither."

"I doubt that very much."

"Why can't you be nice to me?"

"Not my nature. I'm a hunter, I don't get close. It becomes your weakness. It's bad enough to hunt with family."

Julia nodded. "I know how you feel. My mother died at the hands of something evil. My father swore to avenge her death. And he did. He was born into this life. He never knew anything different. My mother, however, she didn't pick this. She had no idea. I was only a baby when she died. So my father took me with him. I studied with him. I grew up knowing about demons, monsters—"

"Everything that goes bump in the night."

"Yeah. I guess. There are a lot of people like us. A whole group of people we work with. We meet up every month and pool our resources. You would be amazed what you can get done in groups. Demons sure, but vampires, easy to wipe out with a group of a hundred hunters."

"Wait a minute, you know a hundred hunters?" Dean stopped caressing her thigh for a moment.

"Yup. So if you're hunters and we're hunters, why haven't we heard of you?" Julia asked.

Dean shrugged. "My father taught us to be on our own. He always said other hunters are fine for some jobs. But in order to keep moving, best to be by yourselves."

"I guess so. Still strange though. We have an entire network of people and you've never come up." Julia cocked her head to the side, looking at Dean.

"Like I said, best to be on your own."

Dean's cheeks flushed. He grabbed Julia by the wrist and pulled her on top of him. He held her head in his hands. She stared into his eyes.

"Why do you need the scrolls?"

"I can't tell you that."

"My father knew that he was destined to do something good for people. Then, when they started finding the Dead Sea Scrolls, he knew that he had to find the one scroll his mother always told him about. The ultimate battle plan for the war between good and evil. Hundreds of people have been waiting thousands of years for that scroll to appear. And your brother has it in his bag in a flour can."

"Could be worse, I guess." Dean shrugged.

"You really piss me off, you know that?"

"Yup."

Dean gave her a long kiss. Her lithe body relaxed on top of his. He pulled her sweater up over her head, and ran his hands over her sinewy back. She quickly undid his belt buckle with one hand. Dean raised an eyebrow, impressed. He kissed her again.

TWENTY-FIVE

When Dean woke the next day, Sam was standing in the doorway. Silent. He made a face. Dean shrugged. Sam soundlessly closed the door behind him.

Dean looked at Julia still asleep beside him, then levered himself carefully out of bed. He grabbed his jeans and leather jacket, then struggled to get his boots on. He left the room and walked across the gravel parking lot. Sam was nowhere to be seen. Dean muttered curses under his breath. He needed coffee and Sam had wandered off like a kid at Disneyland.

Then Sam swung into the parking lot. Dean gulped as he saw his brother was driving a brand-new green-and-white 1953 Oldsmobile Fiesta. It had a large chrome grill like a duck bill on the front, white wall tires, 170 horsepower and two-tone seats. Only four were made in 1953.

"Do you know how much one of these is worth?" Dean said excitedly.

"Keep your voice down. The sticker price is $5,700. I found it in the glove compartment."

"One of these sold at auction for 150 K, just last year. Well, you know, in fifty-five years. Man, I wish I could bring this back with me!"

"Speaking of which. Let's get on the road. I have an idea that Don will know to look for us in Waubay."

"Sure."

Dean got into the passenger seat.

"You don't want to drive?" Sam asked.

"Didn't get much sleep." Dean smirked. "By the way, they have a network of like a hundred hunters."

Sam looked at his brother in surprise.

"You're kidding me. We've never come across that big an organised group before. What do you think happened to them?"

Dean shrugged. "And supposedly, they all know about the scroll. Specifically the War Scroll."

Sam looked stunned. He pulled the car out onto the two-lane highway and headed north.

"How do they know about it?"

"I don't know. A whole group of hunters all believing the scroll has a meaning. Sounds sort of like a cult. But they know about it, that's for sure."

"Do you think Julia and Walter told them?"

Dean looked out of the window. "Whether they did or not, we'll be long gone into the future by the time they find out."

For the first time since they were flung back to 1954, Dean felt a squeeze of regret. Sure he had spent loads of time with plenty of women. But it was true that very few of them meant anything to him. Somehow Julia seemed different. Not only did she know the life that Dean had grown up in, but she was similar to him. Dean never had trouble being himself around people—that insecurity type thing wasn't his bag, there were too many other more important things to deal with—but Julia made Dean want to be better. Just being around her made him want to not be such a jerk. He'd been fighting it since they met. But somehow Julia had an affect on Dean. *Oh my god, am I turning into Jack Nicholson in that Helen Hunt movie?*

Dean swallowed and noticed there was a lump in his throat. He looked down at his sweaty hands leaving imprints on his jeans.

Sam glanced over at his brother.

"What's your problem?" Sam raised a curious eyebrow.

"Nothing. Shut up."

For about a hundred miles Dean stared out of the window. He kept going over and over in his mind the first time they had met. He didn't feel guilty about leaving her. He had a job to do. He'd left plenty of women while they were sleeping.

So why was he feeling guilty now?

Seven hours later they pulled into Waubay. The town didn't look much different in the 1950s, everything just looked fresher, the paint wasn't peeling and the roads were newly paved. The bar where they would meet Don was basically the same, except the building didn't have as many cracks in it.

They took a booth in the back and ordered two beers.

Sam brought out the flour can with the scroll stuffed inside.

"Put that away," Dean hissed, scowling. "If Don zaps us back to 2010, we don't want to accidentally leave the scroll behind."

"So, I have a thought. If in the future only the last pages of the scroll are missing, what do you think happens to the rest of it? We know it eventually ends up back in Israel. How do you think it gets there?"

Dean shrugged. "Maybe Eli the garden gnome shows up again and takes it there. Who knows? I don't care. We have the scroll, we've got what we came for."

The Winchester brothers finished three more beers apiece. Still no Don. Dean was getting agitated. Local patrons had come and gone. The bartender had already given them complimentary fish sticks. But still Don was nowhere to be seen.

"You think we should use the sigil?" Sam asked.

"No, that will invite every angel that's on Earth right now. We've flown under the radar up until now, let's not draw attention to ourselves."

"Good point."

The bar closed at twelve. The brothers thanked the bartender, a large gruff guy in a plaid shirt, and told him that if anyone showed up looking for them, they'd be at the motel down the road. The bartender nodded.

The next day, the boys resumed their vigil in the bar, still waiting for Don to zap them back to 2010.

"What the hell is taking him so long?" Dean growled.

"I don't know. There really isn't anything else to do but wait."

"Great. Waiting around for another angel, exactly what I wanted to spend my life doing. At this rate we'll be seventy by the time he shows up." A cloud passed over Dean's face. "You don't think he'll leave us here that long, do you?"

"I don't know. But think about it this way—you could spend the rest of your life with Julia. Happily ever after."

Dean knuckle punched Sam's arm. "Shut up."

He tried to change the subject. "Why don't you just study up and translate the scroll? Maybe we can get out of here that way."

"I've been trying. It's beyond what I can translate, Dean. It's ancient Aramaic, written in Aramaic script. It's half language, half symbols. I have no idea what it says. Without Don we have no chance of finding out the final battle plan for Lucifer."

"Well, can't you learn?"

"I could, but we would need to go to a large university, like Chicago or Berkeley. The texts that would teach me ancient Aramaic aren't just lying around the Waubay Library. And then I would need to study for months to be able to understand even the most elementary of symbols. I mean, look at it."

Sam made sure no one in the bar was taking notice. Then carefully pulled out the scroll and smoothed it onto the table top.

"Look at how complicated this is. It's not like learning an alphabet. There is a symbol for every word. And a sound that goes with every symbol."

That was the end of the discussion.

On their third day of waiting around in Waubay, Dean got out of bed and looked out of the window at the foggy summer morning. They had to do something. This was ridiculous.

"Sam."

No answer.

"Sam, *wake up*."

Sam rubbed the sleep from his eyes. "I'm up. What?"

"We've got to call Julia and Walter. We need Walter to translate the scroll. It doesn't matter anymore if he knows what the scroll says. Someone else will have to know what the last pages say besides us, right? We have to call them."

"Dean, we have no way of getting in touch with them. They don't have cell phones. I can try Walter's office back at the Biblical Society in New York, but I doubt they went back there. What do you suggest? Besides, are you sure this isn't because you just want to see Julia?"

"No, Sam, it's not. We have nowhere else to turn. If you have a better idea, I'm all ears."

Dean did in fact want to see Julia. Every fiber of his body wanted to, but his mind kept telling him, "No."

In truth though, Julia and Walter were the only people they knew in 1954 that could help them. If they translated the page, they would have an idea how to defeat Lucifer. At least with that information they could call the angels to help them.

Sam and Dean had—very reluctantly on Dean's part— ditched the Oldsmobile Fiesta and hotwired an old Chevy instead. It didn't go very fast, but they didn't want to draw attention to themselves anyway.

They rolled into a local electronics store. It was filled with black-and-white TVs. In the center of the store, on a raised platform covered in a green shag rug, was a color television. Mesmerized kids sat in a cluster in front of it. Even the adults couldn't look away.

A guy in a brown suit approached Sam and Dean.

"Looking to buy a new television set, gentlemen? Look at this beauty, a hundred dollars, top of the line. Technicolor they call it. Look at that picture. It's like you're really there."

"Thanks Crazy Eddie. Do you have CB radios?" Dean asked.

"Of course, all brand new. Biggest craze yet, huh? Right over here."

Crazy Eddie led them to the back of the shop, where a series of CBs and ham radios were set up. None of them were plugged in.

Dean looked at Sam. Sam looked at Dean. Eddie went back to the customers crowded around the color TV. Sam and Dean grabbed some equipment and hid it in their leather jackets.

As they walked out, Dean patted Crazy Eddie on the back.

"Thanks, think we'll pass."

"Anytime," the man said genially.

Back at the motel, Sam and Dean set up the ham radio and CB.

"How do you know they'll even be on a CB or ham radio?" Sam said as he plugged one of the units into the wall socket.

"Guess we'll just have to chance it. How else is this group of hunters communicating?"

Sam and Dean spent the next couple of hours putting out feelers on the radio units.

"Breaker, breaker. Looking for Papa Bear and Baby Bear. Ten, thirty-five. We're up in the land of the Walleye. Anyone read?"

Sam and Dean had no idea what Julia and Walter's handle would be. But they had an idea that they would be monitoring the airwaves.

About six hours later, Julia's voice crackled over the CB radio.

"This is Baby Bear." Dean could tell from Julia's tone that she wasn't happy with his moniker for her.

"Is this Dopey? Come in Dopey?"

"Yeah Baby Bear, this is Dopey. You and Papa Bear want to meet up?"

There was silence on the other end of the radio.

Eventually, "What's your twenty?" Julia asked.

"Two Pines Motel," Dean said.

"Be there in twelve hours," Julia responded. "Over and out."

The radio was taken over by static. Dean looked at Sam.

"Aren't you the least bit pissed that we didn't know they were hunters?" Sam asked.

"What else can we do? Besides, does it matter? Let's just get out of here as soon as we can."

TWENTY-SIX

Exactly twelve hours later, there was a knock on the motel room door. Julia and Walter stood in the doorway, wearing what looked like fishing gear.

"Were you fishing?" Dean asked.

"Trying not to draw attention to ourselves," Julia said tersely as she pulled a large shotgun out of one leg of the rubber waders she had on. "Plus, it's a good way to carry around firepower."

Dean nodded.

Walter walked into the room and sat on the bed.

"So, you ditch us and now you need our help?" He stared pointedly at Dean.

Dean gulped. Had Julia told her father they slept together? Dean met Julia's eyes. She looked away. That was an affirmative. *Crap.*

"So you can't translate the scroll on your own. Just like you couldn't have gotten it on your own. And now you need our assistance. Again," Walter said.

"Yes," Sam said. "It would take months. Can you help?"

"You've ditched us twice now. There is a hoard of demons looking for us because of you. I'm not quite sure what's in it for Julia and me."

"I don't think that's because of us—" Dean interrupted.

Walter held out his hand to stop him.

"Regardless, now you come begging for our help."

"I wouldn't exactly say begging," Dean said.

"Boy, let me finish."

Dean was about to tell Walter he reminded him a lot of their friend Bobby, but he decided to keep his mouth shut.

"Let's get started," Walter said.

Walter laid a large suitcase out on the bed. It was filled with loads of dusty texts—most looked even older than the ones he'd had in his office in New York.

"From my own private collection," he said.

"Where did you get all of these?" Sam asked. He was amazed at the array of books. There were sixteenth-century Bibles, dozens of books in ancient Greek, even some old parchment scrolls.

"I've collected them since I was a boy, in anticipation of this very moment. We have a safe house south of here, and I locked them up in a bomb shelter there. I always knew they would be important." Walter grew somber. "I've known about the existence of the scroll since I could talk. I knew I would one day hold it in my hands. It was my destiny. I'm part of the link in the chain to ultimately defeat evil. And that destiny is coming true."

Sam and Dean exchanged a look but said nothing.

Walter pulled out the bedside table in between the twin beds, so it stood halfway down the beds. He then took the round side table and put that next to the bed on one side, and took a chair and put that on the other side of the other bed.

"Can I have the scroll?"

Sam reached into his bag and pulled out the steel flour can. Walter reached for it gingerly. He took out the scroll and gently laid it on the round side table. He spread the scroll out, end to end. The last couple of pages came to a rest on the chair.

"Walter, can we start from here?" Sam indicated. He knew exactly where the translation of the scroll in modern times had left off.

"Why? It's a twelve-foot scroll."

Sam looked at Dean. This time, a whole unspoken discussion passed between them. They couldn't explain that they already knew what the first ten feet of the scroll said. Sam looked back at Walter.

"Legend has it that it's a battle plan, right? So let's start from the end. Eisheth is already on our tail. Let's just cut to the chase. We can always go back."

"You have a point. Okay. Let's get started."

Walter opened up each and every one of the books that he had brought. Leaning over the parchment, he traced a symbol with his finger then started paging through a book looking for its match.

"Grab one, this is how it's done."

Sam sat down on the floor, grabbed a book and started thumbing through it.

"I'm going to go get some air," Dean said.

"Me too," Julia agreed. "Dad, you okay?"

Walter waved her away.

Dean and Julia stepped outside. There was an awkward silence.

Julia broke first. "I bet you don't call a lot of women after you spend the night with them."

"Not usually. No."

"So this is good, you can use my father just like you used me."

Dean looked her in the eyes. "I didn't use you. And as far as your father is concerned, he's a grown man. He knows the deal. You're hunters, right? Sometimes you use people for information—just like you used Sam and me back in New York."

"That was different, I needed to find out who you were."

"Well, now you know."

"I'm not sure that I like you, now that I know the real you."

Dean walked away from Julia across the parking lot.

"I wasn't untruthful." Julia followed him.

"You weren't exactly forthcoming either." He spun around. "All that bullshit about your father being a scholar, and then you show up here with an arsenal taped to your back. What else are you hiding? I mean, I like a girl with a hint of danger, but you're far and away the most dangerous piece of ass I've ever had."

Julia slapped him hard across the face.

"My father was a scholar. He *is* a scholar. But we have another life."

Julia looked up at Dean with tears in her eyes.

"I have no choice. Don't you understand that? Look at every other girl my age. They're married, have a house, a husband. Kids. Do you know that by the age of nine, I knew I would never have that? Ever. That is not a normal existence. So excuse me if you didn't get all the information. I had other things to do."

"Like saving the world?"

"We don't know what's on the scroll. Maybe there is a part for me to play. I hope so. I don't know. But I don't have a choice. Do I?"

"No, you don't. Nobody does. I'm finding that out."

Standing next to Julia, watching the grass swaying in the warm evening breeze, Dean felt a brief moment of happiness. *Strange as that is*, he thought.

"I didn't mean to slap you."

Dean lifted her chin gently in his hands. He gave her a slow, deep kiss.

"You're forgiven," Dean said.

"That wasn't an apology," Julia huffed.

"It'll do. Let's get some coffee."

Sam and Walter worked diligently into the evening translating the text. Walter knew a lot of symbols that weren't in the books. It would have taken Sam a lot longer if he had done it on his own. But still, the process was laborious.

* * *

Dean and Julia sat in the café across the street from the motel.

"So, no picket fence for you?" Dean said, stirring his coffee.

"Don't think so," Julia absent-mindedly scribbled on a napkin. "So what about Eiseth, what can we do about her?"

"I don't know. She's supposed to guard the scroll that essentially tells the secret of how to destroy her husband. She's going to go after it with everything she's got. That's why it's so important that we find out what it says. If she shows up again, I have a feeling that she's going to have made a lot more friends."

A few hours later Dean and Julia headed back to the motel room.

Sam and Walter were wide awake and still working hard, though Sam's hair was wet, so he must have just taken a shower. Walter peered at his daughter and Dean as they stood in the doorway.

"Shut the door. The scroll shouldn't be exposed to the elements," he said.

Dean sat down.

"Have you found anything?" Julia asked.

"Yes, and no," Walter replied as he peered through a magnifying glass at the scroll.

"What does that mean?" Dean said with a hint of sarcasm.

"Well, the text on top says that the battle lines are drawn with people's faith. The believers versus the non-believers. In order to defeat Lucifer it says this, 'The Adversary's undoing lies in a trail of blood across the ages. All that become hosts must become ash.'"

Sam looked at Dean. They knew what hosts becoming ash meant.

Oblivious, Walter carried on. "But often the writers of ancient scrolls tried to hide something beneath the actual text. They would create a chemical reaction which would reveal the true text. Sam and I finished and the text seemed pretty cut and dry. But then, Sam took a shower."

"He always makes a mess, doesn't he?" Dean said.

"Yes, he does. But the steam coupled with the water droplets coming off his body as he reached for another towel... Well, it produced this."

Walter gently held up the last pages of the scroll. Though Aramaic script could be seen plainly on the page, another page seemed to be underneath it.

"It looks like a list," Julia said.

"Yeah, it does." Dean looked closer at the parchment.

"Can you tell what it says?" Julia asked.

"They're names," Walter said.

"Names?" Dean said, alarmed—your name on a scroll that Satan was trying to protect. Well, it couldn't be good.

"But that's not the most peculiar thing," Walter said. "Some of the names belong to angels."

"That's weird." Dean looked at his brother. Was there something more? Sam was eyeing Dean. Dean knew that look. It was the *We gotta talk* look.

"I think I have something in the car that can help," Sam said. "Give me a sec."

Sam and Dean walked outside to the parking lot.

"So, what did you really find?" Dean asked as soon as they were out of earshot.

"Walter's right, they're names—paired up with the names of angels."

"So what, that's what Don wanted us to find? A list of angel names."

"Don't you see, Dean, if the angels don't have vessels, there's no war. Yes, our names are on the scroll. But there's more. It's basically a roster of all the soldiers in a battle. But we're here for a different reason."

"That was his plan? No vessels, no fight?" Dean punched a car hood. "That's ridiculous. I'm going to kill him when I see him."

Sam nodded. "The demons aren't going to kill these people... Abaddon sent *us* to do it..."

TWENTY-SEVEN

The four of them sat in the motel room largely in silence as Walter transcribed the names, slowly but surely teasing out the angels' most monumental secret.

The scroll associated each angel with the bloodline of his or her potential vessels. Sometimes only one host was listed, sometimes many. When Walter got to the line that read, "'Castiel—borne by the progeny of Ishmael: Gregory Novak, who begat James Novak, who begat Claire Novak,'" Dean's jaw clicked shut. Sam looked over at his brother. They had met Castiel's vessel, Jimmy Novak, and his daughter Claire, while Cass was being interrogated in Heaven.

The process dragged on, as each name required Walter's deliberation. Meanwhile, Sam had surreptitiously started translating from the bottom of the page, where the very last name seemed to read: "Michael—borne by the Sons of Light, John Winchester, who begat Dean Winchester." It would take Walter another hour to get there. *And then,*

Sam thought, *they'll know everything.*

"Stop," Dean blurted out suddenly.

All eyes turned to him.

"Stop writing."

Walter let slip an exasperated breath, but continued to scan his magnifying glass over the tiny sigils.

"Every minute the scroll spends exposed to moisture degrades the pigment," he muttered impatiently.

"Good," Dean said, "'cause we're not doing this." Grabbing the battered and fragile parchment away from Walter, Dean made for the door.

"What are you doing?" Julia asked, hurt in her voice. "We finally get a chance to read the thing, and you want to walk away?"

"Are you not paying attention? Damn thing wants us to butcher a thousand innocent people."

"More," Walter corrected simply. "At least 2,000."

Dean held the parchment up to the light. "We're in this to save lives, not end them. This list—these people haven't done anything wrong."

Walter never took his eyes from the scroll, as if breaking his gaze would cause it to crumble.

"They're angelic vessels," he said calmly. "Both sides in the final battle are angels… and with no hosts, they can't fight. No Apocalypse. One of the people on this list will be Lucifer's host on Earth, and we have the chance to kill him."

Dean looked to Sam to back him up, but his younger brother was looking away, lost in his own thoughts.

"Dean, remember why we did this. All of us." Julia stepped closer to him, her hand beginning to reach out for the scroll. "We want the same thing, and this is how we get it."

Dean's mind was racing. After all, their points were entirely valid. One way or another, the angels were ultimately responsible for the Apocalypse, and killing their vessels would rob them of their foothold on Earth.

It would also rob the entire Winchester family of their lives.

"The price is too high," Dean said softly, despite his thoughts to the contrary. *If only dying was enough.*

"What happens to mankind when Lucifer rises?" Walter demanded. "'And they came forth, winging from Heaven and Hell to the place between. The fates of men hung on their swords, in a place called Armageddon.'"

Dean recognized the curious quote from one of the more gruesome editions of *The Book of Revelation* that John Winchester had carried.

"Billions dead," Walter said.

Lost in his thoughts, without acknowledging the others, Sam pulled himself out of his chair and left the room. Dean stared after him, imagining how he must be feeling. *A 2,000-year-old scroll just told him his family has to die so that he can't destroy the world. Probably not feeling great.*

"I know the figures," Dean said to Walter. "Planetary enema, half the world on fire, all of it. That doesn't change what's right and wrong."

"None of it is right. But there are two options, and one of them is a lot less wrong." Walter's lower lip trembled with emotion. "Three *billion* strangers versus 2,000 strangers."

"The difference is who kills them," Dean shot back.

"I don't want to kill anyone," Walter said. "But I can't live out the rest of my life knowing the end is coming, and… and not *do anything*."

"What if it's wrong?" Julia said hesitantly.

Walter stared at her for a moment, not understanding.

"What if the list is wrong, and none of these people are vessels?" she persisted.

Walter huffed at her, incredulous. "This document was written *millennia* ago, and it lists a 'Craig Masterson' and a 'Danny Fuller'. Do those names sound ancient to you?"

"So they were clued in to the future," Dean said. "The future can change."

"No, it can't," Walter replied. "*Destiny* does not change."

"My life hasn't been decided, buddy," Dean blurted.

Walter paled, his frown deepening.

"There will be another way to stop Lucifer," Dean insisted. "There has to be."

With a nod, Walter sat back down. "When I was eight years old, my father bought an automobile. The first in our town. Every boy in my class wished their father could do the same, but… for most of them, it would be years before they could afford it. Two weeks later, my father was the first person in town to crash a Model T. First person to die in an automobile accident."

Dean didn't know where the old man was going with the story, but decided he was better off listening than interrupting. He knew from experience that "dead dad" tales were a sensitive subject.

Walter continued. "My mother told me, 'This is what God wanted for him.' That there was a plan. But deep down, I knew there wasn't. It was senseless and stupid and unfair. For years, I hated her for saying that. And then, after I'd grown up a bit, I learned the truth. It hadn't been an accident. My father had been killed by a demon. Protecting me while I slept." Walter paused for a moment, observing Dean's muted reaction. "There was a purpose to it. A plan. He gave his life for mine, so that I could be here for *this*."

It was all Dean could do not to roll his eyes.

"This moment, this choice, it's what my mother warned me about. It's fate—"

"It's bull," Dean snarled. "That's a swell sob story, but I've got one just like it. Only my dad didn't give his life so I could go on to murder innocent people, he gave his life so... so I could get a fair shake. That's it." Thinking about John Winchester was always difficult for Dean, especially when he was forced to marginalize his sacrifice. "If he could have kept me from this life, he would have. Same with my mom. I'm sorry to say it, but just about everyone in this line of work loses someone to it eventually."

Julia shot Dean a cold look, but he soldiered on.

"It doesn't give you a special destiny. It gives you attachment issues and a manageable drinking problem."

Frustrated, Walter tried another tack. "This is bigger than all of us. We have to at least let the others weigh in."

"Others?"

"The rest of the hunters, at our headquarters."

Dean's confused look drew suspicion from Walter.

"You weren't kidding about doing things your own way. Never heard of a hunter that didn't report in at least once in a great while."

"We've never been to… 'headquarters.' And we don't plan on going now."

"I can't let you walk off with the scroll, Dean."

"And I can't let you kill those people!"

Walter looked Dean in the eye and said with calm authority, "Hand back the scroll, or things are going to get ugly."

From beneath the table, Dean heard the unmistakable click of a revolver's hammer pulling back.

He had no choice but to comply.

Sam kicked at the dirt of the parking lot, watching the dust fly up into gloomy clouds that reflected his mood perfectly. He could hear Dean inside, talking to Walter and Julia, but didn't want to be anywhere near that conversation. The idea that Sam's death could halt the Apocalypse in its tracks wasn't a new one—in fact, he himself had thought of it almost immediately after learning that he was Lucifer's chosen vessel. To have it be Abaddon's promised solution, however, was devastating. Sam had long ago given up on any hope of a normal life, but giving up on life entirely, along with all of those unknowing souls? He remembered what he had read about Abaddon back in New York. *I should have known this would turn out badly, I should have warned Dean.* He had wanted to find another way so badly that he had allowed them to walk into this trap.

When Dean exited the motel room and ambled toward him, Sam made a concerted effort to reign in his emotions.

"Sammy…"

"You don't have to say it. You're going to figure something out, we'll stop them from committing mass murder, I know."

"No, just… I'm sorry. I know how much was riding on that being the thing to get us out of this mess. And now, it just gets messier."

Sam nodded toward the motel. "Where'd you leave things?"

"At gunpoint. Walter's convinced this is his destiny, like he's the Luke Skywalker of the Apocalypse, and that list is going to bring down the Emperor."

"Well, it would," Sam offered. "I mean, the plan would work, right? Cut off the angels from their vessels, they can't fight the final battle—even using backups."

"You're not actually thinking about this, are you?" Dean asked, his brow furrowing.

"I'm… I don't know. What I do know is that if it came down to it, we'd both…"

"We'd do what we had to do," Dean said. "Hell, we've both died before. But we're not there yet. And this isn't just *our* lives we're talking about, it's 2,000 people, probably mostly children. People that have no part in this besides drawing the short straw, genetically speaking."

Sam nodded his agreement, but his heart wasn't in it. Part of him had always wished for an easy way out, and sudden lack-of-existence would certainly do the trick. He tried to change the subject.

"What are they going to think when they get to the end of the list, and there we are?"

"Let's not even go there," Dean replied. "What I don't get is why Abaddon would send us here in the first place. Says he wants to defeat the Devil and go on sipping pina coladas for the rest of eternity on Earth. But think about it, if we destroy all the vessels, that means his, too."

"So he'd be stuck in Hell."

"And he said that he wanted Lucifer to be destroyed entirely, but this would just keep him locked up," Dean added.

"With Abaddon stuck guarding him," Sam continued.

Both of them paused to reflect on the pretzel that was temporal mechanics. Then Sam chimed back in. "He must not have known exactly what was on the scroll…"

"Or he's just another angel douche, playing us for fools," Dean said bitterly.

"Where does that leave us?"

"Screwed, as usual," Dean said.

"What if… what if we're the ones who destroy it?" Sam ventured.

"Back up."

"In 2010, history records that the last page is missing or destroyed. What if *we're* the ones who destroy it? To stop Walter from fulfilling his… destiny, or whatever."

"Then we're going to have to fight our way past Walter to get it," Dean answered. "He's not going to let that thing out of his sight again, not after we got the slip on him the last time."

Sam looked at Dean seriously. "Could you do it?"

"Kill Walter?" The words rolled a little too effortlessly off Dean's tongue.

Outwardly, it seemed as though the notion didn't faze Dean, but Sam knew it did. Dean would never admit to having a soft spot, but right now, it was the exact size and shape of Julia. In fact, it was a novelty for Sam to be on the other side of their usual dynamic—instead of being the lovestruck kid brother falling for the wrong woman, he was the protective one waiting for the right time to intervene. After what had happened with Ruby, Sam doubted if he'd ever again be able to have a healthy relationship with a woman. *Not that it matters, since I'll probably be dead soon. God, that wasn't morbid at all.*

Dean stared back at the motel room.

"No. Probably couldn't," he conceded.

"Guess we need another plan," Sam said, relieved by his brother's candid response.

"Yeah." Dean kicked at the dirt, billowing it into a gloomy cloud, matching the one Sam had made earlier. "I think I've got one."

Later that evening, Dean went looking for Julia. He found her scrubbing the bands of her car's CB radio, listening for any hint of voices in the static. Before alerting her to his presence, he took the opportunity to watch her with her guard down. He imagined that she carried herself differently when she thought no one was watching—that he could see the 'real' Julia underneath the layers of defenses.

"I know you're watching me, Dean, and it's creepy."

Guess that theory's shot.

"I came to see if we could mend some fences," Dean said.

"Nothing to mend. You made it pretty clear what your intentions are regarding the scroll."

"And now we share the biggest secret that anybody's ever kept. The key to stopping the Devil. And that means we're going to have to work on our trust issues."

Wearily she looked at Dean. "I don't have the energy to get into all of our issues."

"The way I see it, I have no choice but to trust you."

"Why's that?" she asked.

"Because without your help, I'm not going to be able to stop your dad from murdering a lot of innocent people. And the only way I'll be able to convince you to help me is to tell you the complete God's honest truth, and that means trusting you not to flip out when you hear it."

"I'm a big girl."

Dean sized her up. "Not that big."

"My dad has been working toward this his whole life. What makes you think I can convince him of anything?"

"You're his daughter. That's how daughters work. Look at Paris Hilton, she runs around showing off her hoo-ha and her dad just keeps refilling her checking account."

"Who?"

"Right. See, that's the problem. Different frames of reference."

"Get to the point, Dean."

"Fine. You and I are both hunters. We both have

missions to complete, it's just that… mine has taken me a little farther from home."

"How far?"

"Fifty-six years."

Dean could see that Julia was trying to process the information, but she gave no indication as to whether she believed it was true or not.

"Let me go back to the beginning," Dean said.

"That would be helpful."

"With a father like yours, you must know the story of Lucifer and Michael. Lucifer loves God more than anything else, but can't stand his creations. Us. He doesn't think we deserve to live in Paradise. He rebels, and big brother Michael has to put him down. Sweet family story."

With a flick of her wrist, Julia turned off the buzzing CB radio, focusing her attention on Dean.

"Lucifer spends all his time in the pit gearing up for the rematch. But, it's not that simple. First, he has to be let out. Second, the rematch has to take place on Earth, so he has to find the perfect meatsuit to jump into, and Michael has to find his. And here's the kicker, their vessels… have to be brothers. 'So it is in Heaven, so shall it be on Earth.'"

Realization began to dawn on Julia's face. Dean hurried to finish before the inevitable questions started.

"A battle for the fate of Earth, fought by two of the names on that list in there. And it's true, if all those bloodlines were cut, the angels would be all dressed up with no place to go. But Walter's wrong about one thing. They're not strangers."

"You…"

"…and Sam. Hounded by this crap since birth. And fifty-five years from now, Lucifer will be freed. The Apocalypse will start. And we'll find a way to stop it. *Without* killing hundreds of people."

Julia turned away, pushed one step too far.

"So, let me get this straight, you're a time-traveling angel-vessel from the future."

"I'm *the* angel vessel. Michael's."

"And Sam… is Lucifer."

"His vessel. Yes. But angels, even fallen ones, aren't like demons—they need permission to come in. And Sam won't give it."

"If you really believe that, you wouldn't be so desperate to find another way to stop him."

"I trust my little brother."

"You don't trust anyone, Dean. Even now, you're thinking of ways to take back everything you just said."

"What makes you think that?"

"Because that's what I'd be doing. This line of work isn't designed to let people make friends. Even if they're family."

"Well, Sam's all I've got," Dean said. "And if you think I'm going to let Walter murder him…"

"If your story's true, you've seen the start of the Apocalypse. And as a hunter, you're not willing to do whatever it takes to stop it?"

"There's another way. We'll find it."

"We go out every day and put our lives on the line for other people. This is the single biggest evil sonofabitch there ever will be, and that's not big enough for you to lay down in front of?"

"Hunters don't lay down. If I'm going down, I'm going down swinging."

Julia's mouth curled into a half-smile. "Okay." She turned away from him. "Right answer. But… what makes you think there's another way? Chances like this don't come twice…"

As earnest as he'd ever been, Dean moved to look her right in the eye.

"I have to believe that there is. Your dad… he *wants* his destiny. Sammy and me, we don't. Most days, I wake up and feel like running. But this is what we're saddled with, so we're going to find our way out from under it. But fifty-six years from now. Not today. Not like this."

"You said you'd put your trust in me, but you're asking me to put a hell of a lot of trust in you. I'm supposed to trust my grandchildren's lives to you being able to punt your way out of this."

"I thought you didn't want the picket fence."

"I want it, Dean, I'm just smart enough to know I'll never get it," she said sadly.

Dean was entirely spent. There was nothing else he could say to her that hadn't already been said, so he went back to the beginning.

"Talk to Walter."

She nodded, but didn't say a word. Her facial expression was unreadable.

"We save people. We don't murder them."

"Let me sleep on that," she said as she walked away.

* * *

It was late, and Dean forced himself to go to bed. There was nothing for him to do besides wait, putting him in an uncomfortably passive position. As a hunter, his tactic had always been to keep moving, to keep testing every option until he found a solution, but that rarely involved letting a woman 'sleep on' the most important decision of her life.

Sam was already asleep in his bed. Instinctively wary, Dean locked the door to their room and checked the windows were sealed. He trusted Julia; he had to. But now she knew that, in theory at least, Sam's death could save the world from the Apocalypse, it didn't hurt to take some precautions.

Despite all of the thoughts swirling in his head, the comfortable mattress and backlog of sleep deprivation quickly took its toll, and he fell asleep with his shotgun beside him.

When Dean awoke, the sun was shining brightly in through the motel window. *It's got to be least 10 a.m.*, he realized.

Swinging out from under the covers, Dean noticed the empty bed next to his. He had a moment of panic—where was Sam? But he pushed it aside, *Sam always wakes up early. He's probably grabbing some coffee.* Stepping outside, he felt the cool morning breeze on his skin. It would have been refreshing, if he wasn't in such a hurry to hear what Julia had to say.

Stopping outside her door, he raised his hand to knock, then thought better of it. *Serious morning breath. Should have brushed before I came over.* He and Julia obviously had no future together—since her future was in the distant past—but that didn't mean Dean had given up entirely.

As he turned back toward his room, Julia's door swung open.

"Dean," Sam said, framed in the open doorway, a broken look on his face. "We have a problem. They're gone, and they took the scroll."

TWENTY-EIGHT

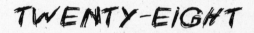

Throughout Dean's life, he'd been betrayed by anyone who had got close to him. With Julia he had allowed himself to hope, even though, Dean realized, it was an idiotic notion to fall in love with someone born fifty years before him.

A burning anger bubbled up within him. He returned to their room and headed straight for the closet.

"They said they weren't going to make any moves until we talked about it some more," Sam said.

"Well, they lied. Seems like Walter's plan to play a part in saving humanity means he's going to do whatever it takes."

"Aren't we as well?"

Dean stared at his brother. "We're not killing people, Sam."

"How are we going to find them? We have no idea where they've gone."

Dean held up the cord of the CB radio.

"We're going to track them as we go."

Twenty minutes later, they pulled into the electronics store.

As they raced inside Crazy Eddie was there, smiling broadly.

"Good morning gentlemen. Can I hel—"

Dean put his hand in his face.

"We're taking some equipment."

Dean pulled a CB converter off the wall, and Sam grabbed a large extendable antenna. They left without saying another word to the store clerk.

"You've got to pay for those!" Eddie called after them.

Sam assembled the gear as Dean drove. The plan was to find the signal that Walter and Julia were using, and quickly, before they could tell anyone about the list. But chances were slim. They had no idea which direction Walter and Julia had gone in. Moreover they had no idea what kind of hunter network they were a part of. John Winchester had always taught his boys a sort of code: they might have to kill the bodies demons inhabited, but they don't kill people. From the conversations they had had last night, it seemed that not all hunters thought that way. To Julia and Walter, the greater good was worth sacrificing some human life.

Dean gripped the steering wheel; all these things flying through his mind as they burned down the freeway.

Sam regarded his brother. Sam was pissed. Dean knew better than to get involved with someone, especially another hunter. Just at the time when the outcome of the Apocalypse would be determined by whether Sam and Dean could find away to keep Lucifer and Michael at bay, *Dean decides to get involved with a chick*. Sam knew his brother would never let him get away with that if the tables were reversed. Example, Ruby.

Sam fiddled with the CB radio, but all they heard were truckers all over the Midwest; not one spec of evidence that Walter and Julia were out there.

Dean pulled over for gas. They had been driving south in a crisscross fashion for hours. The new Oldsmobile they had hotwired was a gas-guzzler.

Dean hit the head at the rest stop. Staring into the mirror in the men's room, he wondered if they would ever be able to leave 1954. Would they run into their father at some point? Would this mean that they would never be born? How long could they live in the past? Would they even age? Dean took off his jacket and set it on one of the sinks. He ran some water over his face. As he reached for his jacket, he noticed a small piece of paper hanging out of the inside breast pocket.

It was a napkin from the café across the street from the motel. On it was scribbled a little drawing that Julia had doodled while they were having coffee the previous night. It was an arch, with little stick people figures underneath it. Dean had teased Julia that she was terrible at drawing, and that he would never pick her to be on his Pictionary team. She didn't understand the reference, but she did give him the drawing. The arch looked like it could be the Gateway Arch in St. Louis. Dean could be totally wrong, but it was the only lead they had.

"They're in St. Louis." Dean jumped into the driver's seat.

"How do you know?" Sam asked.

Dean held up the napkin. "Julia drew this, sort of looks like the St. Louis Arch, right? I wasn't paying attention to what she was doing. I bet that's where they're based. When we called them on the CB, it took them twelve hours to get to us. It's a twelve-hour drive to St. Louis, especially in these old cars."

"They have a twelve-hour jump on us. Let's get going."

Dean hit the gas and headed due south.

Around eight hours later, as they reached the outskirts of St. Louis, they turned on the CB again.

Dean nodded toward the radio. "Flip through, see if you can't get a higher frequency for any emergency calls."

Sam did as he was told. Surveying the upper frequencies of the CB might lead them to any emergency calls coming into the St. Louis Police Department. If Walter and Julia were serious about killing off some of the angelic bloodlines, there probably would be some witnesses to the violence. Unless they were really, really good.

In a quiet residential street, Dean pulled over to the side of the road. It was around eight p.m., the sun was going down and several families were out for an evening stroll.

Sam diligently switched through the frequencies, going all the way up and then back down again. Then he caught it. It was faint, but they had picked up the local police radio.

They listened for more than an hour. All the police calls were for public drunkenness or the occasional domestic dispute. Dean leaned back and closed his eyes. It was going to be a long night.

Dana Mey Smith was on her hands and knees looking underneath the bed for Bertrand.

"Found him!" She appeared back at her son's bedside with the erstwhile missing bear. "Don't let him drop down there again," she said with a sincere maternal voice.

Dana smoothed down the blond cowlick of her son's hair; ever since he was born, the absurd tuft of hair had adorned her son's forehead. If it hadn't smoothed out in five years, she was certain it was never going to. But at least the hair's disposition fit the popular hairstyles of the times.

"I won't," Cory said as he closed his eyes contentedly and turned over.

Dana tiptoed out of his room and down the stairs. At first she didn't notice anything out of place. It was still hot in her small two-story Victorian, though she kept all the windows open all the time when it was the middle of summer like this. And she didn't lock the door because Greg would be returning home from his shift. So it wasn't unusual to have the long curtains move in the breeze. But as Dana turned toward the kitchen, she saw a figure outlined in the curtain. The figure was tall and dressed in black clothing with a ski mask on his face. She screamed.

He moved toward her. She screamed again and tried to run toward the back door. The man tackled her to the floor. She tried to knee him in the groin, but he was far too fast and too strong.

Dana felt her head hit the floor. A hot tingling feeling ran from her ears to her eyes.

"I don't have any money. I don't have any money," she cried through her tears.

The figure put his hands around her throat and started

to squeeze. She struggled at first, pulling at the fists around her neck. In a matter of thirty seconds her body went limp.

The man got up off the floor and pulled the dead body into a pantry inside the kitchen.

"Ma!" a small voice called from the front of the house.

The figure turned, his eyes shifting around the living room. He peeled off his ski mask. The man's sandy blond hair was matted down with sweat. He put on a smile and approached the stairs. On the top of the landing was a small boy, about four or five years old. He was in his pajamas.

"Ma, Bertrand fell again." The little boy's eyes focused on the man in black, standing at the bottom of the stairs. "Who are you?"

"I'm a friend of your mom's." The man said through a plastered-on smile. "Can I help you find Bertrand?"

"Okay."

The man had just stepped onto the staircase when the door flew open. A policeman stopped in his tracks, and surveyed the situation. The man opened his mouth as if to offer some excuse. That's when the cop tackled him. Cory screamed and ran back to his room.

The man drew a knife and plunged it into the cop's soft belly. The dead weight collapsed onto him, but he managed to roll out from underneath.

A second, younger cop appeared at the door, gun drawn. The intruder rose to his full height. The cop let loose three bullets, but two went wide, with the third passing straight through the man's shoulder. He turned and took off through the back of the house. The cop dove over his partner in pursuit, but the man had apparently vanished into the summer night.

He returned to his partner's side and fell to his knees. The prone cop opened his shirt to reveal the deep stab wounds. He tried to speak, but a stream of blood poured out of his mouth. His eyes rolled back. He was dead.

Sam and Dean had heard the police call. Following the patrol car to the scene, Dean left Sam waiting outside, while he headed around the side of the house.

"Dean, he's coming through the back!" Sam yelled.

Hearing his brother, Dean jumped a fence and went around the back. That's when he saw the man in black sprint out of the house across the backyard. Dean took off after him.

The man vaulted over a six-foot wooden fence. Dean was close behind. He reached for the guy's black sweater. It half ripped as he pulled away, but the small delay allowed Dean to punch him in the back of the throat with his right hook. The man fell to the ground. Dean flipped him over and started pummeling him in the face.

"You a hunter? Hey, you a hunter?" Dean growled.

"Go to Hell," the man spat.

"Been there, done that." Dean punched the guy in the ear, knocking him out.

"Dean?" Sam hissed.

"Over here."

Sam appeared with a flashlight. "Let's get out of here."

Sam took the guy's legs and Dean wrapped his arms

underneath his shoulders. They made their way to the car, opened the trunk, swiftly bound the guy's hands and feet and roughly folded him inside.

Then they jumped into the front seats and took off.

The brothers pulled into a motel, checked in, and, under the cover of night, carried the guy into their room.

Dean threw a cup of cold water at the man's face. He opened his eyes and tried to move.

"Hey, get these off me!" He struggled against his bonds.

"You need to answer some questions first," Dean said.

"Screw you. You have no idea what you're dealing with."

Sam leaned over the guy menacingly. "You just murdered two people. We'll be happy to let you go. I'm sure the police will completely understand as they tear you limb from limb. They have the death penalty in Missouri, Dean?"

"Please, it's 1954, of course they do."

"Fine, what do you want to know?" the man hissed.

"What were you doing in that woman's house?" Dean demanded.

"I was asked to do a job. I did it."

"Who asked you?"

"I don't know, never saw the guy. He called me up and said he wanted some skirt laid up, and I told him my price."

"Which is?"

"Normally I don't like to kill ladies. But he offered me a grand."

"A grand to kill a woman? And the kid?"

"I didn't know there was a kid. I wasn't going to hurt

him. Honest."

"How were you going to collect the money?"

"The guy said to call him and we would meet up."

"You really think you were going to get paid? Do you even know where this guy lives?"

"I'm not an idiot. I got a bead on him. He's some old guy."

Dean's face hardened; deep down he was still hoping their suspicions were wrong and Julia and Walter weren't behind this. But he had a bad feeling they were right.

"Call him." Dean grabbed the telephone off the night-stand and forced the receiver into the guy's face.

"Um, hello? Hands are tied."

"What's the number?" Dean held his hand over the rotary telephone. "Come on."

The guy recited the number. Dean put the receiver to his ear. On the other end of the line it rang, and then there was a female voice.

"Hello? Hello?"

Dean scowled—it was Julia. She and Walter had hired someone to kill the first of the angelic vessels.

"Hello? Is anyone there?" Julia said impatiently.

Sam quickly took the receiver from Dean, and put it up to the guy's ear. He motioned for him to speak.

"Hey, it's Grant. Deed's done. When can we meet up?"

"One second," the end of the line was silent for a moment. "Rick's Drive-In. One hour. I'll see you."

There was a click. The guy looked up at Dean and Sam.

"Can you loosen these ropes now? I can't feel my dick."

Dean punched him hard in the face.

TWENTY-NINE

It was around midnight, and the drive-in was hopping. Dean pulled the car into the darkest corner of the parking lot. They had bound the guy in the backseat, and tied him down.

"Hey, I can't see. How are you going to find her?"

"We'll find her," Sam said.

Dean noticed a young couple making out in the car nearest to them. The windows were all steamed up.

"Very *American Graffiti*," he spat.

Sam leaned back and stuffed the nose of the gun into the guy's stomach.

"Remember, if you mention one word about the kid to them, you're dead. You understand?" Sam's face and voice made it clear that he was completely serious.

"Yeah, man. I get it. It's cool man," he grunted.

A couple of minutes later, Julia and Walter pulled up in a station wagon. They took an end parking space, closest to the exit. If Julia looked in her rearview she might see them, but she was engrossed in surveying the people milling under the bright lights of the drive-in's carport.

Dean reached into the back of the car with his hunting knife and cut the cords on the guy's wrists.

"Go get your money, scumbag." Dean opened the back door.

The man scrambled out of the car and approached the back of Julia's on the driver's side. She swiveled around as he approached. Twenty yards back, Sam and Dean watched from inside their car. The guy touched his face, where Dean had repeatedly punched him. From afar, it seemed like he was making some excuse for his appearance. Julia passed over an envelope. The guy glanced back at Sam and Dean and then started walking at a rapid pace through the crowd around the drive-in.

"You're just going to let him go?" Sam asked.

"We have bigger fish to fry," Dean said coldly.

Dean watched Julia pull the car out of the parking lot. They followed slowly behind.

Julia turned right onto a main street and headed for downtown St. Louis. Dean stayed two car lengths behind her; he didn't take his eyes off the station wagon.

"Dean, try to calm down. We'll figure this out," Sam said as tactfully and gently as he could.

"Leave me alone, Sam." Dean gripped the steering wheel even tighter. "She just murdered an innocent woman. She's a liar. Who knows how many other people died tonight? I'm not going to let any more people get killed because of this God-damned Apocalypse."

Sam was silent. They drove for the next twenty minutes without speaking.

Julia pulled into a large brick industrial-era warehouse on the outside of town. She drove the car around back, so it was hidden from the street. Dean idled the car at the curb. He was perfectly still.

"Do you want me to go in?" Sam asked.

"No," Dean said, shaking the cobwebs away. "I'm good. I got this."

They took two shotguns, one salt-filled and one they had loaded with regular bullets, and of course Ruby's knife.

"Let's go," Dean said.

He headed off into the dark toward the looming building. Sam followed close behind. They crept around the back of the structure and spotted half a dozen cars. There were no lights. But it didn't look like anyone was lurking around. A large steel door was cut into the back of the building. Dean tried to push it, but it was locked from the inside. It would probably make too much noise to open it anyway. He spotted a six foot-long transom window, which was about nine feet off the ground and swung open from the top.

"Sam, give me a lift."

Just then a large bear of a guy careened around the corner and barreled headfirst into Sam. Sam went down in a heap.

Dean swung at the guy with the end of his shotgun. It connected right under the guy's chin, but only sent him stumbling back a couple of steps. Dean picked up a handful of gravel and threw it in the guy's face, momentarily blinding him. He threw a blind swing and went down on his ass. Dean leap on top of him, and landed elbow first, smashing into the big man's kidneys. He curled up like an infant. Dean put both hands round the guy's throat, constricting his airway until his face turned purple. Just before the guy passed out, Dean let go. *That should keep him down for a little while.*

Dean held out his hand to Sam. "Come on, let's go. Stop laying around."

"Do you think there are more of them?" Sam asked, rubbing his head.

"That guy was big enough to be three guys. Come on. Alley-oop."

Sam held Dean by the knee. Pushing his weight up, he managed to grasp the ledge above. In an impressive rock-climbing move, Dean swung his leg onto the cement ledge underneath the window, pulling himself so he was half inside the building and half out, balancing on his stomach.

He disappeared into the black interior of the building.

Sam was glad that the little bit of action had made Dean communicative again. When Dean was silent and brooding things could get rough.

A couple of minutes later, Dean pushed open the large steel door.

"This place is a fortress. Not good," Dean said as he slid the steel portal closed behind Sam.

Inside the building, there was a steel staircase that led up one side. In the centre was a very large open space, and for the first time Sam noticed a pair of railroad tracks that led underneath the massive steel door. On the tracks sat an old steam engine, facing toward the door as if ready for a quick get away. The building was a large repair station for many Midwest rail lines. It didn't look active to Sam.

Dean motioned for Sam to follow him as he slid against the wall and peered over a railing. Beneath was a basement. One side was open and the other was underneath the cement and steel floor. It allowed for about ten feet of space from the ceiling to the floor. Old steam engine parts had been pushed up against the walls and a long steel table had been placed in the middle of the basement structure. About fifty people milled about, crowding around something on the table. When the bodies parted, Sam caught a glimpse of the War Scroll laid out on the table.

A wooden door opened and Julia and Walter appeared. Dean's eyes turned steely.

When Julia spoke, everyone quieted down.

"Thank you all for coming. First off, I'd like to say that I appreciate your sacrifice. And it will be a sacrifice, because as we go into this battle, despite our precautions, some of the people standing next to you may die. You may die. And though what we are embarking on is bloody, it is necessary. We are faced with the destruction of the Earth. To stop it there are actions that we as people, and as hunters, need to take. As you see, we have the last bit of the War Scroll, the sacred scroll written by the Essenes outlining the battle plan for the Sons of Light to overtake the Sons of Darkness."

A murmur rose from the group.

"We were brought together decades ago for this express moment," Julia continued. "Many of you knew my grandfather, and my grandfather knew your great grandfathers. We have waited for this moment for generations. And now it is here. We are all meant to play a part in defeating evil for the very last time. The Apocalypse we know will come. The Mayans weren't far off; though the threat to end the world will come three years earlier than they thought. I unfortunately have intimate knowledge of this. But with this scroll we can stop it. What you see written behind the main text of the scroll is a list of names."

All heads bowed once again to look at the scroll.

Up above, hiding in the darkness, Sam peered at his brother. Dean didn't take his eyes off Julia as she moved around the room, almost military style. If she hadn't been rousing people to murder, it might have been impressive.

"This is a list of names, each is a bloodline which will produce the vessels for the angels to fight Lucifer. We know that these bloodlines have been cultivated over 3,000 years by the angels, all for the impending fight with Lucifer. But, if the angels don't have the vessels, there is no fight. Do not think of this task as extinguishing a heavenly light in this world. That's not what we are doing. We are preventing that from happening. We are preventing the greatest fight man will ever know. We will be saving a billion lives."

Dean watched Julia as she handed out a list of names to each hunter.

"On these pieces of paper there is a list of about fifty names, all are within your specific regions. Pass them to everyone you are working with. My father and I have already started and we have the name of Lucifer's vessel and intend to take the appropriate action. Be careful, crafty. Dip into the funds if you need to hire someone in your stead. Do it quickly to avoid prolonged hysteria. We would like to extinguish these bloodlines by the end of the month. That gives you about ten days.

"Go out there and do this for the love of man. Good luck."

One hunter pounded the butt of his shotgun on the table. Then another and another. The sound was a somber drum beat of death echoing through the large building. Then silence. Maps were laid out on the table. The people split into groups and the planning began.

As Julia spoke to a tall older man, she looked up into the darkness of the building, almost directly at Dean. Dean's breath caught in his throat. Julia's face registered a half second of recognition and then she looked back to the man in front of her.

"Let's get out of here," Dean whispered.

"We're just going to let them do this?" Sam asked.

That's when Dean heard it; it was far off in the distance, but the sound was unmistakable. It was the chugging of a train. The tracks below the brothers started to shake. Dean looked around—there wasn't a Devil's Trap to be found. How could Julia be so stupid?

Downstairs, the group fell silent, then *en mass* they grabbed their guns and ran up the staircase like battalions exiting u-boats.

"Turn on the lights!" someone called.

There was the clunk of a large switch being flipped and all the lights flickered on. That's when Julia spotted Dean and Sam standing above her. Dean's eyes met hers; Julia's immediately welled with tears.

Outside, the engine had reached the outer edge of the train yard. It flew through the chain link fence, flinging cars out of the way like falling dominos.

The engine crashed into the steel door with such force that a six-foot-high span of bricks above the door cracked and fell to the ground. The door folded in half like an envelope. The hiss of the engine blew steam into the rafters forty feet above.

A silhouette appeared at the top of the engine.

Dean whispered, "Eisheth."

THIRTY

70 A.D. Khirbet Qumran, West Bank

The evening wind blowing in over the Dead Sea was, appropriately, as cold as death. Eisheth detested it, it whipped open the tents, and sand would kick up and cut into faces like glass, sending humans running for cover. She just about detested everything about life on Earth. After what she had seen, no one could blame her. Within the Lord's Kingdom there was no bad weather, no wanting for food—and there certainly were no foul-smelling goats. Which wasn't the case when living amongst the Essenes.

Her host was a girl of only eight years. At that age, children naturally demonstrate enough idiosyncratic behavior that no one noticed a little bit of demonic possession. *That's one positive thing about my new life*, Eisheth thought, *no more begging and pleading with vessels*. "Please, it's for the greater good," she used to say. "It's God's Will. Say 'Yes.'" The life of an angel required constantly asking for consent, and constant capitulation to the whims of others.

Demons didn't have to ask. They took what they wanted, when they wanted it, used it up, and left what remained to rot. It suited her personality so much better.

Yet, what Eiseth wanted most, simple as it was, she could not take.

Sick of the biting gale, for after all she was in a human body and hated when it was uncomfortable, she sought shelter within one of the many canvas-walled tents that made up the majority of the settlement. The colony was substantial, but dwindling. Thousands of people, mostly men, gathered here to celebrate their shared faith... that unfortunately required them to remain celibate. How they intended to keep their faith alive into the next generation, Eiseth wasn't sure. Her "father" had settled here after his wife died in childbirth, believing her death was his punishment for selfishly valuing his own pleasure over his God. *Humans.*

Inside the tent, Abaddon was already waiting.

"I don't have long," he said.

It took all of Eiseth's considerable willpower to maintain her composure.

"Did he send word?" she asked. Abaddon avoided her gaze.

"Of course. The Morning Star sends his deep affection…"

Not his love, she thought.

"…and wishes to know what you've found."

Eiseth nodded, her cracked lips quivering.

"The prophet finishes his work as we speak."

One half of Abaddon's face pulled into a smile, while the other remained eerily blank.

"Where is he?"

Prophecy was laborious and frustrating, coming in fits and starts, with no set schedule and no guarantee that the results would make sense. Eisheth hated being here among the zealots of the day. Despite that, she had dutifully watched the group… for him. Finally, one of the men she was particularly close to had written something of interest. She had immediately called Abaddon.

Abaddon and Eisheth entered the cave slowly, their human eyes adjusting to the dim surroundings. The prophet sat with his back against the rock wall, a small fire burnt to embers in front of him. At his side, a set of clay jars waited to be filled and sealed.

Fear flitted across the prophet's face as Abaddon approached.

"Who… who…" he stuttered.

Without a word, Abaddon reached out and touched the man's forehead. He collapsed to the ground with a dull thud, his mind wiped completely of a year's work.

"I can't stand small talk." Abaddon picked up the completed scroll, admiring the intricate lettering. "We should use him more often—beautiful penmanship."

"What now?" Eisheth asked, looking for her reward. "He's happy with what I found, isn't he?"

Abaddon moved to pick up one of the clay jars, hefting it and feeling its weight, then putting it back down.

"Oh, very. Tickled," he said as he clapped his hands together. For a moment, nothing happened. He looked around the cave, surprised, apparently waiting for something to appear. Once again, he clapped loudly.

From outside, a low rumble filled the air, reverberating around the cave walls and shaking loose dirt from the ceiling. A swell of black smoke surged in through the cave's opening, dancing through the air before finding its way to one of the clay jars.

"Who was that?" Eisheth asked as Abaddon placed the lid on the jar, sealing the demon inside. "Anyone I know?"

"An insurance policy," Abaddon responded. "Something to help you find your way."

"My way?" she asked.

"Do you remember Lilith's hobby?" Abaddon asked with a dark grin, clearly aware that Lilith's name would provoke a strong response from Eisheth.

"How could I forget," she replied, memories of Lilith's pet fresh in her mind. It was one of many lines that Lilith had crossed that Eisheth was unwilling to. Torturing an animal, twisting it into something unnatural, for no reason other than her own amusement. "The dog." She hated the dog.

"I love that dog," Abaddon said.

"So does Lilith. Why would she give him up?"

"Because he asked her to."

Eisheth swallowed reflexively.

"He knew you'd need it."

The pieces weren't connecting for Eisheth. She had read

the prophecy, though she didn't fully understand the text. She knew that the battle it described was thousands of years in the future. What she didn't know was the role that she was destined to play.

"I want to see him," she said, desperation seeping into her voice. It had been years. How many, she didn't know. It felt like thousands. "I *need* to see him."

"I'm afraid you have a different destiny."

Words had never had a more sinister edge. Eisheth backed away from Abaddon as he lifted the lid from another jar. His finger circled the rim, searing an Enochian sigil into the clay. Eisheth recognized the angelic script instantly. It reminded her of home—her first home. Heaven. Looking at Abbandon, this was beginning to feel like a terrible mistake.

Perhaps wholly trusting Abaddon wasn't a wise move, he was a fallen angel after all. They were crafty, not single-minded like herself, a demon. Perhaps she shouldn't have had her lust move her feet into blind submission to Abaddon's direction.

In that moment, she pondered the extent of God's forgiveness. If he could forgive humans for their vanity, their cruelty and their lust, surely he could forgive her. Surely love wasn't so abhorrent a sin—

The thought ended there with a flick of Abaddon's wrist. Eisheth's soul, blackened by its union to Lucifer, jetted out of the young girl's mouth in terrible, choking spasms.

Husband, why have you forsaken me?

She wouldn't get her answer for nearly 2,000 years.

1954 A.D., St. Louis, Missouri

Didn't see that coming, Dean thought.

Standing atop the engine, the demon's eyes flared crimson—it was as if the blood pumping in her host's veins was visible through her pupils.

Sam and Dean exchanged a harried glance, both understanding that any chance of peacefully defusing the situation had perished with the arrival of Eisheth and her horde.

From within the train, her demonic followers began to appear. First, a pair from the conductor's hatch, clambering out and over the twisted steel that once was the building's door. Next, a bald-headed man leapt with inhuman agility out of one of the cargo compartments. A veritable flood followed them—Dean counted about a hundred demons, every one of them moving into position around the assembled hunters. Reflected light from the glowing fire glimmered in their ebony eyes.

"Everybody stay back," Dean shouted, trying his best to take command of the situation before someone tipped its delicate balance. His thoughts flipped quickly between regret—for having created the quagmire in the first place—and anger, directed squarely at Julia and Walter for fanning the flames.

To Dean's chagrin, Walter shoved his way through the crowd of hunters and stood before Eisheth.

"You don't know what you've walked into, demon," he called out to her.

Chuckling, Eisheth squinted at Walter.

"Aren't you a sad little creature," she cackled. "Puffing out your chest like a man."

If he was offended by the jab, Walter didn't show it.

"Seems to me, this is about the worst place you could find yourself. Going head to head with the only people on this Earth who know how to kill you."

Behind him, over a dozen of his compatriots formed into a rough phalanx, preparing for the inevitable fight.

With a look to her followers, Eisheth indicated for them to move forward.

"I am willing to find an equitable arrangement," she said. "Give me the scroll, and we'll only kill…" She trailed off, scanning the crowd, finally pointing a threatening finger at Julia. "Her."

Dean bristled, and jostled his way through the crowd to stand next to Walter.

"Listen, bitch, we've heard about enough from you," he growled.

Sam followed him out of the throng, taking up a defensive position next to his brother. Walter noticed and immediately stepped away from him. *Julia must have told him everything*, Dean realized. *Of course, by now he's had time to translate the entire list, so he could have found out about us on his own.*

"Samuel Winchester," Eisheth snarled. "I thought you, of all people, would understand what a mistake this is. Do you honestly believe you'll be allowed to succeed?"

"We're not afraid of you," Walter said. His eyes shifted

nervously between her and Sam, betraying the bravado in his words.

Eisheth ignored him, and continued to address Sam.

"As if *your* name isn't on that list. Do you really think the *angels* will let you destroy their entire stock of vessels?"

Sam remained silent. Now it was Julia who stepped forward.

"We don't give a damn what you or the angels think," she said. "This is our planet, and we're not going to let you destroy it."

"Samuel. I'm speaking to *you*." Eisheth glared at him. "Not the riff-raff."

Behind Sam, Walter nodded toward several of the hunters. They pointed their rifles at Sam. Another set raised theirs toward Eisheth and her horde.

"Ah. I see. We have ourselves a little intraspecies squabble." Eisheth smiled at Sam. "And you were such fast friends the last time we saw each other. What happened? Somebody find out your little secret?"

She addressed the group. "You really should be bowing before him, not pointing guns at his back. Do you realize how perfect a specimen he is? Do you know what kind of strength it takes to house an *archangel*?"

"He's a freak," Walter declared. "Just like you. Now why don't you take your little circus and leave town? Can't promise not to catch up with you, but I'll give you a head start."

"Things sure have changed since I was bottled up," Eisheth said. "2,000 years ago, people had so much faith that they refused to marry. Thought it would take up too much of their prayer time. Now look at you."

"You want to talk about faith?" Walter cried furiously. "You're a monster! A blight on God's creation."

"If you cared about God's creation, you'd let Him do with it as He wished. If He wants to take His ball and go home, let Him. Except in this case, He wants to smash His ball to pieces."

"He wants me to save it," Walter said with fervor.

"Please," Eiseth said exasperated. "You? Look at you! You think *you're* important enough to be part of God's plan?"

Blood rushed to Walter's face. Dean could see the fury in his eyes, every taunt bringing him closer to breaking point.

"Enough!" Sam shouted, stepping between Eiseth and Walter. "Walter, you think you've figured out what part you have to play, but trust me, *you don't want to play a part*. It's hell. And it's not fair. I don't want anything to do with Lucifer, and I'm going to do my damnedest to avoid it, but those are the cards I was dealt. Maybe the cards you got let you sit this one out. Maybe you have something else to do with your life, besides throwing it away trying to stop the inevitable."

Dean shot Sam a look. *Inevitable? What was he saying? That he knew he'd have to say yes to Satan eventually?*

"Glad you've accepted that, Sam," Eiseth stated.

She stepped off the roof of the train engine and dropped, landing with a thud on the cracked flooring.

"If you wish it… I will spare them."

Sam and Dean both recoiled in shock. *What did that crazy broad just say?*

"In exchange for one thing."

Of course, Dean thought. *Of course there's a catch.*

After a moment's hesitation, Sam said quietly, "What?"

"When the time comes, and Lucifer is finally freed... I want you to kill Lilith. *Before* you say yes to Lucifer, considering you won't have much of a say in things after that."

Sam's face went slack. *Was she serious? Did she really not know?*

Shaking his head, Sam backed away from her.

"No. I—I can't."

Eisheth fumed. "Fine. Don't say I didn't give you a choice."

She held up her hand, getting the attention of the demons around her. Then she brought her hand down, toward Walter and Julia's army.

"Wait! Sam. Sammy," Dean cried out. "You can reconsider, right? Seems like killing Lilith might be something you're into." He shot Sam a big-eyed look, hoping that his little brother would realize how stupid he was being. *Lie to her, dumbass! Give Walter and Julia a chance to tuck their tails between their legs and run, then we can deal with this the old-fashioned way.*

Eisheth motioned to her demons, stopping them, and waited for Sam to respond.

"Why do you care?" Dean asked, trying to draw her out while he figured out a plan.

"Guess my story didn't make it into your copy of the Bible," she barked angrily. "I was an angel. I was supposed to be up there, among the Heavenly Host, deciding all of your pathetic little fates. But I made one mistake. Loved an angel I wasn't supposed to, and look where it got me." She indicated the pack of fiends behind her. "Lilith, a damned human, comes in and pushes me out, so I ripped out my grace and became human for him, too. But even that wasn't enough. It was as if Lucifer only had space in Hell for one of us."

"Sounds like Lucifer's not your biggest fan then, if he let that happen," Dean said.

His words caused Eisheth's jaw to grind. "You don't know what you're talking about. She did what humans do. She manipulated, schemed, and back-stabbed until she had the support of his… caretaker." She paused, then added, without much conviction, "Lucifer never stopped loving me."

"I bet."

"When this was discovered, it was *I* who brought it to Abaddon's attention," she said, pointing at the list which was still laid out on the table, "because I was the better wife. More loyal than Lilith. *I* gave everything up for him. I told Abaddon that."

"Wait, Abaddon?" Dean said, his head reeling. How could that be true? Who was Abaddon loyal to—Heaven or Hell?

Eisheth smiled cruelly. "You know him?"

Dean looked at the floor, considering the options. One: she was lying. She was a demon, after all. Two: Abaddon was a spy infiltrating the bad camp 2,000 years ago, and that's how he knew Eisheth. Three: Abaddon was bad and always had been, or his true motives were too complicated for Dean to ever figure out, and he was best left going with his gut, which at this juncture was telling him to kill Eisheth and run.

"You'd remember him if you'd met him. He's not exactly a charmer."

"I don't doubt that," Sam interjected. "But what does he have to do with the scroll?"

"Look who's chatty now," Eisheth said. "Abaddon was the one that told me I would be in Lucifer's favor for showing him the scrolls. He was the only link I had to a very absent husband. And he's the bastard who sealed me in the jar."

Sam and Dean shared a wary look. At the moment, they were facing a firing squad on one side, a bitter old demon and her lackeys on another, and if they ever found their way home, an angel gone bad would be waiting for them. So, it was a lot like any other day.

"I spent 2,000 years in that damn jar, puzzling over what it all meant, why my husband would let that happen. And I think I've figured it out."

"Yeah? What's that?" Dean said. As Eisheth related her story, he was busy scanning the room for something that would give them an advantage. But as he currently saw it, there were over a hundred demons, and just over fifty hunters. The hunters had guns, the demons were almost impossible to kill. If Eisheth was anywhere near as powerful as Lilith, the advantage was certainly on her side.

"The task I've been given, it's a test. I stop you, and I've proven my worth. Lucifer wants nothing more than to have a fight. I'm here to make sure he gets it. The vessels must be preserved."

"After all he put you through, you're still doing his chores?" Dean asked.

"I love him." It seemed that to Eisheth, it was as simple as that. No matter what had happened to her, what she had been forced into, her mind was made up.

"This is insane," Dean said with vitriol. "We're talking about thousands of lives. It's not a test; it's not a special destiny. It's about right and wrong, and damn if the demon isn't right this time. I have no intention of letting Michael and Lucifer fight it out, not with the whole world hanging in the balance, but I'm not going to give up on doing the right thing just to take the easy way out. There's an easy fix for all of us. Walk the hell away—"

Before Eisheth could respond, Walter stepped forward and placed a rock salt shotgun firmly to her temple.

"Dad! No!" Julia cried out, rushing toward her father, but it was too late. In a blur of motion, Eisheth slammed her fist into his ribcage, instantly shattering it. He reeled from the blow, his shotgun blasting uselessly into the air as the demon dove at him, gripping him firmly by the neck.

With a sickening crack, she ended his life. His body went limp and she let it drop to the floor. For all his talk about destiny, Walter had ended up deciding his own fate.

"Kill them all. Except for Samuel."

THIRTY-ONE

Dean fired a round of bullets at the surrounding demons, creating a haze of smoke and salt. Bodies keeled over. Sam slashed a couple with Ruby's knife. The demons' wounds flashed a hellfire orange as they were dispatched into nothingness.

While Eisheth was distracted, Dean ran to Walter's body. Figuring the old man would not have let go of those precious last pages of the scroll, he patted him down and sure enough found them in his breast pocket.

"Sorry old man. I hope it was worth it," he said, carefully pulling out the papers and pocketing them.

The fight raged around him, the air filled with shotgun blasts and the screams of hunters as the demons overcame them. The hunters were fighting back but there were just too many demons. *It's a massacre*, Dean thought, *and there's nothing we can do to save them*.

Through the chaos he spied Julia. In a rage of grief she

was drop-kicking, stabbing and shooting at demons from all sides, but they were closing in. Fighting his way through the maelstrom, Dean grabbed hold of her. She struggled against him as he pulled her down the steel staircase to the room underneath the engine work floor.

Sam stood at the bottom of the staircase and shot rounds of salt over their heads.

Eiseth turned back around and saw Dean disappear down the staircase.

"Come on Winchesters," she cried, standing tall and bloody amongst the dead and dying hunters, surrounded by her horde. "I just want to talk."

They barricaded themselves in an ante-room which led off the basement.

"So now what?" Sam asked.

"Is there another way out of here?" Dean asked Julia, who stood immobile, staring at the floor.

He grasped her by the shoulders.

"Julia! Is there another way out of here?"

She looked up. "I killed him."

"No, you didn't. Walter died for what he believed in. No one was going to convince him otherwise, not even you. Now we have to find a way out of here."

Dean looked around the room. "What is this place?"

Crates and sacks were stacked up against every wall of the rectangular room. A distinct pungent odor hung in the air. The only fresh ventilation was coming through a large grate in the ceiling.

Dean pried open a crate and looked inside. Dynamite.

"That explains the reinforced steel door," Sam said, looking over his shoulder. "I bet this was used as some sort of hub when they built the Atlantic Pacific Railroad. They'd need explosives to grade earth and create suitable terrain for the rail lines."

"Now I feel bad about taking away your Thomas the Train toy." Dean glanced witheringly at his brother. "This stuff must be like seventy years old. Do you think it still works?"

There was a loud bang at the door, then another. The demons were trying to get in. Each impact dented the steel a bit more. It was only a matter of time.

"We're not going to have time to find out," Sam said, guarding the door. "Let's get these things unpacked."

Minutes later the trio were hard at work. Julia was stringing detonation wire between the crates of dynamite, and Sam and Dean were ripping open all the various sacks of chemicals and gunpowder. By the time they were done they were knee deep in explosives.

The demons continued to work on the steel door, it was beginning to tear like tin foil.

"Let's get out of here," Dean said, unscrewing the bolts on the ventilation shaft.

A faint scratching sound could be heard coming from above.

"Did they get inside there? That's our only way out," Julia said nervously, looking up into the darkness between the metal slats.

"We've got no choice now. I'll go first. Julia second. Sam, you cover the back and lay the wire as we go."

Dean stood on a chair and lifted himself into the vent. He pulled Julia up behind him. Sam managed to bury the denotation wire in the explosives below. The demons were almost all the way through the door when Sam lifted himself up into the shaft and hastily put the grid back on it.

They crawled through the ventilation shaft on their hands and knees. It ran underneath the engine work floor and every twenty feet or so it changed direction. They soon felt like they were going in circles.

"Are you sure you know where this is going?" Julia asked.

"It has to lead somewhere," Dean said. The enclosed box shape of the duct-work made Dean uneasy, it reminded him of being stuck in a coffin after his death. "This is so not good for my claustrophobia."

Sam was bringing up the rear, sliding his shotgun in front of him and then crawling up to meet it. The action made a lulling swish-swish sound. But then he heard the distinct screech of metal scraping against metal.

"Dean, I think you need to speed it up a bit," Sam called ahead.

"I'm going as fast as I can."

"I think they just got into the vent."

"Damn it."

"Hurry!" Sam called. He could hear the demons getting closer.

Sam took the right turn behind Julia, but his leg wouldn't move. He looked back. A demon, a man in overalls, smiled a toothless grin at him.

"Where you goin' pretty boy?"

Sam flipped onto his back and shot the man between the eyes in one motion. The salt pellet burned into the demon's head. Smoke escaped from his mouth, sped across the top of the ventilation shaft and disappeared out of the grate.

"Dean, we need to get out of here!"

Dean slid underneath the grating that led to the outside. He crouched down then pushed it with his back. It wouldn't budge.

"It's stuck!"

"I have a whole load of demons on my ass. Figure something out!"

Dean pushed again. The grate gave a bit, then a little more. He scrambled up and disappeared outside.

Another demon quickly crawled toward Sam. He spun and shot it in the heart.

Julia clambered out of the grate ahead of Sam.

Sam managed to follow her, squeezing through the opening just as more demonic black eyes appeared out of the darkness.

He found himself standing on a grassy patch about fifty yards away from the engine warehouse.

Dean started shooting salt rounds into the hole Sam had just vacated. He yelled at Julia over his shoulder.

"Get that car over here." He pointed at a car parked on the street twenty feet away.

"Let's get the grate back over it," Sam said, indicating the hole.

They pulled the iron grate onto the hole just as three

more demonic faces appeared below them.

"Suck it, bitches." Dean smiled.

"I don't think that's going to hold," Sam said.

An engine roared. From behind the wheel of the car, Julia motioned for them to get out of the way. She stopped directly over the grate. They could see the demons trying to push the grate open, but it would only move so far up against the undercarriage of the automobile.

Sam pulled the detonation wire about ten feet from the car.

"Find some cover," Dean called to Julia.

Julia exited the car and took cover behind another car parked on the dark street.

Sam looked at Dean. "Let's hope this works."

Sam lit the detonation wire. It sparked, then fizzled out.

"Aww, come on! Let me try." Dean took the Zippo from his younger brother and tried lighting the wire, but it refused to ignite.

"It's too old," Dean said. "Eiseth's still in there. Let's light that bitch up."

"Someone has to go in and light it some other way. I'll do it," Sam said.

"Sam, no. No telling what Eiseth will do to you if she catches you."

"Let me do it. I started this."

"It's a suicide mission."

"It's not like that. We need to kill Eiseth, she's leading the charge in there. Those poor possessed people are already dead. We need to put them out of their misery."

Dean nodded his head, his brother was right.

Sam took the Zippo from Dean.

"Wish me luck."

He ran off toward the warehouse.

Sam peeked through a dusty window—the warehouse was crawling with demons. Eiseth had somehow recruited yet more. The bodies of the hunters were littered across the floor, not one of them was still standing. *Poor people*, Sam thought, *all of them thought they were on their way to fulfilling some sort of destiny, and they all died today. Because of me.*

Sam kicked open the window and climbed inside. He stealthily made his way to the steel staircase. The basement was full of demons all still fighting to get into the anteroom where they had been holed up. Sam looked around for something to light. He saw an old piece of rope and an empty beer bottle. Sam took some oil from a can and poured it into the beer bottle, then he dipped the rope into the oil and shoved that into the top of the bottle.

"I was hoping we would get a little one-on-one time," a voice said.

Sam spun around to see Eiseth leaning suggestively against the dead body of a hunter splayed over a piece of machinery. She smiled and sauntered toward him.

"I have to say, Lucifer did well. He always had good taste. You'll soon find that out." Eiseth reached her hand up to touch Sam's face. "We are going to have such fun together."

Sam pulled away. "You disgust me. You should've stayed in your genie bottle."

"Oh, come now, Sam. Aren't you even a little bit happy

to see me? I'm happy to see you. I was cooped up for so long in that jar. I had plenty of time to fantasize about what vessel Lucifer would pick for himself when he rose. And, my oh my, I am glad it's someone so tall. You know… when Lilith wasn't around," Eisheth pressed up close to Sam, "Lucifer and I did some wonderful things together. Would you like me to show you?"

She trailed her fingers over Sam's chest and down toward his belt buckle.

"Maybe in my next lifetime."

Eisheth laughed. "You are a comedian, aren't you? Don't you understand? I'm your future wife. Maybe not in this body, but I'll make sure she's really nice and young. You'd like that, wouldn't you? In fifty years, when Lucifer is out and inside you… Well, let's just say I can't wait to get back to playing our old games."

Eisheth leaned in to kiss Sam. Sam took a step, spun around and simultaneously lit and threw the bottle into the basement and right at the ante-room door. A couple of demons were blown apart in the quick flare up. It would only be a matter of time before the entire room went up.

Eisheth grabbed Sam by the neck, and threw him up against a wall.

"You think I care about a hundred lesser demons? Burn them all. I just care about you, Samuel. I want you to be safe."

Sam pushed himself up and lunged at Eisheth. With the demon knife, he slashed at her belly. She moved away with a quick step.

"Silly boy, you can't kill me. I'm over 2,000 years old."

Eisheth threw up her hand and Sam went flying fifty feet through the air, landing at the base of the steam engine. His head cracked against the iron.

"Now look what you made me do. I didn't want to hurt this perfect specimen."

Eisheth strode toward him.

THIRTY-TWO

"What's taking him so long?" Dean asked.

Dean and Julia were hidden behind a car, waiting for the four-story brick building to blow.

Without warning, the windows blew out, and hot mercury-colored glass shot in all directions.

There was a rumble, and then another blast as more fire exploded from the windows and roof of the building. Its seven-story smoke stack started to sway. There were a series of smaller percussions which rattled windows in the surrounding buildings. Then everything was silent for a moment.

A sizzling noise came from within the damaged structure, like a thousand tons of bacon frying. A blast like a mini atom bomb shot up into the air, crumbling the fifty-foot walls and sending flaming debris a hundred yards in all directions.

Dean looked at the destroyed shell of foundation.

"Sam?" he said in a small voice.

Then, against the light of the burning inferno, a

silhouette appeared. *Sam?* The figure gradually revealed itself to be Eisheth. She strode up to them, dragging Sam's body behind her.

Dean leveled his shotgun at her.

"He's not dead, don't worry. I'm as upset as you are. His body is so magnificent. I told him I can't wait until I get to explore it *all over.*"

"Put him down," Dean commanded.

Eisheth dropped Sam face first onto the gravel.

"What would you like to do now? I did my job. I stopped all those holier-than-thou hunters from killing the vessels."

"You killed my father!" Julia shouted.

Eisheth regarded Dean with a smirk.

"Really, this whiney little mouse is attractive to you? Okay, listen sweetheart, I had a job to do. I had to stop all you blood-filled air suckers from thinking you are doing God's work. If you only knew. From my perspective, God created a hot, dry, dusty, famine-filled world for you. Why would you ever want to help his cause?"

"Hey, Sigourney, can you stop playing Gate Keeper for a moment, and let's get this over with," Dean shouted over the roar of the fire.

"Just one more thing, then I'll get out of your hair. I need the last pages of the scroll. My job is to protect those names, and I'm not letting anyone else get any crazy ideas about killing off the vessels, especially now I've met my husband's. I'm talking to you, mouse."

Julia stepped out from behind the car and leveled her gun at Eisheth. A lightning quick unseen force pulled

Julia toward Eisheth. She flew through the air and landed unconscious at Eisheth's feet. The demon knelt down and picked her up by the hair, examining her face.

"Nice face, but a little petite, don't you think? Oh, and by the way, thanks for this. It's like a token from my homeland. Makes me nostalgic for all those sacrifices people used to do."

Eisheth held the demon knife at Julia's throat.

"I know. She's definitely not like me, but she will bleed regardless. I'm going to have so much fun with this knife. Do you know what I'm going to be able to do with it?" Eisheth dropped Julia and began ranting and gesticulating with the knife like it was a piece of chalk held by a professor. "I can kill off all Lucifer's precious little demons. I'll be able to slaughter each and every one. Then he'll have to listen to me."

Dean had to think fast.

"What's your plan?" he said. "You reckon killing demons is going to make your absent husband take you more seriously? You can boil little bunnies Glenn Close-style all you want, Lucifer has bigger fish to fry. You're just a distraction to him. Second fiddle. He's Tiger Woods and you're just another cocktail waitress to text message."

"Are those the last words your true love is going to hear you say?" Eisheth spat. "Fine with me."

Grabbing her hair, Eisheth lifted Julia's body off the ground. She pushed her neck back and held the knife to her throat again.

"What if we could make you a deal?" Dean asked, eyeing the glinting blade as she pressed it to Julia's skin.

"What could you possibly have that I would have the slightest bit of interest in?"

"We can take you to Lucifer. Now. You won't have to wait."

That made Eisheth pause.

"It seems like you haven't had a face-to-face with your hubby in a long time. Maybe now is the time to try to get into couples therapy?"

"I don't like the way you talk."

"You're a smart chick. Despite those 2,000 birthday candles on your cake, I know you get it." Dean smirked.

"Someone broke the seals?" Eisheth asked.

Dean looked at Sam. Seemed everyone thought it was impossible.

"Someone broke the seals. Lilith did, to be exact, and she's gone."

Eisheth's eyes glowed brightly, the thought of her husband unfettered, free of his favorite wife, was the consolation and redemption she had been waiting for.

Dean needed to rope her in quick.

"Lucifer is walking around just like you and me. But there's a catch—it's fifty-six years in the future. But we have a way to get you there."

"How?"

"All things come to those who wait. You need to do something for us first."

"I don't do favors."

Dean looked at her steadily. "You'll do this one. Just let Julia go."

Eisheth looked down at Julia's limp body.

"Fine," she said, dropping her to the ground. "What do I have to do?"

"First things first, we have a couple of stops."

"Where'd you say you found me?" Leanne Keeny asked.

"Wandering around St. Louis. You don't remember anything?" Dean shot her a sideways glance as he negotiated the country dirt road.

"I thought I went to New York. I got a job, I think. It was my first day. That's the last thing I remember."

"You're a lucky girl. Is this it?" Dean turned the car up a long driveway leading to a white clapboard farmhouse. "Nice place. I'm sure your parents will be happy to see you."

"They weren't expecting me until Christmas."

"Leanne, do me a favor. Stay here on the farm. Raise a family. You don't need to go to New York to have a good life."

She shrugged. "Guess you're right. Besides, New York was awfully expensive."

"There you go. Smart girl."

Leanne flashed him a big smile as she got out of the car. She shut the door and leaned in through the open window.

"So," she hesitated, "maybe you and me could go get a float sometime."

"Sorry sweetheart, I'm not the settling-down type." Dean winked, put the car into reverse and peeled off down the driveway.

Leanne Keeny took a long look at her parents' farmhouse and then ran inside.

Hours later, Dean pulled into the Twin Pines Motel in Waubay. He parked the car. Julia appeared in the doorway of a cabin. Dean couldn't take his eyes off her.

"Where's Sam?" he asked as he shut the car door.

"He's in a cabin. Sleeping, of all things. Are you sure about all this?"

Dean shrugged. "I'm never sure about anything. But we had to take the risk. Besides, she had a knife to your throat."

"Thank you for saving my life." Julia looked up into Dean's eyes.

He put his arms around her waist and gently pushed her into the cabin, closing the door behind him with his foot.

Dean gently slid onto the bed, pulling Julia with him.

"I'm so sorry for everything," Julia said as she smoothed her hands over Dean's chest. "Everything I believed in, everyone I've ever known… is gone."

Dean gazed into her eyes for a moment. It was true that Julia's life was forever changed. She had lost her father, all of the hunters who were her friends; she had lost her way of life. Dean thought about how hard it would be to go back to living a normal existence. Would there always be an itching to be on the road? Dean didn't know any other life. But Julia, she was different.

"You're free, Julia. You're now free to do what you want."

Julia pulled back to look at him. "What I want is to be with you."

"That can't happen. You know that."

Julia nodded sadly and laid her head on Dean's shoulder.

In the early dawn, Dean woke up. As quietly as possible, he crept out of bed, gathered his clothing up off the floor, lingered a moment at the door, then left.

He walked into the other cabin, where Sam was apparently still sleeping.

"You awake? We need to do this."

Sam sat up in bed. He was already dressed. He nodded and followed Dean out into the parking lot. They walked west into a field by the motel. Dean took the last couple of pages of the War Scroll from inside his leather jacket. Holding them up by one corner, he lit his Zippo and the flame caught the parchment. In a matter of seconds the pages had curled up like black tongues licking up the fire.

As the last bit of the War Scroll disappeared into ash, there was a bright flash of light.

THIRTY-THREE

Castiel had told Dean many times about the difficulty of moving objects through time. How it exhausted him, and left him barely able to think, much less fight. Dean was beginning to learn, from first-hand experience, that it was also true for the traveler. As the 1954 world flashed out of existence around him, a deep, gurgling something bubbled up in his stomach. He mentally prepared himself for the possibility that he'd puke when they got back to 2010. *God, I hope it comes up as puke, not out the other side.*

When the world re-formed, Dean was no longer standing. He was sitting in the back booth of the Waubay bar, a cheeseburger and a freshly poured beer waiting on the table in front of him. Sam was seated next to him, uncomfortably close.

"You want to give me some breathing room?" Dean scooted sideways slightly.

Sam didn't respond. He just tapped the glass in front of him, as if it wasn't real.

"Hey, you want to sit on a guy's lap, wait till Christmas," Dean said.

Finally, Sam slid out of the booth and stood up, surveying the rest of the room.

"Do you see him?"

Dean looked around the bar. Don, or Abaddon, or whoever the hell he was, apparently hadn't stuck around to greet them.

"Dude zapped us back. Gotta be around here somewhere." Remembering their earlier encounter, Dean looked toward the back of the bar. "Check the bathroom. Guy has a woman's bladder. Then we'll check outside."

Unfortunately, the bathroom's only occupant was a large Peruvian man, who incidentally did not like having his privacy invaded. Sam learned that lesson very quickly, much to Dean's amusement.

As they left the bar, Dean saw something that nearly brought a tear to his eye. The Impala, in all its glory, rested under a nearby oak tree.

"Aren't you a sight for sore eyes," he said, running his fingers over the cool metal of the hood.

"Why are you stroking a car?" Sam asked.

"Give me a break, I haven't seen her in weeks."

"Her?"

Dean was distracted when he noticed a white spot on the windshield. That's when it hit him—something was seriously wrong here.

"Didn't park it here," he said, mostly to himself.

"What do you mean?" Sam asked.

"I left the car at the motel. We… we got zapped back from the motel, not the bar. The Impala shouldn't be here."

He pointed at the white spot. "And when have I ever parked her under a tree, where birds can… *do things* on her?"

"Sorry about that, Dean. I moved it for you," Abaddon's voice called out from behind them. "Thought you'd appreciate a welcome home meal, rather than a stuffy motel room."

"That's awfully nice of you, Donny, but why don't you cut the crap?"

Abaddon hung his head, as if in shame.

"Ah. So I take it your trip didn't go well?"

"You know exactly how it went. You knew all along what we were going to find, and what we'd have to do when we found it."

"You know, Dean, you really should let your baby bro get a word in edgewise sometimes. I think he'd really appreciate it." Don looked amused.

Sam was apparently speechless with anger. His face had contorted in rage at the sight of Abaddon.

"See, he looks a little… piqued."

"Don't worry about him," Dean said. "Worry about me, and what I'm going to do to you. What the angels are going to do to you when they find out you've been batting for the other side."

"Oooooh. I'm scared." Abaddon shielded his face in mock alarm. "Don't tell Daddy on me. Oh wait, my dad's dead. Gone to wherever omnipotent but lazy deities go when they finally get bored with their creations and abandon ship."

"So what, now you kill us? Put us through the funhouse and then slit our throats when we find our way out?"

"Buddy, you're not getting the lesson at all."

"What can I say. I'm a drop-out."

"That's fine, since it's not really for you to get, anyway. It's for our good friend over here." He nodded toward Sam.

"Tell me if you've heard this before: You're going to say yes. And it's not because you'll be tricked, or because you'll be forced. It's because the other options don't work. Not for you."

"You don't know all our options," Dean retorted.

"I just gave you a great one. And what did you do? You went out of your way to keep things the way they are. You got your friend killed to save Lucifer."

"We didn't kill anybody."

"Honestly, it's a win-win for us either way," Abaddon continued. "If you'd tried to kill all those vessels, you would have failed. You would have moped and felt terrible for trying, and we would have ended up in this exact same place, only you'd be one step closer to damnation. Like it or not, all three of us know that the fight is inevitable. And that's why you did what you did."

Sam could no longer hold his silence.

"You pretend that you thought of everything, that the outcome was determined before you set things in motion."

Abaddon turned to Sam, a little disconcerted by his calm tone. And there was something else in his voice as well. Abaddon frowned slightly.

"But you've left a loose string," Sam said. "You forgot about my destiny."

"Your destiny… is with Lucifer." Abaddon seemed suddenly uncertain.

Sam smiled broadly. It was so out of character in that moment that it even rattled Dean.

"That's more true than you know," Sam said. "And when I'm finally returned to him, I'll be sure to tell him how easily you were fooled." Sam's eyes flashed red.

"Eisheth." The truth hit Abaddon heavily. It looked as if the air had been pressed from his lungs.

Dean's heart was racing. They had taken an awful risk, and so far it had paid off. With any luck, Abaddon had been weakened enough by transporting them to be an easy target for Eisheth. Whether Eisheth behaved herself in Sam's body was another question.

"I'm going to make you suffer, Abaddon," Eisheth said. "For at least 2,000 years."

She flew at Abaddon, supernaturally propelled at an impossible speed. Bones crunched as they slammed against an oak tree. Abaddon was up in a flash, fiercely pounding Sam's body with his fists.

"Careful with my brother," Dean shouted from the sidelines.

Without looking up, Eisheth lifted Abaddon off his feet and threw him clear across the parking lot. He struck the metal dumpster outside the bar, crumpling its sides like an empty beer can.

The possibility that the fight would go on for hours was

very real. Dean had no idea how powerful either creature was, but he knew the human bodies they wore would be destroyed long before the twisted souls within them. *Alright, time to figure out an endgame.*

As Abaddon lifted himself from the buckled dumpster, Dean made his move. He ran full-tilt toward the bar's front door, swerving to avoid the scuffle. Abaddon landed a solid blow across Sam's face just as Dean entered the bar.

"Phone. I—I need to use your phone." Dean's pale face and desperate tone were enough to convince the bartender to immediately grab the receiver from below the bar.

"It's not long distance, is it?"

"Well, I'm calling Heaven…"

Thirty seconds later, Castiel picked up his cell phone. "Hello?"

"Cass. It's Dean. I need your help. Right now."

"Dean. Your absence has been… concerning me."

"That's great, man, I'm touched, but I need you to get your ass moving. Waubay, South Dakota. It's the only bar in—"

Castiel appeared next to him. The bartender and his pack of regulars looked on in awe.

"—town."

"Where's Sam?" Castiel asked.

"Look outside," Dean said. "I think we might need some backup."

Within a minute, Cass had assembled a mixture of odds and ends he had found in the bar's tiny kitchen. Herbs, a pile of toothpicks, and an assortment of other seemingly random ingredients that apparently formed a potent magical cocktail.

"You're the MacGyver of magic, Cass."

"I need blood," Castiel said, as if he was asking Dean to pass him the salt.

"Whose?"

"Yours. That's what will attract the angels. They'll be looking for any sign of you."

At that very moment something—or someone—was thrown against the side of the building, knocking knick-knacks off the walls. Dean took that as a sign. He grabbed a knife from behind the bar and opened a deep gash on his palm.

"A sigil," Castiel said. "Quickly."

Outside, Sam's face was bloodied, his body bruised and beaten, and the fight was nowhere near over. Eisheth used Sam's good left arm to smash Abaddon across the face, toppling him to the ground.

"I trusted you," Eisheth said coldly. Sam's fist pounded down against Abaddon's cheek, sending blood spilling out of his mouth.

"You were never his favorite," Abaddon hissed, barely able to move his lips. "You were no more than a pet. Why'd you think we put you—"

Eisheth punched him in the face again.

"—with the dog?" Abaddon cackled, blood pouring down his face and onto the dirt. A second later, his manic smile froze. He had seen something behind Sam that terrified him.

Eisheth turned and saw it as well. Five black specks dotted the otherwise clear sky. Within a heartbeat, they filled the heavens—five men, held aloft by invisible wings, fury in their eyes.

The angels descended on them in a flash, knocking Sam aside and plunging their heavenly daggers deep into Abaddon's flesh. As he writhed in pain, Dean and Castiel rushed forward.

"Cass, get us out of here!" Dean cried as the angels turned from Abaddon to Sam.

Castiel and the closest angel were both speeding toward Sam. For Dean, time seemed to slow. If Cass didn't reach him first, the angels would show Eisheth no mercy. Sam would die as collateral damage.

The next thing Dean knew, he was standing outside a greasy burger joint.

"What happened?" he asked, looking around.

Next to him, Sam stood, much the worse for wear, but alive. Castiel stood on his other side, having teleported them clear of the fight.

"Abaddon was destroyed. They'll… Excuse me, but why is there a demon inside Sam?"

"It's a long story, Cass."

Castiel narrowed his eyes at Sam, studying him closely.

"Don't. Don't start anything. Just… let her go."

Eisheth turned to Dean, surprised. "Let me go?"

"That was the deal. You save our asses, we save yours."

"Dean, this is not just any demon," Castiel said gravely.

"I know. And it could very well bite us in the ass. But that's what's happening."

Five minutes later, they were sharing an odd farewell with Missy Fuller, former employee of Burger Junction, current bride of Satan.

It had been a strange few weeks.

Sam and Dean recounted their journey to Castiel over burgers. Sam noticed that Dean left out a lot of details, most of them concerning Julia.

That there had been a list of angelic vessels wasn't news to Castiel. He'd heard rumors over the millennia that the list existed, but no one in Heaven had ever known its exact location.

"Except Abaddon," Sam pointed out. He was still in considerable pain, despite Dean having patched him up and forced a cocktail of painkillers down his throat.

"His deception will have caught Heaven off guard. The angels are not going to blindly trust each other nearly as much as they once did."

"So at least we've accomplished something," Dean said with a touch of bitterness.

After eating their fill, Castiel helpfully teleported the Impala to the Burger Junction, then disappeared. He was off, once again, to try and find his absentee father. Sam and Dean both empathized.

As they climbed into the Impala, Dean frowned. "What do you think it'd be like? Having a home base like Walter and Julia did? Hunter HQ?"

"We've got Bobby. Besides, it didn't work out very well for them."

"I can't shake this feeling… that our lives could have been different if they were still around. They were organized. They were everywhere."

"Dad didn't report in to anyone, and he got by just fine," Sam said. "That's what made him Dad."

"What if they could have stopped Yellow Eyes. Saved Mom."

Sam didn't answer. He already felt the weight of the world on his shoulders. He didn't particularly want to feel any more.

EPILOGUE

Dean's footsteps creaked on the ancient wood floor of the Rustic Pines Retirement Community. It smelled like a hospital—every surface regularly wiped with disinfectant chemicals, stale processed air. Old people.

At the end of the hallway, a woman was waiting for him. She introduced herself as Betty, the resident coordinator. As they walked toward the East Wing of the building, she rattled off a list of facts that left Dean's consciousness as soon as they entered. He really didn't care about the bingo schedule. He was here for something else entirely.

They walked past a dozen rooms, all of them occupied. The faces inside looked friendly, content, which comforted Dean. Not a terrible place to grow old.

"The storage area is downstairs," Betty said with a glued-on smile. "Excuse the conditions. We don't usually bring guests down here."

She wasn't kidding. The basement was damp and

unwelcoming, to say the least. Dean imagined he could feel the chill of the bare concrete through the soles of his shoes.

"Just through here," she indicated.

A large door blocked their path. Its hinges were rusty and groaned loudly as she tugged on the metal handle. Inside, a sea of musty, ancient boxes greeted them. *The remnants of entire lives,* Dean thought. *Like in the pyramids.*

"I believe the articles you're looking for are over here."

With practiced swiftness, Betty navigated the maze of boxes and pulled out one in particular. The cardboard sagged at the bottom from the weight of its contents.

"Tell me again, what was your relation?"

Dean struggled with his answer. In the moment, with that box right in front of him, he couldn't remember what he had told her on the phone. He took a stab in the dark.

"She was my great aunt."

"She never talked about family. And no family ever visited." That last sentence contained a jab directed squarely at Dean. An accusatory "Where were you?" was definitely implied.

"Yeah. Things were strained."

"Better late than never, I guess. Although, for Julia, I guess not." With that, Betty left Dean alone with the box.

He opened it delicately, almost afraid to touch the material inside.

Once Betty was definitely out of earshot, Dean whispered quietly, "I'm sorry you didn't get your picket fence, Julia."

Sam waited outside, leaning wearily against the Impala. *Things are finally back to normal,* he thought. *More or less.* Not that normal was good. In fact, Sam found himself missing 1954. For all of the tragedy, it had been nice to experience a time when things had been less complicated for a while. No Apocalypse. No horsemen. No impending battle to end all battles.

Dean walked slowly down the front steps of the retirement home, carrying a single piece of paper.

"You found her stuff?" Sam asked.

"Yeah. Let's get moving." Dean's voice was gruff. Sam recognized his I-don't-want-to talk-about-it face. Not that Sam ever let him get away with it…

"Dean, come on, what did you find?"

Dean stopped at the driver's side door.

"Nothing worth yapping about."

In one swift movement, Sam reached over the hood and snatched the piece of paper from Dean's hand.

"Hey!"

"We're gonna talk about it eventually. I'm just skipping a six-hour car ride with you brooding the whole way." Sam unfolded the paper, finding a list written in blocky handwriting. *A guy wrote it*, Sam realized. *Specifically, Walter.*

Sam held in his hands Walter's transcribed list of bloodlines. At the very end, the words "Michael" and "Lucifer" were written on two consecutive lines. Next to each—nothing. The paper had been cut, Dean and Sam's names removed from the list.

"She kept it," Dean said after a while. "Don't know what that says."

"But she took our names off," Sam said. "I think that says a lot."

Dean opened his door and sat heavily in the driver's seat. He exhaled loudly enough for Sam to hear it.

"You… You think you could drive?"

Those words were so seldom spoken that it took Sam a second to register them.

"Are you sure?"

"Yeah. I've been in the driver's seat a little too much recently."

Reluctantly, Sam rounded the front of the car and swapped seats with Dean.

"Where we heading?"

In the passenger seat, Dean had already closed his eyes.

"Surprise me."

As night approached, the Impala motored onto the open road. Toward—for better or worse—their destiny.

THE END

AUTHOR'S NOTE

I was pleased to be asked by Christopher Cerasi to write a novel for *Supernatural*. Since the deadline conflicted with my impending wedding, I asked David Reed if he wanted to collaborate. I owe him great thanks for picking up the ball and running with it when I was crying over the cost of chair rentals. Also much thanks to Christopher for the support and fun phone calls; he has turned out to be a great friend and believer in the show. Thank you to Cath Trechman, who exhibited patience and professionalism throughout this process, and whose love for the written word shines through in her impeccable work. — Rebecca Dessertine

ACKNOWLEDGMENTS

The authors would like to thank the creator of the show, Eric Kripke, and the exec producers for continuing the most gutsy, rockin' show on TV.

Rebecca would like to thank her husband Jason, for his support and love, and her sister Carrie, without whom she wouldn't understand how deep the love runs between siblings.

David would like to thank his wife Mairin, for almost never complaining about the insanely late nights that come with writing a novel while also holding a full time job. He'd also like to thank her for baking really great cookies, pretending to be excited about new *Halo* games, being an amazing mom, and a million more things that make her a great person to be around. In addition, David would also like to thank his son for being so gosh-darn cute.

ABOUT THE AUTHORS

DAVID REED grew up without cable TV, but still turned out all right. After completing nearly half of a computer science degree, he realized that programming computers is way less interesting than watching them turn evil and murder people on television. With that in mind, he set off with his then-girlfriend for Los Angeles, where he got his break working on *Battlestar Galactica*, subsequently writing the comic book miniseries *Battlestar Galactica: Final Five* with Seamus Kevin Fahey. Since then, he has branched out from robot mayhem to general mayhem, writing the Syfy Original Movie *Lake Placid 3* and the story for the *Supernatural* episode "Hammer of the Gods." He lives in Los Angeles with his wife and infant son.

REBECCA DESSERTINE wrote her first screenplay in fifth grade. She was very disappointed her sequel to *Stand By Me* was never optioned. After attending NYU at sixteen, she transferred to the University of Virginia, where she finished a degree in drama that turned out to be quite a waste of money after she moved to Los Angeles and discovered she wasn't a good actress. She has worked for *Supernatural* for three years. As a writer she co-wrote the second series of the show's comic *Supernatural: Rising Son*. She also co-wrote the story for the episode "Swap Meat." Outside of the *Supernatural* realm she produced an independent film, *Loveless in Los Angeles*, that can occasionally be seen on Comedy Central. She currently lives in the Los Angeles neighborhood of Echo Park with her husband, dog, and two cats.

ALSO AVAILABLE FROM TITAN BOOKS:

SUPERNATURAL
THE UNHOLY CAUSE
By JOE SCHREIBER

Way back in April 1862, Confederate Captain Jubal Beauchamp leads a charge across a Georgia battleground... Fast forward to the present day and a civil-war re-enactment on the same site becomes all too real. When Sam and Dean head down South to investigate, they discover that the past really isn't dead...

A brand-new *Supernatural* novel that reveals a previously unseen adventure for the Winchester brothers, from the hit CW series!

WWW.TITANBOOKS.COM

SUPERNATURAL™

THE OFFICIAL SUPERNATURAL MAGAZINE

features exclusive interviews with Jared and Jensen, guest stars, and the behind-the-scenes crew of the show, the latest news, and classic episode spotlights! Plus, pull-out posters in every issue!

TO SUBSCRIBE NOW CALL

U.S. 1 877 363 1310
U.K. 0844 844 0387

For more information visit:
www.titanmagazines.com/supernatural